D1188391

Tough
Cookie

M. Ruth Myers

Published by Tuesday House

ISBN:-10: 0615732615
ISBN:-13: 978-0615732619

This book is a work of fiction. Names, characters and incidents are products of the author's imagination or are used fictitiously. Any resemblance to actual events or persons, living or dead, is entirely coincidental.

Cover design by Alan Raney

ALSO BY M. RUTH MYERS

Maggie Sullivan mysteries

No Game for a Dame

Other novels

A Touch of Magic
Costly Pleasures
A Journey to Cuzco
Friday's Daughter
Captain's Pleasure
Love Unspoken
An Officer and a Lady
Insights
A Private Matter

ACKNOWLEDGMENTS

I would like to express my appreciation to members of the Dayton Police History Foundation, Inc. for preserving a rich and fascinating segment of Dayton history. Their dedication helps keep the past alive.

My particular thanks go to that organization's secretary-treasurer, retired Dayton police sergeant Stephen Grismer. His patient and insightful answers to my questions add great richness to the Maggie Sullivan mysteries.

Any inaccuracies are entirely my own.

ONE

I was at my desk improvising a game of jacks with a rubber ball and spare slugs for my .38. The bullets wobbled a lot, but it was cheap entertainment. It beat trudging through slush and ice from Dayton's last snowfall to spend three cents on the *Daily News* only to learn Herr Hitler was still bamboozling leaders in Europe.

The knock that interrupted me at pigs-in-the-pen was self-important. Three precise raps.

"It's open," I said to the frosted glass panel.

I caught the ball and set it down with the slugs so I'd appear businesslike. A man in a fine gray fedora came in flicking sleet from his sleeves. He had ashy hair, a prominent overbite and a fussy air at odds with his age, which I put at early forties. He looked around and his brows drew together.

"I'm hunting Miss Sullivan's office."

"I'm Maggie Sullivan." I rose with a smile so bright it risked blinding him.

He was too busy glancing left and right again to notice. His lips pursed with suppressed disdain.

"Oh my," he said. "I expected you to be bigger."

"Gee, is there a height requirement for private eyes? I could stand on my tiptoes."

For the first time since entering, he favored me with a real look. It was the same one nuns nail you with while waiting for you to confess to a lie.

I remembered my bank account was nearing empty.

I remembered I'd been eating sardines for dinner all week to get by.

"Ah, you mean you expected a secretary," I said sweetly. "Most people prefer the privacy of a one-woman operation." There might have been good reason why those nuns so often suspected me of stretching the truth. I gestured to the chair in front of my desk. "Won't you sit down, Mr.–?"

"Hill. James C. Hill."

He looked at the chair as if debating whether to dust it. He sat. Having already removed his hat, he placed it on his knees and tucked a pair of kidskin gloves fastidiously beneath it. He wasn't acting like most of the people who walked through my door. Most were nervous, or maybe angry, but in one way or another always keyed up. The man in front of me seemed merely miffed at being here.

"David Rike says you're to be trusted," he announced abruptly.

"I'm glad to have earned that trust."

I'd worked as a part-time floorwalker in David Rike's big department store while I was in high school, then gone full-time and gotten promoted. Three years ago, he'd lent me the money to hang out my shingle.

"He says you handled a somewhat delicate personal matter for him."

"I never discuss what I may or may not have done for someone, Mr. Hill."

His mouth compressed in displeasure at my evasion. He surveyed me a moment. He was fairly good-looking, but gave an impression of setting great store by correctness in every aspect of dress and manner.

"Does the name Ferris Wildman mean anything to you?" he asked.

"Local tycoon, made his millions investing in businesses, building projects, that sort of thing." It was all I recalled from the papers. I added some bait. "Seems to be well regarded."

My final comment was almost guaranteed to make prospective clients either feel good about coming to me, or to spew out a beef against the person in question. Hill's condescending smile indicated I'd given an approved answer.

"I work for Mr. Wildman. I'm his business manager. His assistant." He paused in case I swooned at having such an eminent visitor. "Mr. Wildman would like for you to dine with him tonight. He wishes to engage your services."

Hill's position suggested he enjoyed some status in his own right. He wasn't accustomed to playing errand boy. But judging by his fine coat and kidskin gloves, he was too well paid to tell his employer no. Or maybe Ferris Wildman hadn't been willing to entrust a task of this nature to anyone else.

"I'll need some idea of what it concerns."

Hill's lips pressed primly together.

"I'm not privy to that information."

So I'd guessed right. He resented being here. Compounding that was resentment at being left out. His pale gray eyes were analyzing every aspect of my office: The calendar from my DeSoto dealership showing their new 1939 models. My framed diploma from Julienne. The photo of my father in his police uniform. Hill's expression hinted he found the surroundings only slightly better than a tenement. Maybe he hadn't noticed the fancy pot with a dead plant decorating one corner.

"What time will Mr. Wildman expect me?" I asked.

"Half past seven. You'll be compensated for your time, of course." He stood. He gave his hat a shake to free it of rain. Or dust.

"You'll need to give me his address."

But Hill's composure had slipped. He was staring at the pile of bullets, which my telephone had hidden while he was seated. Uncertainty teetered in the gaze which jumped to meet mine. I smiled and lowered my voice to share a secret.

"I like to take them out and polish them now and then. Makes them shoot faster."

He drew himself up.

"It has always been my experience that those with an untidy desk do untidy work," he said stiffly.

"Mr. Wildman's address?" I prompted.

"Mr. Wildman will send his car. He knows where you live."

"I'll need an address anyway. If he wants to see me."

James C. Hill stood still as a stone for a moment. I sensed the two of us weren't likely to become great pals.

Good thing he wasn't the one who wanted to hire me.

* * *

When I'd heard the elevator go down I stood for a minute and listened to the steam knock in the radiator. Then I went to the window and looked out.

A navy blue Cadillac town car twice as long as the other cars parked along Patterson glided to a stop in front of my building. Twelve cylinders, judging by the length of it, maybe even one of the sixteens. Once the Depression sank its teeth in deep, even most rich folks had shied away from cars like that. A driver in livery jumped out into leftover snow to open the door. Apparently he didn't do so fast enough for James C. Hill, who had come forward beckoning impatiently with his finely gloved fingers.

It was pretty clear Hill liked his fine job and the importance it gave him. I had a hunch he and I would end up going a couple of rounds if his employer hired me.

To celebrate the prospect of a fatter fee than those from the small, routine employee background checks that had kept me solvent this past month, I opened the bottom drawer of my desk and took out the necessities for a gin and tonic. I'd drink it with my pinkie extended to get in practice. Then I'd dig up whatever background on Wildman I could in the next few hours.

I wondered what sort of trouble had prompted someone like Ferris Wildman to send for a private investigator. I wondered what people like him served for dinner.

Whatever it was, it was bound to beat sardines.

TWO

Since I didn't keep a dress at the back of my closet for when I dined with the Rockefellers, I went to Genevieve, who lived two rooms away from me at Mrs. Z's.

"You won't shove a gun in the pocket and stretch the poor thing, will you?" She quirked a brow as I slipped into her close-cut black velvet jacket, admiring its tailoring.

"If I need one I'll have the butler bring it to me on a silver platter," I kidded. She didn't need to know about the .32 automatic in my evening bag. I hadn't told anyone I still got the jitters from having a killer who'd stood almost as close as Genevieve try to shoot me a few months earlier.

Genevieve laughed at my answer. She was a good ten years older than the rest of us girls in the rooming house, but the two of us were pals. I surveyed myself in the mirror on her wardrobe door. The jacket was a little roomy, but add it to my moire skirt, silk blouse and pearls, and I looked pretty good for five foot-two of cop's kid who hadn't yet turned twenty-five.

Excited knocking sounded at Genevieve's door. Against all etiquette usually observed by residents at Mrs. Z's, it burst open before Genevieve had a chance to speak. Three of the other girls crowded in, wide-eyed.

"There's a car downstairs for Maggie!" Constance said breathlessly.

"It's a limousine!" said her sister.

The usually unflappable Genevieve quick-stepped to the window with them at her heels.

"Oh, my," she said. "That's not a car, it's an ocean liner."

I knew it must be the big Cadillac. Slipping into my coat I headed downstairs with one eye peeled for Mrs. Z's tomcat, who had a nasty habit of sinking his teeth into passing legs.

The liveried driver I'd seen from my office window that afternoon was standing ramrod straight beside the big blue car. He stepped forward to open the door as I drew near.

"Good evening, miss," he said with a nod. "There's a robe in there if your knees get chilly."

I thanked him and off we went. My attempts to chat him up didn't bear much fruit.

We were almost to Webster when a truck shot out of a side street. It was big – impossible to say what kind since its headlights were off. The engine revved and it came straight at us, picking up speed. Through a little window in front of me I saw the chauffeur try to wrestle his oversized chariot out of harm's way. A crash of metal on metal sent me sliding across the seat as I grabbed for a handhold. I heard tinkling glass. The Cadillac fishtailed. Before my head cleared enough to realize we'd stopped, someone was opening my door and speaking urgently.

"Miss! Miss! Are you alright, Miss? Don't try to sit."

I did, of course.

"Holy Mother!" I scrambled out past the uncertain hand the chauffeur raised to deter me. My breath made large, uneven puffs in the cold air. The truck had vanished.

"They meant to hit us." I gripped the top of the door to steady myself.

"Yes. I–" He swallowed hard. "It looked like they did."

We stood for a minute breathing and gathering our wits.

"It would have been a bad hit if you hadn't turned this whale as fast as you did."

He smiled wanly. "It's a responsive car."

"What's your name?"

"Rogers." He pressed a hand to his cheek bone.

"You get hurt?"

"Hit my face on the steering wheel. I've had worse."

He started around to inspect the damage. I tagged along. It was going to take a headlight and a new fender and maybe some work beyond that to restore the car to its former elegance.

"Any idea who did this?" I asked.

"Who did it?" He looked startled.

"You drive Mr. Wildman places. You hear things. Probably get a sense when things aren't right."

He shook his head vehemently. "No idea."

Several porch lights had come on, prompted by the sound of the crash. No doubt plenty of faces were peering out behind curtains, with the fancy car adding extra interest to neighborly concern. A door opened and a man came toward us.

"Do you need help?" he asked. "Is anyone hurt?"

"Thank you, no," Rogers said. "The car looks driveable. I'll inform the police and come back to meet them if they wish. But first I need to get the lady to her destination."

The man who had offered help gave an awkward nod in my direction. Probably thought I rode around in the Cadillac on a regular basis. Rogers gestured and I went around and slid into the back seat again. But not until I'd noted which house the helpful man returned to.

* * *

Ferris Wildman lived in Oakwood. His driveway curved up a small hill, but with only the Cadillac's single headlight cutting the darkness, I couldn't tell much about the house itself. The glow from the windows was just enough to let me see it was three stories, with a crenelated balcony roofing a wide front verandah, and some kind of six-sided tower at one end. We stopped by the tower and Rogers accompanied me to the front door.

"Tell Mr. Wildman I need to speak to him for a moment. There was – an accident," he said to the black-suited man who opened the door.

"Of course," said the man in black without even a blink. He was medium build with an oblong face and traces of gray in his hair. He gave a small bow of apology. "If you'll be so good as to wait just a moment, miss."

A maid in a black dress and frilly white apron stepped forward and took my coat. Rogers stood at parade rest, one arm curved to hold his hat and the other arm tucked behind him. Before I could notice much more than the hall where we stood being large enough for roller skating and that a staircase flared like a cornucopia to the left of the entrance, a tallish man with silvery hair and a nose resembling an eagle's beak appeared.

"Miss Sullivan, I'm Ferris Wildman," he said with hand outstretched. "Are you all right? I understand there was some sort of accident."

"Perfectly fine, thanks. Your man Rogers is an exceptional driver."

He smiled absently, more reflex than anything else.

"If you'd show Miss Sullivan to my study, please," he said to the butler. He turned away, attention now on the chauffeur. So far his manner conveyed concern, not anger.

Wildman's study turned out to be in the tower room. The outside wall held a beautiful little fireplace with Delph tile decorating the face and edge of the hearth.   There was a drop-front mahogany secretary but no desk. I could hear the buzz of voices in the hall, too indistinct to make out what they were saying. I hoped Rogers wasn't getting a dressing down.

A few minutes passed. Ferris Wildman entered the room, speaking over his shoulder. "Just give Smith the approximate location. He'll take care of formalities with the police. They can come here if they have any questions. And have Mrs. Tate give you a glass of something bolstering with your supper."

He advanced on me with a smile of apology.

"Do sit down, Miss Sullivan. May I offer you something to drink? I'm partial to whiskey, though I'm told the sherry is also quite good."

"Whiskey, then. With a splash of water."

The butler went to a cart and removed the top from a silver ice bucket. I sat on a Queen Anne chair. The ease with which Wildman sank onto the divan across from me made me suspect it was his spot of choice.

"You're sure you're not hurt anywhere?" he asked. "Rogers says the collision was hard."

"You've got a sturdy car."

He chuckled. "Yes. A terrible indulgence." He didn't sound at all repentant.

I waited while the butler set our drinks down and departed.

"Did Rogers tell you they rammed us deliberately?" I asked.

"He said they might have."

"Any chance it's related to whatever problem you brought me here to discuss?"

For the first time since I'd met him, Wildman looked worried.

"I ... shouldn't think so."

He took a neat drink of whiskey. I sipped a taste. It was fine brew. I waited.

It gave me a chance to study the man more closely. His silver hair was thick, and on the long side, and swept back from a clean-shaven face. The lips beneath his humped eagle's nose were thin.

"I appreciate your coming to see me on such short notice–" he began abruptly.

The telephone rang. Wildman looked up expectantly. The butler knocked and came in.

"Your call from Texas, sir,"

Wildman excused himself. I enjoyed the fire. And my whiskey. By the time he returned it was nearly an hour past the time originally set for our meeting. I hoped my stomach wouldn't start growling.

"I must apologize," Wildman said, freshening his glass and offering the same for mine, which I declined. "That call was supposed to come through this afternoon. I'm a shareholder in a drilling venture. They were sinking a test well."

I guessed he meant oil. "The burdens of a tycoon."

He looked briefly amused. "Something like that."

He sat forward.

"I am a wealthy man, Miss Sullivan. I've gotten that way by being shrewd at investments. Sometimes they pay off. Occasionally they do not. When that happens, I take my loss like a man. It's part of business. Winning and losing."

We were getting to why he'd invited me here. I nodded.

"Perhaps they'll get oil from that test well. Perhaps not. That winning and losing is – as you put it – part of the burden of being a tycoon."

His features had hardened. For the first time I noticed the darkness of his brows, which, as he leaned forward further emphasized his nose, giving him more than ever the look of a bird of prey.

"I do not object to losing. Occasionally. I do object to being cheated. I object to lies. To being swindled–"

Screeching anger outside the door brought us both to our feet as it slammed open. A blonde with a gun in her hand lurched toward us. Behind her I saw the butler make a wary – and unsuccessful – attempt to grab her arm.

"You sonovabitch!" she screamed at Wildman. "You've ruined my life!" She let off a shot that shattered a lamp a foot from where Wildman stood. "Make a move and the next one goes into your head!"

The gun veered toward me. Her eyes were glassy and brimming with hate and I caught a glimpse of her finger hovering on the trigger.

"Who's this?" she slurred. "Your latest floozie?"

THREE

I put a hand to my throat and staggered sideways a step.

"I – I think I'm going to faint," I gasped. As I sagged toward the carpet I caught Wildman's startled and vaguely disappointed look.

Midway down I bunched my muscles and pushed off on one foot, pivoting. My shoulder, with all my momentum behind it, drove into the side of the woman's knee. It didn't catch her as far behind as I wanted, but drunk as she was it was enough to bring her down. I landed on her and scrambled for the gun. It jarred loose her grip, but she managed to hang onto the butt of the gun.

Despite her inebriation she fought like a cat. The gun went off again, its report roaring in my ear. I became aware of others joining the attempt to restrain her. Rogers had appeared from somewhere and was at her head. He managed to pin her shoulders. The butler caught gingerly at her left wrist. Her other hand still waved the gun unhealthily close to Rogers' head. I pulled back and socked her hard in the jaw.

It didn't knock her out. Instead she started to weep.

"Father! Father! Are you all right?"

A skinny boy of eight or nine burst in. Seeing us on the floor, he skidded to a stop. A woman ran in behind him, grabbing his shirt.

"Sorry, sir–"

"Is that a gun?" The boy's eyes were wide.

"Shouldn't you be doing your arithmetic, Stuart?" Wildman asked woodenly.

The woman hustled the little boy out.

Sitting back on my haunches, I finally got a good look at the woman I'd tackled. She'd been pretty once. Still was, maybe, beneath too much makeup and too much anger and the bloating that came from too much booze. She was blonde with the flawless look of weekly salon visits. I made her to be about ten years younger than Wildman, who stood watching impassively.

I picked up the gun, which had finally tumbled free when I hit her. I set it aside after checking the chamber. The chauffeur and butler lifted her deferentially to her feet. Her sobs grew louder in the otherwise silent room.

"You bastard," she gasped. "You smug, self-important bastard. Why do you have to humiliate me?"

Rogers, I noted, was keeping a tight grip on the woman's arm.

"Put her in her car and drive her home," Wildman directed tersely. "Keep her keys.

The butler slipped a hand under the woman's elbow and he and Rogers escorted her from the room. I was still on the floor, resting back on my heels. Wildman hadn't budged an inch since it all began. Now, coming unfrozen, he helped me to my feet.

"With a tackle like that, you could be playing for Pittsburgh," he said.

He was shaken. His effort at lightness showed it. Sports didn't interest me much, but I knew enough he meant football. I managed a smile.

"Are you all right?" he inquired.

"Yeah. Fine. Thanks." I was kicking myself for not having my automatic in some kind of shoulder rig, but it was a little early in the year to be shooting somebody anyway. At least I hadn't turned sissy when I found myself staring at a gun again.

"I could do with more whiskey," Wildman said abruptly. "You?"

He poured it himself even though the butler returned just then accompanied by the girl in the frilly apron who'd taken my coat. She carried a dustpan and brush with which she made short work of the broken pieces of lamp. Within minutes the butler had added a log to the fire and carried the frame of the lamp out ahead of her. Just like that, all traces of the recent unpleasantness were eradicated.

"I take it you know the lady who came calling," I said as the door closed behind the two servants.

"My sister." Wildman grimaced. "She's been indulged all her life; can't be bothered with reason. Married a man who's an even bigger spendthrift than she is. Our father left her portion of his estate in a trust, which I administer. Wise on his part, as she'd otherwise have spent every penny. She resents it."

"Enough to have set up that truck ramming into your car?"

He gave a mirthless laugh. "Dorothy never looks far enough ahead to plan anything."

"She might have killed you just now. And damned near did."

He knocked back the rest of his whiskey and didn't answer. As I hefted my own glass I realized an inch or two on the underarm seam of Genevieve's jacket had pulled apart. I touched a finger to it absently.

"I'll replace your jacket, of course," Wildman said, noticing. "I do apologize. Now let's have dinner and get back to the reason I asked you here."

*   *   *

The butler and maid bustled in and set up a table for two in an alcove. It happened as fast as debris from the shooting had disappeared. Starched white linen, comfy dining chairs, a silver bucket on a pedestal for wine. There was even a rose in a bud vase. The first course was prawns on ice with tiny little points of toast.

"As I was telling you earlier, I accept the fact that now and then I'll have to take a loss on my investments," Wildman began. "But I will not tolerate being conned. I will not tolerate being played for a fool. In my sort of business, reputation is a valuable asset. It's money in the bank."

I had trouble thinking of what Wildman did as business. It felt more like putting one pot of money up to make more money. I kept on listening.

"When I invest in a project, Miss Sullivan, it's enough to bring others along. Other investors. Perhaps a bank loan. It's because I am known for ... shrewdness. Good judgment. An ability to spot problems or weaknesses others miss, as well as opportunities." He paused to sip water and blot his lips. "Perhaps I sound vain. The point is, I value my standing as someone prudent, someone with a very hard head for business."

"Yet someone's snookered you," I guessed.

His smile was a civilized reflex hiding something more ruthless.

"If you wish to put it that way," he agreed.

"Let's start there then."

Wildman thought a minute. "About six months ago I got wind of what seemed to me a very promising investment opportunity. A manufacturing venture. Its details are unimportant. The channel through which it reached me was entirely trustworthy. The reputations of other investors involved were as sound as my own. The integrity of the man who was putting the whole thing together was unimpeachable. Or so I thought."

We were working our way through veal birds now. They'd come with asparagus tips that had to be from a greenhouse and walnut sized buttered potatoes. There was half a tomato for garnish. I hoped it was okay to eat that too.

"Then what happened?" I prompted.

Wildman sipped some wine. It was white, which was just all about I know about wine. His eyes grew piercing, once again reminding me of a bird of prey.

"In short, the man behind the deal disappeared. Anyone who'd put up money lost it."

"Including you."

"Yes."

"How much?"

He chuckled mirthlessly. "You're direct. I wish more people were. The s.o.b. stung me for eighteen thousand dollars."

I whistled silently. Wildman leaned forward.

"I don't like losing that kind of money, Miss Sullivan – but I can afford it. It will not affect how I live or my business dealings, except perhaps to make me even more cautious regarding the latter than I already was. It's the principle of the thing. The fact that someone made a monkey of me. I asked you here because I do not intend to let that go unremedied."

The wad he'd lost might not be a lot of money to him, but I couldn't even imagine all it would buy. Nevertheless, Wildman had a right to be sore.

"What's the name of the man I'll be looking for?"

"Harold Draper."

He filled in details. Draper had worked his way up at a top-notch firm that dealt in commercial realty. Half a dozen years ago he'd stepped out on his own, putting together investment deals to not only buy property but also develop it. At a time when a quarter of the country was out of work and plenty more stuffing their shoes with cardboard and managing on potatoes and tea twice a day, if they had even that, Draper's profits – and his reputation in the business community – had risen.

"I'm guessing you haven't reported his con game to the police," I said slowly. "It's not the sort of thing you wish made public."

He inclined his head.

Apparently Wildman had some sort of hidden bell or buzzer for summoning servants, because the butler came in then with a heavy silver coffee service and asked if I took cream or sugar. I said no. We waited a minute while the maid replaced our plates with footed dishes containing some sort of concoction of ladyfingers and pastry creme and fruit and such.

"Since you want to keep mum about Draper's swindle, what exactly is it you want me to do?" I asked slowly.

Wildman set his dessert aside untouched and leaned toward me.

"I want you to find the man in question, Miss Sullivan. I want you to bring him to me."

"Then what happens?"

"I will show him he chose the wrong man to gull."

I set my spoon down. I hated to walk away from the layers of creme and pastry. I'd hate to walk away from Wildman's sizable fee even more. But I didn't like the way his hawk eyes had hardened.

"I don't hunt people down so they can be killed, Mr. Wildman."

"There are punishments far more satisfying than killing someone, Miss Sullivan."

The answer was as chilling in its own way as the threat of violence, and better suited to the thread of ruthlessness suggested in the man across from me.

"I'll take you at your word, then. I'll turn over every stone I can to find Draper. I'm guessing your name carries plenty of influence in this city, but if I bring you Draper and he turns up dead, people I know will ask questions you don't want to answer. They won't back down and they'll make your life a misery."

I hoped he believed it.

I wasn't sure I did.

FOUR

Food and facts both stick to you better first thing in the morning. Over my daily breakfast at McCrory's lunch counter, I concluded I had more oatmeal in the bowl before me than useful information about my latest case.

I knew Harold Draper, who dealt in real estate and once had been on the up-and-up, had swindled my client and other smart men out of considerable dough and then disappeared. My client, Ferris Wildman, had sent word he wanted to hire me, a few hours after which his car – with me inside – had been deliberately rammed. When he'd barely begun to explain why he'd sent for me, his sister had burst in with a gun and tried to shoot him.

Either my client wasn't too popular or someone didn't want him talking to me.

Wildman had pooh-poohed the idea his sister might have played any part in the swindle. She seemed awfully keen to have him out of the way, but I was inclined to believe her performance last night was mere coincidence, unrelated to his sending for me. She'd been too drunk to be reliable, to herself or anyone else, if her goal had been to prevent an outsider from hearing details of the lucrative con.

"Thanks for the magazine. Give me something fun to look forward to Saturday nights," murmured Izzy, the thin little waitress who'd brought my breakfast and sometimes my lunch for years.

I nodded, but she was gone down the counter before she could even see my acknowledgment. I'd slipped her a third-hand copy of Black Mask. She was raising a kid on her own, which couldn't be easy.

Sipping the coffee she'd refilled, I decided Wildman's sister could wait until I'd checked out other people. Even if she'd played no role in her brother getting bamboozled, she might tell me something else that proved useful.

The air along the counter to my left was blue with smoke. Now a woman sat down on my right and started a cigarette to go with her toast. I decided to leave, unable to take any more of the smell. It was perfume of the death that had eaten away at my dad, day by choking day.

*   *   *

My office was on Patterson a few doors shy of where it angled into St. Clair, near some railroad tracks and the produce market. The market didn't have much this time of year, just roots and a few winter greens and late apples, but I liked its shouts and the clatter of carts and trucks over bricks all the same. I'd just turned the point of the triangle when a police car headed in the opposite direction pulled to the curb in front of me and its window rolled down.

"Awful fine shoes for this much slush, Maggie Liz. Did you never hear of rubbers?" asked the man with a thicket of white hair who stuck his head out the window.

"Going to give me a ticket for walking without galoshes?" I grinned, going over to meet him.

Billy Leary had been my dad's partner and was one of my godfathers. Behind the wheel Mick Connelly, a cop in his early thirties, nodded formally. He had rusty red hair and a well defined mouth, and even six feet away he stirred something in me that I didn't want disturbed.

"You doing okay?" he asked.

"Yeah. Fine. You?"

He nodded.

On the night I'd had to shoot a man, Connelly had risked his neck to save mine. Trouble was, I'd managed to save it myself at exactly the instant he'd burst in. If he'd been a second earlier, he'd have beaten me to it. If I'd been a second slower, I'd be dead. I'd thanked him more than a few times, but he'd become standoffish since that evening. Things felt stilted between us.

Oblivious to the tension, Billy spoke again. "Awful about the Pope."

"Yeah."

The morning paper had carried news of his fatal heart attack. Even though I'd parted ways with the Church, Pius XI had been Pope for most of my life. He'd shown plenty of spine speaking out against Hitler and Franco for the way they were mistreating Jews, and he'd scolded the U.S. and Britain for not doing the same.

The two cops rolled on, with Billy giving a cheery wave. I continued into my building and up the stairs to my office. I wished I could get Connelly's guarded expression out of my mind.

Hanging my coat on the coat rack, I scooted my chair across to the radiator. I kicked off my shoes and stretched my toes out to warm them. Good thing Billy wasn't around to witness the price I paid for vanity. Wildman had arranged for me to meet with his assistant first thing this morning to get names and backgrounds of other investors bilked by Harold Draper, but I wanted to make a couple of phone calls before I set out.

Instead, I found myself thinking about Mick Connelly. I liked Connelly. He was a good cop, and smart in the bargain, but I wasn't after involvement, and I had a feeling he might be. Why couldn't I just accept that the rift between us was probably for the best?

I got up and lifted the telephone into my lap and made my phone calls.

* * *

Wildman had an office suite in the Hulman Building, Dayton's first skyscraper. The building was just a few years old and was pretty plush. A smooth-as-silk elevator delivered me to the twentieth floor. Some of the doors along the silent hall bore the names of law firms or doctors. Wildman's was identified only by its polished brass number.

When I stepped inside I saw at once why James C. Hill had turned up his nose at my small space. The reception area where I stood was bigger than my whole office and paneled in walnut. Closed doors trimmed with more polished brass opened off it on either side. Behind the middle-aged receptionist and a younger girl who sat clattering away at a typewriter, an open door to another room showed tickertape machines spitting endless strips of paper. A young man in shirt sleeves and vest bent attentively over one of them.

"Miss Sullivan?" asked the receptionist with a pleasant smile. "Sit down and I'll let Mr. Hill know you're here."

My fanny had barely sampled the comfortable chair when she put down one of her phones and directed me through the door to my left. A pretty young woman there sprang up from her desk to take my coat and showed me through another door to Hill.

He was on the telephone, patting the fingers of one hand impatiently on his desk. He nodded a greeting.

"At what time do I expect my standards?" he was demanding. "And how many days a week does that mean? Yet still I don't see them. Perhaps you've forgotten that Mr. Wildman wants his daily report by eleven? You haven't? Good. Please tell me how I'm to accomplish that if I don't receive my standards on time."

The receiver he held smacked into its cradle. He rationed out a lifeless smile.

"Do sit down, Miss Sullivan. I apologize for the unpleasantness. Some employees simply cannot absorb the concept that time is money."

Today he was wearing a fine Harris tweed, subdued but suitable for any setting required by his role as Wildman's assistant.

"You have a nice view," I said. "I kind of thought you might be all the way at the top."

"Mr. Wildman prefers not to be ostentatious," he said with only a hint of smugness.

I'd have to use that to explain my lack of a secretary. A four-bit word sounded more impressive than pleading privacy.

I took the chair Hill offered and got to the point. "Mr. Wildman has filled you in on why he sent for me?"

"Yes. I've prepared a list of other men we know of who invested in Draper's project. I suspect there are others, but these names are certainties."

The papers on his desk were aligned at the edges. The pencils had fresh points. He slid me a file folder. I left it for the moment.

"What's your opinion of this interest of his in finding Draper?"

"My opinion?"

Hill hadn't anticipated the question. He considered as if a single wrong word might precipitate earthquakes. The position he'd risen to probably came from a life of such caution. Or maybe he was just pompous.

"I think it's uncharacteristically foolish of him," he said at last. "Harold Draper's gone, and the money with him. But while Mr. Wildman asks my advice about many matters – indeed, that's a large part of what he pays me for, analyzing demand for commodities, risk assessment, investment possibilities – he didn't seek my advice on this."

"Is that unusual?"

"I think perhaps he perceives it as a personal matter rather than business, so no. In any case, despite the many things which Mr. Wildman confides in me and relies on me for, I am still an employee. If Mr. Wildman wishes to indulge himself, it's not my concern."

Maybe not, but the exclusion stung. I'd heard resentment when he called himself an employee.

"And this bunk deal took place about six months ago?"

Hill furrowed his brow. "Yes. That sounds about right. When it first came to our attention and we started looking into it pursuant to an investment, anyway."

Six months seemed like a lot of time between getting swindled and coming to me. Still, it probably took awhile before people put money up, and longer still before they found out they'd been taken. I filed the thought for further exploration.

"Does anyone have enough of a grudge against Mr. Wildman to want to injure him?"

"One doesn't become a success without making enemies. But no, I can't think of anyone."

"Wildman's son–"

"Stuart."

"Where's his mother?"

"Dead, I'm afraid. Ran off with a musician shortly after the boy was born. Mr. Wildman divorced her, naturally. She killed herself within a year. His first wife lives in Europe. She receives quite a nice allotment. They're on cordial terms."

"His sister doesn't seem to like him very much."

He almost laughed outright. "No. But she generally nurses her grudge with a bottle. As far as I know, she's never waved any sort of weapon around until last night. Are you thinking about the accident with the car en route?"

"Yes. Who besides you knew Mr. Wildman sent for me yesterday?"

"Rogers, certainly, since he was driving. I suppose any of the servants might have, if they were given to eavesdropping. Are you suggesting ... what? That someone meant to frighten you away? Prevent Mr. Wildman from talking to you?"

"Something like that."

He gave a patronizing smile.

"Perhaps it was simply an accident."

A feverish knocking interrupted.

"Yes? Come in."

The young man in shirt sleeves I'd seen earlier hurried in. He pushed a narrow cart whose upright panel held pegs with small loops of ticker tape wound around each. The man didn't look at Hill, and backed up several steps before turning.

"On time tomorrow," Hill reminded the retreating figure. As the door closed he glanced at a clock on the wall. "I have to leave for a meeting shortly, Miss Sullivan. If you wouldn't mind looking over that list to see if there's anything more I can add?"

FIVE

There were five names on the list Hill had given me. I went back to the office to set up appointments. I'd see if I could talk to three that morning, then decide if I wanted to follow up anything from them before I talked to the others.

First, though, I called the *Dayton Daily News* photo department and asked for Matt Jenkins, disguising my voice when the old guy who ran the department answered.

"Oh dear," I sighed upon learning Jenkins was out. "Could you tell him his cousin from Peoria's in town and will be at the Fox at half past twelve if he wants to have lunch?"

Jenkins owed me at least a year's worth of information for the last big scoop I'd gotten him. Not that I expected him to make it easy to collect.

Propping my feet on my desk I began to set up appointments from the names and numbers Hill had given me. On the second one, when I'd introduced myself to the secretary and was halfway into asking to see her boss, I got a surprise.

"I'm sorry. I–" The voice on the other end wavered and cracked. "I regret to say Mr. Preston is ... recently deceased."

I sat up, startled. Alert, too, though I wasn't sure why.

"I apologize for intruding. May I ask when he died?"

"Just day before yesterday. You're not the first to call and ask for him, so please don't worry."

I murmured some condolences and then hung up. Preston had been dead before James C. Hill had come to see me yesterday. And hours before I'd heard the first word about Draper's swindle. That seemed to suggest there was no connection between his death and my investigation. Still, the timing seemed odd. So did the fact that Hill, whose ears were supposed to be pricked for every nugget and rumor in the world of investments, had been unaware of it. Had Wildman been equally in the dark? Surely they'd discussed names when he told Hill to draw up the list and meet with me.

* * *

Chatting with two of the men Draper fleeced would keep me busy enough until lunchtime. Most people weren't likely to see me if I told them my line of work, so I said it was about a business matter when I made the appointments.

The first was with Ulysses Smith. He was thin and bald and stoop-shouldered. His office wasn't as fancy as Hill's – or, presumably, Wildman's – but two large canvases on the wall took my breath away. One showed a narrow street in an old city where a cobbler plied his trade with a cocked head and a twinkle in his eyes that made him look like the next instant he'd kick into a dance. The other was a mother whose knuckles were red and whose face was weary, her smile one of heart-rending tenderness as she brushed her daughter's hair.

"An investigator?" Smith said looking nervously at the card I handed him. "I don't understand. What are you here about? Who are you with?"

"A private individual hired me to locate a man named Harold Draper. Do you know of him?"

"Draper! He's a disgrace – a bounder!" He colored slightly. "That is to say, I knew him slightly through business. He left town a few months ago."

He sank into the chair at his desk. "I'm afraid that's all I can tell you. We weren't really acquainted."

"I'm told he left under something of a cloud."

Smith sighed in resignation. A few pale freckles, or maybe spots, decorated the front of his dome. He waved me toward a chair.

"I suppose that's more accurate. He ... disappeared, in fact. He was putting together some real estate development deal. I'm told that – that he took his investors' money. That he swindled them. Now that's all I know. I really had very few dealings with him."

I waited a moment. "I'm told you were one of the men he swindled."

"That's ridiculous." His eyes faltered. He busied himself with papers on his desk.

"So when you called him a bounder, that was based on hearsay?"

The tips of his lips worked fractionally.

"I ... when you hear the same story from various sources ... trustworthy individuals...." His voice trailed off. All at once he looked at me, his face filling with anger. "One of the men he hoodwinked killed himself. I know for a fact it was because he lost money to Draper. He came to me for a loan and he told me why he needed it. There. Is that proof enough?"

Moisture shone in his eyes. He got up and went to the painting of the mother and daughter. He touched his fingertips lightly to its frame, patting it.

"Charles Preston?" I said softly to his back.

"Yes. I had no idea he was in terrible straits. I thought – he was just somewhat pinched." He shook his head, still touching the painting.

"Who were the others? The trustworthy individuals who talked about Draper? Who might have been duped?"

He turned to face me again. The tips of his lips did their odd little dance.

"I can't recall. It's been some time. Now if you'd see yourself out. I'm sorry I couldn't be any more help."

* * *

My last stop that morning was a man named Frank Keefe. He had wavy black hair and a chin that made no apologies. He held a cigarette between his teeth with the same flair FDR used on a cigar.

"Someone's hired me to track down a man named Harold Draper," I said as we shook hands and I gave him a card.

"If you find him, there'll be a line of men wanting a swing at him, me among them," he said as he read it. "Cigarette?" He offered a chased silver box and nodded me toward a chair.

"No, thanks."

I sat down, aware of Keefe's eyes admiring my legs. He grinned when he saw I'd noticed.

"I don't suppose you're likely to tell me who hired you."

"Sorry, I can't."

"Worth a try." He grinned again. It was a grin that was probably worth a lot in business, and it reached all the way to his eyes. He leaned back in his desk chair. "Draper's a crook. A charlatan. But I figure you know that. I figure that's why you're here. That someone's sore enough about the Champion Works deal that they hired you to run the little s.o.b. to ground. Am I right?"

"Batting a thousand." Neither Wilding nor Hill had thought it important to tell me the name of the deal at the center of Draper's swindle. It wasn't important. But it was handy.

"Whoever it is, my hat's off to them," Keefe said, checking my legs again. "Draper put one over on some mighty shrewd businessmen. Clipped me for ten thousand dollars. One of the men he fleeced hung himself."

"Charles Preston?"

Keefe nodded and blew out a chestful of smoke.

"Decent fellow." He stubbed his cigarette out in an art deco bowl. His light mood had vanished. "What can I do to help you?"

"Tell me everything you know about Draper."

He thought for a minute.

"Widowed for as long as I've known him. No kids. Damn fine tennis player. Used to be on the up-and-up, or at least I've had other dealings with him in the past and never got skinned. Got good returns for what I put in. I don't try to make a killing, just average profits, or a shade above, over the long term. Draper usually put together the kind of deals that gave that. This one promised to do somewhat better."

He winced and started another cigarette.

"A drinker?"

"Not particularly."

"Womanizer?"

"Not sure I make a good judge of that." He grinned. "But no. He'd talk to the wives at parties. Not many do that, me included. Men go off in clumps and talk business; women are left on their own. Draper would sit down and talk with the ladies. I wondered a couple of times if he might be lonely."

"Any pastimes that could have made him need money? Gambling? Racing?"

Keefe spread his hands. "Can't help you there."

"Relatives?"

"None I've been able to sniff out," he said wryly. His cigarette jutted up. He studied me through the smoke. "You looking for him ... these questions. You know something I don't? Is he still in town?"

"Not to my knowledge. To tell you the truth, I suspect this may be a wild goose chase, as long as it's been since he took off. But somebody hired me, so I'm looking. I have names of some of the men he clipped in this deal–"

"That's how you found me."

"Yes. It would help if you told me the names of the ones you know about. Or think might have been involved. If you want him found."

He hesitated. I crossed my legs.

Keefe's breeziness blew itself out. He studied me carefully. The ash on his cigarette grew dangerously long until he decided and flicked it into the dish.

"Oh, I want him found all right. I'd like to wring his thieving neck. Thanks to him I'm hamstrung for the next three months at least. No funds to invest in anything new; just marching in place.

"Charles Preston, the poor soul that killed himself. Ulysses Smith. Arthur Buckingham. Warren Tucker. Those are the ones I know of."

They matched the names on the list James C. Hill had given me. I picked up my handbag.

"And you might try Rachel Minsky. I've heard she invested, but that could be a rumor. Rachel doesn't rub elbows with the rest of us."

"Rachel Minsky," I repeated. "A woman?"

His infectious grin reappeared.

"Cute little Jewess. Built like a pigeon. Ball of fire. Runs a construction company out on Springfield Street."

It was a name I hadn't gotten from Hill or Wildman. A woman's name at that. A woman who ran a construction company, which made it more interesting.

"Inherited it from an uncle, I think," Keefe was saying. "Or maybe she bought it. Some scandal about the uncle or cousin or whoever owned it before her going to jail."

Most likely she just owned it, then. Had someone running it for her. But women often picked up more than men did, because too many people took them for dim, or forgot they even were in the room. Meaning Rachel Minsky could be exactly the source of information I needed. I thanked him and let him help me into my coat.

"One word of warning, Miss Sullivan." He settled the coat on my shoulders. "If you go to see Rachel Minsky, don't turn your back on her. She's a tough cookie."

Then again, so was I.

SIX

"My cousin from Peoria?" Matt Jenkins snorted as I slid into the booth across from him at the Red Fox Grill. "Remind me not to have offspring if there are cankers like you on the family tree."

"Figured you'd guess who it was if I said that."

"And you didn't want Stutzweiler to know who you were because you intend to wheedle some kind of information out of me that you shouldn't have."

"Enjoying that bonus you got?" I asked as a waitress set a cup of vegetable soup and a grilled cheese sandwich before him. I ordered a bowl of the soup while Jenkins' eyes twinkled behind wire-rimmed glasses. He was edging thirty and a halo of red-blonde curls circled the increasingly visible top of his head.

"Glad you asked, because seeing as how I'm flush, Ione and I thought we might treat you to some music at the Carousel Saturday night," he said.

He checked to make sure his big Speed Graphic and other camera gear were safely out of range of any spills and bit ravenously into his sandwich. Good thing he was slim since he always attacked food as if he were starving.

"Ione's anesthetically boring cousin is going to be in town again and you can't find another chump to make up a foursome," I said shrewdly. "Forget it, Jenkins. He rattles on like a jalopy. The rest of us end up needing toothpicks to keep our eyes open."

"The Carousel, Mags. Table at the front. I hear the drummer's really great."

I growled and Jenkins knew he'd won. Lance's Carousel was the hottest music spot in Dayton.

"Now, what do you want me to risk my job to find out this time?" Jenkins asked.

"You won't be risking anything. I just want to know if you remember anything about a businessman named Draper who disappeared about four months ago."

"Disappeared?"

"Skipped town, by all accounts. Owing people money."

"'By all accounts.' You mean it could have been foul play?"

"That's what I want to find out. I'll check back copies at the library, of course, but your pals in the newsroom hear rumors that don't make it into print."

He nodded thoughtfully, his merry eyes now sharp as tacks.

"These last few years, more than a few men just closed their doors and walked away. Most of them probably owed somebody."

We ate in silence, aware some of those men had jumped into the river, or maybe put a gun to their head. The past ten years had been rough. One man in four without work. Families out in the street. Lines a mile long outside soup kitchens. New Deal programs had put people to work, but too many still were in need and too many businesses still were on the skids.

"There wasn't an obit," I said. "But the cops get unclaimed bodies, and your boys on the police beat might remember some around the time in question, or maybe heard hints about someone conning investors and then taking off."

"And that's what he did? Pulled a con?"

I shrugged. The less Jenkins knew about some details of my work, the better it was for everyone. Among other things, it confirmed this tidbit or that if he got the same information.

"I've heard several stories. Could be sour grapes. He'd apparently been a reputable businessman for years."

"You say Draper's his name?"

"Harold Draper. Dealt in commercial real estate. Big projects by the sound of it."

"Yeah, okay. You usually ask for a lot worse."

Sometimes Jenkins and I had to put a fence between our two jobs, but other times we chatted over that fence. I wanted to ask what he knew about Wildman and his gun-waving sister, but that would give him an idea who'd hired me on this. Besides, I knew of a better source.

"Oh, there is one other thing," I said. "When's the best time of day to catch Tilly Sweeny?"

He almost choked on his last bit of soup.

"Why in hades would you want anything to do with that misery?" he asked dabbing his lips with his napkin. "Most of us stay as far away from her as humanly possible."

Tilly was second-string to the woman who wrote the paper's society column. She dug up dirt and was said to be good at it. Some of Tilly's dirt got washed a little and sprinkled in at the end of the news on society parties, but she wasn't the one who got a by-line on the column, and she resented it.

"Perhaps I want to reach out to the lonely," I said, crossing my hands on my breasts like the saints in pictures that had decorated my schoolroom walls.

"Uh-huh." Jenkins gave me a withering look and shrugged into his camera gear. "Or perhaps you need to dig in mud so disgusting decent folk would be overcome by the fumes. She comes in around ten. If you want anything close to reliable information, you'd be smart to catch her before she gets a snootful."

"Which is?"

"When she goes to lunch. And she goes early."

SEVEN

There were two men left on my list of Draper's reputed investors. One was out of town and the other one couldn't see me until Monday. That left Rachel Minsky. A sugary male voice informed me she could see me at four o'clock.

That left me some time to trot to the public library and go through back issues of the two daily papers. I started five months back, which would cover a few weeks before Draper disappeared, just in case anything caught my eye that might have spurred him to take off. By the time I had to leave for my appointment I hadn't found anything, and I hadn't learned much except that Wildman's sister was Dorothy Tarkington and that she'd been picked up for drunk driving. If I'd thought she was able – drunk or sober – to drive a big truck, I'd have put her down as the one who'd bashed her brother's Cadillac last night, but I didn't.

My little DeSoto couldn't hold a candle to Wildman's limousine when it came to plushness, but it had a heater and it started reliably in even the worst weather. It also held the road well, which proved handy on the icy streets surrounding Rachel Minsky's construction firm. The office was in an industrial area. A sign half as big as the front identified a single-story wood building as MINSKY BUILDERS. A coal yard and a warehouse sat across the way while another warehouse flanked one side. A large fenced-in area filled with machines and stacks of lumber and pipe occupied the remaining side.

Some trucks were pulled up by the fence along with a big black Buick. I figured the Buick belonged to Rachel Minsky. Climbing two steps I stamped snow off my shoes and went inside. It was a no-nonsense place. A counter holding several fat ledgers separated people who came in from three desks and their occupants.

"I have an appointment with Miss Minsky," I told a fellow wearing a sweater and corduroy jacket who came to help me.

"Talk to him." He jerked a thumb toward a young squire whose hair shone with Brylcreem.

The young guy's starched collar looked out of place beside the sturdier wear of three other men who bobbed around, spindling papers, writing on clipboards and fielding phone calls. His desk had a blotter and orderly trappings. He looked up as I started over.

"Miss Sullivan?" It was the overly cordial voice from the telephone. He rose elegantly to his feet and hurried to lift a gate in the counter, beckoning me through. "You're a few minutes early, but that's all right. You can go on back. Second room on the right. I'll let Miss Minsky know that you're here."

The place wasn't near as swank as the Hulman Building. A single bulb provided weak light in the narrow hall. The walls were sheets of plywood. The door of the second room on the right was closed.

As I knocked, something hit the wall on the other side. A hard throw. If it was meant as a welcome, I had some meeting ahead. I walked in.

"Jesus H. Christ on a crutch!" spewed a short woman standing behind a cherrywood desk. Her fists were planted on her hips.

She was my age, or near it, with a shape that would have made men drool if she'd been two inches taller. Some probably still did. She was so intent on a document lying before her that she hadn't noticed me.

"Interesting choice of words for a Jewish person," I said.

Her head snapped up. At first glance she looked sweet and doll-like. A cloud of soft black hair floated above a pointed chin. But a pair of dark eyes sized me up with military shrewdness.

"What's wrong with it? He was a good Jewish boy. Who the hell are you?"

"Maggie Sullivan. I made an appointment...."

The phone on her desk jangled. She snatched it up. After listening a moment she banged it back down.

"That miserable little pig turd."

Her secretary, I guessed. He'd waited to tell her I was on my way back, knowing full well I'd catch her off guard.

Her lips thinned into what the unwary might take for a smile. "Doesn't like working for a woman. Doesn't like working for a Jew." She flounced into her chair as if onto a throne. "You're here. You might as well sit."

The dark rose suit she wore had come from the top floor of Rike's, or the needle of an equally expensive dressmaker. She wore a gold pin on the lapel. Garnets decorated her ears.

"A private dick." She tossed aside the card I gave her. "I don't like cops. No reason I'd like a private one any better. What is it you want?"

"Harold Draper," I said. "I'm told you had dealings with him."

She fitted a cigarette into a short gold holder. Using a match from a can on her desk she lighted it deftly. She blew some smoke out, regarding me through it.

"A lot of people had dealings with Harold Draper. So what?"

"So one of them hired me to find him."

"Oh-ho."

I'd never met a woman so sure of herself. It came through in the lazy rotation of her chair left and right. In the way she leaned back. In how at ease she seemed – garnets and all – in the Spartan office where maps of the area stuck to paneling that was only a cut above plywood and rolls of what looked like blueprints overflowed an open cabinet. If she was curious who my client was or what I wanted with Draper, she gave no hint.

"What can you tell me about him?" I asked.

"What I'm guessing you've already heard. He turned out to be a crook. Took off with his investors' money. Made fools of people who thought they were smart. Why come to see me?"

"I heard you invested in Champion Works."

Her lips thinned again. This time it might really be a smile.

"I did – but I started to smell a rat."

"And?"

"I got my money back." Her amusement was unmistakable now. "I was very polite."

"Anything you can tell me about Draper's personal life?"

"We didn't belong to the same country club," she said drily.

"Who else got sucked in by Draper's scheme? Or who have you heard might have been?"

She shrugged. "I'm a Jew. I'm a woman. I'm not part of the gossip chain."

"And even if you were you wouldn't tell me, because you don't like anything resembling a cop."

Her eyes narrowed. She tilted her head.

"Maybe I heard something about the owner of a nightclub called The Mademoiselle. That he'd invested." She measured my reaction.

"Thanks."

She turned back to the document on her desk and I walked out. When I reached the front office I spoke to one of the men who worked at the counter.

"Could I make a phone call? Might save me a trip back."

He lifted one with a long cord and turned it toward me. I called Mrs. Z's. I should still be in time to catch Jolene before she left for her job as a cigarette girl.

"Hey, Jolene, it's Maggie," I said when she came on. "I need information fast. Didn't you tell me once that one of the clubs you used to work at was The Mademoiselle?"

"Wow, you got some memory!"

"What are chances the man who owns it could have put ten grand or so into a big investment deal?"

"*Herbie?*" she shrieked with laughter. "About as likely as Santa Claus being real. I'm still friends with the bartender there, though. Want me to give him a call?"

Five minutes later I walked back into Rachel Minsky's office. This time I didn't knock. I slammed the door behind me to get her attention. Her head shot up.

"What the–?"

"Herbert Warner, sole owner of The Mademoiselle, doesn't have ten bucks to invest in anything except booze – and he usually runs a week behind paying for that."

Anger simmered in her expression. She didn't say anything, just sat nodding to herself and glaring at me.

"You're fast," she said at last. "Impressive."

"Why'd you lie to me?"

"To test you. Make you chase your tail a little. I don't like someone I don't know sticking their nose in my business."

"Draper is my business."

Rachel shrugged. We locked gazes a full twenty seconds. Her eyes were as dark as pools of water at midnight, the surface luminous while something dangerous lurked in the depths.

"Don't turn your back on her," Frank Keefe had cautioned.

I didn't intend to.

Rachel Minsky wasn't going to give me anything useful. I started to leave.

"I might have misstated it, saying he was a good Jew," she said. "Your Jesus fella. The rabbis of the time didn't think so much of him. It might have been interesting to see him in action, though."

Was this a glimpse of how her mind zig-zagged, or did she like to keep people off balance? My hand reached for the doorknob.

"He had a partner, you know."

"What?"

"Draper. He had a partner."

EIGHT

Cozy as Mrs. Z's was, Finn's pub felt more like home. It was the closest thing I had since selling the house I'd grown up in to pay my dad's medical bills. Most who came there were regulars, and whenever you walked through the door someone seemed glad to see you. Grainy photos of carts pulled by ponies, kids playing in front of thatched roof huts, and wild landscapes running down to the sea all whispered longingly of a distant shore. The tables were worn but polished. Behind the bar Finbar Quinn and his wife dispensed dark stout and whiskey and hard cider.

On Fridays, if you got there early enough and knew to ask for it, you could also get brown bread and stew. I was hankering for the brown bread. When I stepped through the door, though, another Battle of the Boyne was underway. I stared.

Billy Leary and Seamus Hanlon were shouting at each other. At least Billy was shouting. Seamus rested a foot on the bar rail, placidly sipping a Guinness. Their uniforms marked them as cops; their unbuttoned jackets and collars showed they were off duty. The two of them were thick as thieves and had been my dad's best friends. I'd grown up with the three of them laughing at our kitchen table while my mother ignored them all or took to bed with one of her headaches. Up until now I'd never before heard the two of them exchange a cross word.

"You're a damned fool!" Billy howled, red faced.

"It's my money. I reckon I'll do with it as I want," Seamus said stolidly.

They weren't quite Mutt and Jeff, but they came close. Seamus was tall and gaunt with a long, battered face that slewed to one side. Billy was short only by comparison, slightly plump, but mostly round in the face. His thick shock of hair was nearly all white now, and his blue eyes ordinarily twinkled.

Billy caught sight of me. "Come talk some sense in him, will you? He's fixing to end up his days in the poor house!"

"What in the name of Pete are you two scrapping about?"

"He wants to go and fritter away all his money."

"'Tis not all my money."

I undid my coat. Seamus slid me a look. I was fond of them both, but Billy had a way of sticking his nose in. Seamus didn't. Since I'd been on my own, Seamus and I had developed a kind of closeness. Both of us alone in the world. There if the other one needed you, glad when we saw each other, but not getting in each other's way.

"And what are you thinking of spending it on?" I inquired. Seamus, as near as I knew, was the soul of practicality.

"A phonograph," he said stoutly. "Been wanting one for a time and now I've found one. Price is fair, too."

I was speechless.

"You see?" Billy fumed. "He's gone daft." He leaned toward Seamus. "What's a man close to being a pensioner want with a phonograph? They're for hoity-toits who want to listen to opera. Or young bucks angling for a way to dance with girls."

"I like girls," Seamus said, almost hiding a grin as he bent to his Guinness.

He was baiting Billy, I realized with fascination.

"You've got a bum knee!" Billy shouted.

Finn looked up from filling a glass to give them a frown. He was probably more concerned that Billy would have a heart attack than that they'd come to blows. Toward the back of the room Mick Connelly, along with half the room, had turned to stare at the quarreling duo. I'd hoped Connelly might be here.

Billy blew out a breath, struggling to regain his temper.

"What makes you want a tom-fool phonograph?"

Seamus turned, his face alight. "Want to play some music in it, is what."

"Then get yourself a radio. You can hear all the music you want, plus Charlie McCarthy and whatnot."

"Don't care much for the funny stuff. Besides, I want to listen to music I like. Patsy Tuohey ... that fiddler Michael Coleman...." He looked dreamy eyed as a girl.

Billy pounced.

"See? It won't stop with the phonograph. You'll keep on spending, buying those records!"

"There's worse vices. And I want it. Mick thinks it's a fine idea."

"Mick!" Billy's color had begun settling back to normal. Now it surged again. "Then maybe he'll toss you a blanket when you're out in the street!"

Jamming his hat on his head he strutted out.

"Stuffed shirt," Seamus said to his back.

* * *

After commiserating with Seamus, I got two glasses of Guinness. I headed warily toward Mick Connelly's table. I wanted to smooth things out, and I wanted some information, but being in a room with Connelly gave me the same sensation I'd had as a kid when I went too high in a swing.

Connelly watched my approach through half-lowered lashes. He had a small cowlick dab at the front of a head of hair that couldn't decide if it was dark red or brown. Marks from childhood pox emphasized the hardness of his cheeks. He lounged back, relaxed, yet with an alertness that never seemed to leave him.

"Peace offering." I slid him the Guinness.

"None needed."

"By way of saying thanks, then."

He nodded. "Think you've done that a few times, though not with stout in hand. Guess my pride just took more of a bruising than I cared to admit. You going to sit down?"

I did, and immediately started to question my wisdom in coming over. I shrugged out of my coat, buying time as I tried to think of a round about way to broach my next subject. It didn't help that Connelly watched curiously.

He had a fine mouth. Well defined. Expressive. One corner quirked and he started to chuckle.

"Jesus. Have I just been reeled in like a great fish?"

"What?"

Nudging aside his nearly-empty glass, he reached for the fresh pint. "You tripped over here to try and worm something out of me the police know and you don't."

"That's a lousy thing to – Will you stop laughing?"

He leaned forward, propping his elbows on the table.

"For the life of me, I can't see how that innocent look of yours fools so many people, easy as you are to see through. I'll spare you the effort of asking me; the answer is no."

Connelly had too good an opinion of how smart he was. I smelled a challenge. I sipped some stout. He did likewise.

"Fine. Think the worst of me, then," I sighed.

I unbuttoned my suit jacket. I slid one arm slowly out, shifted and did the same with the other. The white silk blouse I had on rippled along my skin as I moved.

"I was only going to ask if there was any reason you couldn't tell me whatever you might know about a man named Draper." Raising both arms, I arched my back and lifted my hair. I heard Connelly's breath catch. "He went missing a couple months back."

"Missing?" Connelly had watched every move. His voice sounded strained.

My hair settled back into place. I leaned my elbows on the table a foot from his. He regarded me for a minute, then took a swallow of Guinness.

"That was some performance," he said, raising the glass in salute. "Wouldn't mind seeing it any day of the week."

I deflated, but only a little. I knew I'd won. He considered briefly.

"Only missing person I recall from the last few months was a woman. Husband was frantic. Her parents thought he might have killed her. Turned out she'd run off with a salesman from Louisville."

"Unidentified bodies?"

"Bum who froze to death. Never had a real name, but a couple of fellows knew him from a soup kitchen. Kid hit by a train. Maybe fifteen or sixteen. Most likely riding the rails from some little town in Kansas or such place."

I looked away. Same age as my older brother when he disappeared. Maybe riding the rails. A long time ago.

"Might help if I knew more about the man you're hunting," Connelly's baritone said.

"Businessman. Real estate investments. Had a good reputation until he put together a fake deal and took off with money from some pretty big wheels."

Connelly rubbed his chin.

"I'd forgotten," he said slowly. "Don't know if it's the same man. A month or two back a secretary called to say her boss hadn't turned up for work. She was worried. Said she couldn't raise him at home."

"And?"

He shrugged. "We boys in the street weren't brought into it, so I'd guess there was nothing suggesting foul play. Nor any complaints about being swindled." His eyes traveled over me. They held the ghost of a smile. "If we picked at it over a bowl of stew, could be I'd remember something useful."

I glanced toward the bar.

"I coaxed Seamus into letting me buy him ham croquettes at a joint he likes. I thought he could use a friendly ear."

"Those two old fools squabbling over a phonograph," Connelly said, shaking his head. "Go on, then. I'll poke around, see if I can learn anything else."

"Thanks."

I got into my jacket and coat. When I rose to leave, Connelly stood too. His voice softened. He touched my elbow.

"Those bruises under your eyes that say you're not sleeping – I figure it's the shootout with Beale. The dreams go away, Maggie. It takes time, but they do go away."

NINE

When I got to the office Monday morning my phone was ringing. Experience had taught me that usually wasn't a good sign.

"That man you were asking about? They fished him out of the river last night," Connelly said, low and fast. "Freeze is on his way over."

He hung up before I could thank him. Freeze was a homicide detective. If Draper's body had turned up, Connelly would have felt obligated to tell him I'd been making inquiries. That was okay by me. Connelly was a good cop, and good cops didn't bend the rules.

In any case, he'd cued me in about what was happening. I wasn't sure how I'd play things just yet, but I knew I had to call Wildman.

"This is Maggie Sullivan. Tell Mr. Wildman it's urgent," I said when the butler answered.

I undid my coat while I waited. I was wearing a swell hat, plum colored with a curly pink feather. It looked nice with my gray flannel suit. I'd barely had time to toss the hat on my desk before Wildman came on.

"Miss Sullivan–"

"Draper's dead," I interrupted. "They found him in the river last night. The cops heard I was asking about him. They're on their way to see me. I won't tell them I'm working for you, but they may have names."

"Very good," he said. "Thank you."

No need to draw a picture for Wildman. We hung up at the same time. He could send people scurrying to help him prepare. All I could do was put on my thinking cap. It didn't come with a feather, pink or otherwise. I hung my things on the coatrack next to the window and stood with one eye on the street.

Someone other than Connelly might have told Freeze I'd been looking for Draper, so I'd keep Connelly out of it unless he was mentioned. And as I'd assured Wildman, I didn't intend to tell the cops who'd hired me. Apart from that, I'd share whatever information I had. That included the names of investors Draper might have duped. Including Wildman. He might deny it; I suspected some of the others might too.

A few of the cops, Freeze included, didn't much like me. Sometimes I'd been a thorn in their sides. But when I could, I tried to cooperate with them. This was a murder investigation. Moreover I didn't much like the way it had popped up. Draper, by all accounts, had disappeared months ago. Now, one day after I started asking questions, he turned up dead.

A nondescript black car came down the street and stopped. I guessed it was Freeze. The morning paper still lay on my desk where I'd dropped it to answer the phone. I moseyed over and propped my elbows over it and began to read. I was on page two when the cops came in.

* * *

Freeze was lean and gray at the temples with a nose too pretty for a man. He wore cheap suits and usually had two men at his heels. Today there was just one.

"Good morning, Miss Sullivan. I apologize for the intrusion," he said. He didn't sound particularly sorry.

"Hey, at least you knocked," I said. "Some don't. One guy walked in and caught me tightening my garter."

"Uh–"

Freeze didn't know how to respond. He and I weren't exactly the best of pals. Behind him his sidekick looked from Freeze to me and shifted his feet.

"Sit down." I gestured breezily. "What can I do for you?"

Freeze didn't sit. He took a half-done cigarette from his lips and looked around for an ashtray. I pointed to the dimestore special on top of my four-drawer file cabinet.

"I understand you've been making inquiries about a man named Harold Draper." He tapped ash from his glowing tobacco into green glass.

"That I have. He owes a client of mine some money."

"I wouldn't count on collecting," Freeze said. "We pulled him out of the Great Miami."

I leaned back a smidgen. "Dead or alive?"

"Dead."

"Drowned?"

Freeze just looked at me.

"I don't suppose you'd tell me if it was suicide?"

He didn't answer. He did sit down, though, hitching my client chair close enough to rest one arm on my desk.

"Why don't you tell me what you know about him?" he said evenly.

His toady, following his lead, eased into a chair against the wall and took out a notepad. He was younger than Freeze with a broad face which might have been pleasant if it ever relaxed, which seemed unlikely working for Freeze. I was pretty sure his name was Boike, or something similar.

"Businessman," I began, reciting what was starting to feel like a litany. "Commercial real estate, mostly. Well thought of enough that people with big money to invest coughed it up for a deal he was putting together six months ago. The way I heard it, he waltzed off with the money.

One of the men he bilked hung himself not too long ago. There's some speculation he did it because Draper ruined him."

Freeze regarded me steadily.

"Nothing that we don't already know. What else?"

I gritted my teeth. If he, in fact, knew all that, I'd be willing to bet it was only because he'd talked to Connelly. I'd bet more that some of it was new to him. If the body had been found last night, Freeze and his boys hadn't had time to turn up diddly.

"Yeah, you probably got all that when he first went missing," I said. "I don't suppose you'll tell me who pulled strings to keep that out of the papers?"

I'd pressed the right sore spot. Freeze sat up indignantly.

"Nobody pulled strings. There were no complaints against him. We had no indication a crime was committed."

"In other words, you weren't looking for him. Then how'd you identify the body?"

"He had identification."

My poke had jarred loose a couple of nuggets. Freeze, as if catching on, clamped his mouth shut. Boike was watching us, head cocked. His eyes moved tactfully to the corner, halting as he noticed the dead plant.

Freeze stubbed out the end of his cigarette, which had gotten dangerously short.

"What else do you know?" he repeated tightly.

I thought for a minute. I could flip through my notes but that was likely to make Freeze demand them.

"He was a widower, possibly for some time. No children. Someone said he played tennis."

"You don't seem to have learned very much." He nailed me with a look he probably used to break suspects.

I smiled.

"You're absolutely right, I'm afraid," I said sweetly. "But then I only started asking questions Friday."

Freeze blinked and his steely look slipped. Toes together, I swiveled my chair back and forth a couple of times while he digested it.

"Curious, the timing of his body turning up, don't you think?"

His grunt suggested agreement, and that he no longer thought I was holding back. Freeze was smart. We just got in each other's way too much. Right now I could practically see the gears in his head turning.

"I'll need the names of the people you've talked to about this," he said. "Particularly any who fell victim to Draper's scheme."

I gave him the five names I'd been given, plus Ferris Wildman and Rachel Minsky. At the last name Boike looked up from his scribbling. I couldn't tell whether it was because the name belonged to a female, or because he recognized it.

"And who hired you to find Draper?" Freeze asked.

I smiled.

Our truce was over. His pretty nose thinned in irritation.

"Is there some reason why you choose to withhold information?"

"Because the sign on the door says *private* investigations?"

He let his breath out slowly, seeking control. Pushing the issue would get him nowhere and he knew it. He got up.

"If you think of anything else, let us know." Snapping his hat on, he went swiftly out.

Boike lagged behind, closing his notebook.

"That plant the same one that was dried up six months ago?" he asked, indicating the withered brown specimen.

"Yeah," I said. "They all end up like that. Figured I might as well quit throwing money away on replacements."

I'd dolled this one up in a green and black art deco pot from McCrory's. Clients could see I had taste enough to decorate, but assume I got so involved helping people like them I forgot to water.

Boike nodded as if the answer made perfect sense.

TEN

With Draper turning up dead, Wildman wouldn't be writing me any more checks to trace his whereabouts. Thanks to his advance I still would come out with my bank account looking healthier than it had for a while. Nevertheless, I began to wish I hadn't spent my share of the money to replace Genevieve's jacket.

"How ridiculous even to think of getting another one when a halfway decent seamstress could spend ten minutes on this one and make it good as new," she'd laughed.

That was Saturday morning. Examining the jacket's underarm seams, I'd had to agree. The inch of seam where the sleeve had pulled away from the rest of the lining had been repaired so invisibly I no longer could determine where it had been.

"Besides, brand new it didn't cost half what your client coughed up," Genevieve had insisted, tapping the money. "You and I could each buy a jacket for this amount, and that's what I propose we do. Though it needn't be a jacket, of course – as long as you don't spend all yours on hats. If it will make you feel better, I'll take an extra dollar to cover having my seam repaired."

So Saturday afternoon we'd had a shopping spree. Genevieve got a new skirt and I found a fine little evening jacket, black velvet brocade with lace cutwork. It looked perfect on me, and I didn't have the willpower to take it back, but sitting in my office after Freeze and Boike left, I rued the extravagance.

In twenty minutes I was scheduled to meet with Arthur Buckingham, the investor who hadn't been able to see me on Friday. With my search for Draper at an unexpected end, I should call and cancel. Except I didn't want to. The discovery of Draper's body just as I started asking questions had my curiosity fizzing. Anything I learned talking to Buckingham would be irrelevant now, but it also would make my final – and only – report to Ferris Wildman more complete. If I couldn't deliver anything spellbinding, he'd at least judge me thorough.

The downside was the chance I'd run into Freeze, who wouldn't be pleased that I was still snooping. With one of the men on my list out of town, that left one chance in five that I'd cross paths with Freeze. Not bad odds. I shrugged into my coat.

*   *   *

I didn't run into Freeze, but I didn't learn anything either. Buckingham was as bland as unseasoned potatoes. I didn't tell him the cops would be calling, or even that Draper was dead. That way I hadn't muddied the field for Freeze if he learned when I'd been there.

"Hey, Sis, you look like your dog died," called Heebs, my favorite newsboy, as I crossed Jefferson on the way back to my office.

I lifted an arm, only half aware of him but smiling anyway. On impulse I did an about-face and trotted across to the corner where he spent most of every day.

"Say, Heebs. They found a body in the river last night. A man named Draper. You hear anything about it?"

Some of the newsboys lived on the street, sleeping in alleys and doorways, moving in packs since they didn't have families. Heebs was sharp as a tack. It was a damn waste.

"Not yet," he said with a grin. "What's it worth if I do?"

"Two bits."

"Make it four."

Cocky little devil.

I nodded.

Back at the office I thawed my toes on the radiator. Then I cranked a carbon set into my Remington. It didn't feel right, typing a final report on a case I'd hardly started. I pecked a couple of words, then sat thinking about the visit from Freeze.

My initial thought on learning of Draper's death had been that its occurrence, just when I was starting to dig, was too convenient. That reaction had been nothing but instinct. What I'd pried out of Freeze spritzed some proof on that, or the smell of proof anyway. The police had identified the dead man from papers in his wallet. That meant the paper was still intact enough and the ink unblurred enough to read. That meant the body couldn't have been in the water too long.

I began hunting Draper. Not long after, he ended up in the river. There might not be proof one led to the other, but it seemed to me the condition of the paper he carried pointed in that direction.

Shoving aside the thoughts I wrote my report for Wildman and typed up invoices for several small, routine clients who kept me almost solvent. I was licking an envelope when the telephone rang.

"Miss Sullivan?" said James C. Hill. "Mr. Wildman wants to see you at half-past four."

He didn't give me a chance to r.s.v.p.

* * *

I presented myself at half-past four. The butler ushered me to a small office where a fire blazed merrily in a fireplace whose mantel held photos of Wildman shaking hands with various dignitaries. One of them was Herbert Hoover.

Wildman and his assistant sat in leather chairs by the fire. They were drinking sherry.

"Thank you for alerting me about the police," Wildman said rising to greet me. "They don't appear to know a great deal."

"No, they don't," I agreed.

"Will you have sherry? Mr. Hill and I usually confer at the end of the day. I asked him to stay. He oversees the day-to-day running of things, and I rely on his input. I thought his ideas might be useful as we plan our next steps."

Hill's pale head snapped up. My disbelief just about matched it. I sat down without intending to.

"I don't follow you. You hired me to find Draper, who's turned up dead. That's about as found as anyone can be."

Wildman's hands lay motionless on the arms of his chair. He leaned forward slightly.

"I want to know who killed him, or held something over him that caused him to take his own life. You're no fool. You know as well as I that's what happened. No sooner did you start asking questions than the man you were asking about, a man who vanished months ago, reappeared dead. To suppose it's any sort of coincidence is – preposterous."

Hill, with his love of neatness and order, looked fit to be tied. It took several seconds before his features smoothed. I chose words carefully.

"I agree with all you've said, but now it's become a matter for the police–"

"At best they'll call it a suicide, not a matter for further investigation."

"You can't know that."

"Can't I?" Wildman raised an eyebrow. "Someone brought about Draper's death to prevent me from talking to him. I want to know who. And why."

It might fit with what Rachel Minsky had said about Draper having a partner. If she'd told the truth, which given that I'd caught her in one lie, I had absolutely no reason to think. It was just as likely Wildman simply had a bee up his bonnet, and that this was merely a tycoon's tantrum over not getting the desired lollipop.

Hill's eyes veered back and forth as he followed the conversation. He started to speak then appeared to have second thoughts. In his employer's presence, he couldn't play cock of the walk.

"What do you think, Mr. Hill? Mr. Wildman said he wanted your input."

Hill hesitated.

"Yes, James. By all means."

His assistant avoided his gaze and fortified himself with a sip of sherry. He blotted his lips methodically. He sat erect.

"Very well, then. I think it's madness, sir. Worse still, it appears capricious. Once people hear of it – which they will if Miss Sullivan continues asking questions – I'm afraid ... I think some might start to speculate you're becoming ... dotty."

He sank back as though the reply had drained all his courage. He kept his eyes on the rug. I felt a mite of sympathy for the man.

Wildman didn't look pleased.

"And do you think I'm dotty, James?"

"No, sir. Of course not." The vigor with which Hill knocked back the rest of his sherry suggested his meek tone took some effort.

"No one knows who hired Miss Sullivan to make her inquiries," his employer reminded.

"It's far-fetched, thinking anyone would care if you found Draper," Hill said with surprising stubbornness.

"Maybe not," I said. "There's talk he had a partner."

Both men looked stunned.

Wildman recovered first. "Where did you hear this?"

"A little green parrot."

"Did it tell you a name?"

Wildman's voice warned he didn't like getting the run-around. Or maybe the flippancy. I shook my head.

"Perhaps I need to apologize, sir," Hill said stiffly. "It does seem strange, however, that I never heard so much as a whisper about a partner."

"It's not necessarily true," I said.

"However, it would make any coincidence about Draper's death even less likely." Wildman looked at me expectantly.

"If the police decide they're not interested, I'll continue the investigation," I said. "On one condition."

Wildman frowned. He was accustomed to setting conditions, not hearing them.

"What is it?"

"From now on both of you are truthful with me."

"Truthful!"

Once again I'd caught both off guard. Wildman looked angry, Hill indignant.

"Miss Sullivan, I assure you neither of us—"

"Neither of you bothered to tell me Charles Preston was dead when you gave me that list."

"It didn't occur.... I regret to say it had slipped my mind." Wildman redirected his gaze to the fire.

"I'm afraid I wasn't even aware of it." Hill lowered his head and rubbed at his temples.

"Yet Mr. Wildman relies on you to be up to date on people, deals, opportunities, gossip and rumors."

"Yes! Yes. I was remiss." His hands clamped his head.

"And the list of investors, which you compiled together, made no mention of Rachel Minsky."

Hill looked at me, flabbergasted. "Rachel Minsky! Where on earth did you–?"

"Rachel Minsky? That – that impertinent little Jewish woman whose relatives went to prison? Surely she couldn't afford an investment like Draper's! She – it's absurd!" Wildman sputtered.

Rachel Minsky had told me the truth about one thing: She didn't appear to be included in their social circle.

ELEVEN

I hadn't touched the sherry I'd been offered. Nevertheless, my brain felt slightly off-kilter as I drove home past trolleys letting off weary passengers and street lamps haloed by mist-laden darkness.

I'd gone to Wildman's thinking it was the end of a case. Instead, one with twists and complications which I hadn't yet had a chance to contemplate seemed to be opening before me. That was assuming my client knew what he was talking about when he said the police weren't going to be interested in Draper's death. If he did, I was going to be plenty mad. It would mean Wildman had an in somewhere up the ladder which ordinary people didn't have. I didn't like rich people having more pull than salesmen or waitresses.

As I came down the quiet street where Mrs. Z's two-story white house snuggled under a linden tree, I saw my favorite parking place was occupied by a car I didn't recognize. Probably a boyfriend calling on one of the girls. I parked on the other side of Mrs. Z's sidewalk and got out. A man stepped from the shadows, startling me so that I swore.

"Jesus, Connelly! What are you doing skulking around like a burglar?"

"Waiting to talk to you. Have you had supper?"

"No. Why?" I said warily.

We'd met up under a street lamp. By its yellowish glow I could tell from his coat that he wasn't in uniform.

"Because I have information on Draper. I reckon you have some too. I thought you might like to go somewhere and compare notes. What do you say? Share and share alike?"

It wasn't like any cop to offer to cough up information but I took about half a second deciding.

"Yeah. Sure. Okay."

With a grin I could see in the street lamp, he grabbed my hands.

"Let's see the crossed fingers."

I jerked away with guilt burning my skin. What made him think he'd catch me pulling a kid's trick? I'd only been crossing them mentally.

"Were you that fresh with girls back in Ireland?" I asked indignantly. "Catching hold of them whenever you took a notion?"

"Yeah, probably. Can't recall any of them objecting, either." He gave me a wink, completely unfazed. "So. Fancy a plate of stew or the like?"

"As long as I buy my own."

"If that's how you want it."

* * *

We went to a joint on Fifth that had been there since before the Indians. A long bar led from front to back, but we went through to a room on the right. It was raining again, midway to freezing, and the long windows in the brick wall facing the street let in plenty of chill. We settled ourselves at a table back by the fireplace instead.

"So." Connelly swirled his whiskey and water. "How likely do you think it is Draper was killed?"

The bluntness of it surprised me, as had his earlier offer to divulge information.

"You're the cop. You tell me."

"No way of knowing, at least not for sure. The back of his head had taken quite a knock."

"Before or after he went in the river?"

"There was water in his lungs, so he was alive when he went in. But it could be he was unconscious. If the poor soul came to at all he was too befuddled to save himself."

"Not that many manage to save themselves if they go in accidentally." A series of dams built after the big flood of 1913 tamed fluctuations in the Great Miami's water level. They also created patches of turbulence.

"I think Freeze would like to look at it closer. But nothing we've turned up gives good reason."

"And no one's even willing to implicate him in a crime." It was more statement than guess.

Connelly lounged back and rubbed a hand up the back of his hair.

"Right on the money. Only one fellow on that list of names you provided would even admit to Freeze that he'd been swindled by Draper. Freeze figures him for the same one who hired you."

I was silent a minute.

"Frank Keefe?"

He nodded, grinning.

"Nope."

"Shite." The grin faded.

It didn't surprise me that Wildman hadn't acknowledged his loss to Draper. He might be leery of looking guilty, but I suspected it had more to do with the reason he'd hired me: protecting his reputation.

"Freeze send you to see what you could pry out of me?"

"He did not."

"So why this invitation to chat?"

He crossed his arms on the table and leaned forward, so close I could feel the energy crackling from him.

"Because you're smart, Maggie, and you may know things we don't. And I know whatever you choose to tell me will be true. Festooned with malarkey around the edges, most likely, but somewhere there'll be a grain of truth."

I sipped some gin, as much to escape the heat he gave off as how well he assessed me.

"Freeze is okay," he said. "Has a poker up his backside, but he's good at his job. I know you two tangled some in the past, but now he appears to trust what he hears from you. More or less."

"'More or less'?"

He saluted me with his glass again. "As much as any sane man should."

I tried to hear the compliment about Freeze's opinion, but Connelly's amusement ruffled my feathers.

"Wouldn't hurt you having Freeze in your corner now and again," he said.

"And what do you get out of us exchanging tidbits?"

"The pleasure of your company, pretty Maggie." He winked. "And down the road, when there's a promotion slot comes empty, maybe I'll have earned Freeze's good opinion."

We paused while our meal was delivered.

"The man who hired me is convinced Draper was murdered," I said at length. "He thinks once I started hunting Draper, someone shut him up so he wouldn't spill something."

Connelly looked up sharply. "About what?"

I shook my head. "I have no idea, and I don't think my client has either. As near as I can tell, he's sore because he got hoodwinked. He thought if he found Draper it would show the business community that neither Draper nor anyone else could make a fool of him. I guess it was, in his eyes anyway, a matter of honor."

"Ah, yes. Honor. The lives that's cost."

Connelly's eyes were like stones, seeing far away. All the way to Ireland, perhaps. His voice was uncharacteristically harsh.

"He seems to believe the police will write Draper off as an accident," I said after a moment. "So he wants me to find out who killed him, and why. That hadn't come up when I talked to Freeze."

Connelly grunted. He seemed lost in thought.

"Freeze said you identified him by papers found in his wallet."

"Then had his secretary come in."

It hadn't occurred to me to talk to someone at Draper's office. Then again, I hadn't even worked my way through the list of names I'd been given before he was inconsiderate enough to turn up dead. I picked at a morsel of crust and made a decision.

"There's one thing I didn't tell Freeze this morning. One of the people I talked to said he had a partner."

"Draper had?" Connelly frowned. He gave it some thought. "Why would only one person mention it?"

I wondered too.

Rachel Minsky didn't have any reason I could think of to help me. She could have plenty of reasons to hinder me.

TWELVE

It irked me that I hadn't so much as thought of talking to Draper's secretary. When Wildman had told me the man had disappeared months earlier, I'd assumed Draper's office had been locked up, and that anyone who might have worked with him had moved on. That was sloppy on my part, and I didn't like it. Right after my oatmeal next morning, I set out to correct my mistake.

The frosted glass on the door to the office said Draper Development. When I tapped, the voice that invited me in sounded startled.

Draper's secretary was a circumspect looking blonde in her mid-thirties. The eyes that sized me up were tired and slightly apprehensive.

"I'm Maggie Sullivan," I said handing her a card. "I'm very sorry about your employer."

"Oh, mercy," she said, looking from the card to me. "Now what?"

Her manner was that of someone absolutely wretched. I smiled to reassure her.

"I know this must be awfully tough. Mr. Draper disappearing, and the scandal–"

"There wasn't any...." she began loyally, but she couldn't finish.

"– and then him drowning. Worse, with you having to deal with it all yourself, I expect." With the cops asking her to identify the body, I had a good guess the last part was true. She didn't contradict me. "I won't bother you much," I assured. "It's just that before Mr. Draper died, someone hired me to find him. Since I couldn't do that, I thought maybe I could at least learn a little more about him disappearing."

She shook her head curtly, not to dismiss me, but because she was fighting tears. Fumbling in her pocket she brought out a hanky. It had a violet embroidered on one corner. She dabbed at her eyes.

"One of the men he owed money." Her voice was tight. "That's who wanted to find him, I suppose. I'm sorry. There's nothing I can tell you. He always treated me very well...." Her voice cracked. "He – people liked him. No one ever appeared dissatisfied with any of their business dealings. And then one day he – he just didn't come in–"

The crack in her voice became a break and she sobbed. She hadn't offered me a chair, but I sat down anyway. I'd been softening her up when I offered sympathy about her being left on her own to deal with Draper's mess. Now I saw the strain she'd been under and figured she deserved a shoulder to cry on. I guessed that yesterday had been a nightmare for her, but as her sobs wound down and she rested her elbows on the desk as if exhausted, I recognized the entire interval since Draper took off had taken a toll.

"I'm so sorry," she said at last. "I managed to hold myself together yesterday when the police were here asking questions. Even when they asked me to – to look at the body. I'd never had to do something like that. Well, when my husband died, of course, and that was awful, too, but he'd been ill...." A few remaining tears welled up. She was too tired to fight them.

"You're not exactly needed to type any letters or take dictation," I said, getting up. "Why don't we go somewhere and get a cup of tea?"

"Oh.... Yes. I could do with that. But there's a hotplate in that little closet. I can make–"

"You sit still. I'll do it." I patted her shoulder.

It took a while for the water to heat, but I figured she could do with some time to compose herself. When I brought out the tea she was powdering her nose.

"I think everything must have caught up with me," she apologized. "The – the enormity of it. I'm sorry Mr. Draper's dead, of course I am. But I'm afraid I was having a wallow in self-pity, too. With him gone, with it definite now, I-I'm out of a job. And it's not just me to think of. I have a son."

Setting her tea down, she dabbed at her eyes again. This handkerchief was fresh, with no embroidery.

"How long had you worked for Draper?" I asked.

"Ten years. Almost since he started his business." She managed a smile. "I'm Cecilia, by the way. Cecilia Perkins."

"You were pretty loyal, sticking around for going on four months after your boss went missing." Something nudged me. "How'd you manage to keep this office open? Who paid the rent and such?"

"Oh.... Mr. Draper. He'd paid ahead."

Cecilia Perkins studied her teacup. For the first time I suspected she was lying to me.

"Three months in advance?" I said slowly.

She bit her lip.

"Doesn't seem like much of a way to run a business, tying up that much money when it could be invested – or might even be needed."

When she raised her eyes, they were pleading.

"Mr. Draper had paid in advance, but only for two months. I thought – hoped, really – that it meant he'd be coming back. When men started showing up demanding to see him – angry men – I knew there was some kind of mess. I thought maybe he'd just gone somewhere until he could straighten it out."

It seemed optimistic, but when you're desperate you can believe a lot of things.

"And after two months?" I asked.

She picked her hanky up again, but instead of dabbing her eyes she held it tightly.

"I paid it. I used one of his checks. I know it was wrong, but I'd started to realize I'd have to find a new job. I wanted to buy some time."

"So you forged his signature on blank checks he kept on hand to pay bills?"

"No!" For the first time since I'd come in, a touch of color reached her cheeks. "I didn't forge anything! See? Look." With jerky movements she opened a drawer and took out a checkbook and pushed it toward me. The top three checks in the pad held Draper's signature.

"Mr. Draper didn't like having to sign things. Actually, it was having to undo his cufflink that he didn't like. He was always fretting he'd get ink on his cuff. He liked to sign all his correspondence at once, every morning. And every few weeks he'd sign a batch of checks for me to fill in for the usual expenses. Supplies, donations to charity, dues for this and that, even cash when he didn't want to go to the bank."

The fact that Draper had paid in advance did suggest he'd intended on coming back. Or maybe he'd only wanted to make it appear that way while the trail grew cold. Either way, for the first time I was actually getting some cards to shuffle to find an answer to this case.

"What about your salary?" I asked. "Did you write checks for that too?"

She nodded miserably.

"Two rather large ones. But only for what I'd be owed. You can check the ledger. I suppose – I suppose it was stealing all the same. But please, *please* don't tell the police! My little boy is ... he's not right. He'll never learn like other children, or-or talk very well. I pay a woman to stay with him, and she's wonderful, but if I don't have a job ... and if I went to jail–"

"I'm not looking to get you in any trouble with the police. As far as I'm concerned, you were a loyal secretary, keeping things going."

I heard her sigh of relief. She took a sip of tea. The cup rattled.

"I have been looking," she said. "For a job, I mean. Answering advertisements. Sending out letters. I started as soon as I realized it was ridiculous to think things would change. But you know what times are like. So many need jobs. And without an employer I have no letter of reference, and when someone who might hire me realizes I worked for a crook–"

"No one's likely to know that unless you tell them. No one knows but the men your boss swindled, and none of them want it known they fell for his bait."

She digested it for a moment.

"Are you saying the police don't know what he did?"

"They know, but since no one lodged a complaint, they can't do anything. Did he have any relatives?"

"A sister in Cleveland. They weren't very close."

"Girlfriend?"

"No, I don't think so. I'm sure he didn't." She smiled sadly. "I had hopes last spring. A woman called him here several times. She never gave her name, but he always seemed happy after they talked."

"You've no idea who she was?"

"I'm afraid not. She had the loveliest voice, though. So soft. I didn't even notice when the calls stopped. They just did, at some point."

I had more questions she might have answers to, but I'd already put her through plenty. She'd been scared to death about what she'd done, left in a rotten spot and toughing it out on her own. Right now she was probably feeling the utter exhaustion that hits after you've survived an ordeal and can finally let down. I'd get more from her in the long run if I went easy now.

"You going to be okay?" I asked. "Here by yourself?"

She nodded, looking grateful.

"I'll start closing things down here as best I can, I guess. Call the firm that owns the building and tell them we won't be needing the space. Things like that."

"Okay if I stop by tomorrow to see how you're doing? I know a couple of people who can use a good secretary now and again. I'll ask around."

"That's awfully kind. Thank you."

Liking somebody's not the same as trusting them. Not when I'm working at least. I went down the hall and around a corner to where I had a view of Draper's office as well as the elevator. I'd give it half an hour, just in case Cecilia Perkins came tearing out to report to someone, or someone, alerted by a frantic phone call, stepped off the elevator and went in to see her.

THIRTEEN

No one came or went to cast any doubts on Cecilia Perkins' innocence in the con game that had mucked up her life. As far as I could tell it had hurt her more than the men who'd been swindled, except for maybe the one who'd killed himself. Heading outside, I decided to walk along the river while I thought over what I'd learned these last few days.

The Great Miami had brought the first settlers straggling up from Cincinnati, and like most river towns, the city had grown up along it. Most of downtown nestled cozily in the crook of its arm. Small tributaries went south and sharply north. It always seemed peaceful to me, but the year before I was born a flood had gobbled along it swallowing buildings and people and horses.

It wasn't a big enough river to carry barge traffic. No landings or warehouses lined its shores. Instead, a grassy verge lined both sides. This time of year the grass wasn't green, but it was peaceful for walking and thinking all the same, with the grand Masonic Hall and the Art Institute rearing up on their respective corners across the way, and Deeds Park whispering of summertime pleasures.

Unfortunately, it proved cold as the dickens today. Away from the shelter of buildings the wind was damp and raw. In about five minutes I abandoned my stroll in favor of hot-footing it to the library. I wanted to do some digging there anyway. I could think without freezing.

Once I'd settled myself and my fingers had thawed, I got out my steno pad and tapped my teeth with a pencil. Then I started to list all the people who might have been motivated to kill Harold Draper. All the men he'd swindled, obviously. Scratch off the one who had hung himself. Check that one really had been out of town as his office said. Add Cecilia Perkins? I didn't think so, but I listed her anyway. Rachel Minsky? She'd gotten her money back, but she might hold a grudge. And Draper's partner. If he existed.

Which ones were capable of bashing a man on the back of the head and throwing him in the river?

I thought about it and pecked out a little tune on the table until a man the next table over cleared his throat and glared.

Ferris Wildman, the man who'd hired me, could most likely kill someone. He planned and was sure of himself and there were traces of ruthlessness in him. But I didn't figure him for the kind who'd bash his victim in the back of the head. He'd want them facing him, knowing he did it. Frank Keefe had made no bones about wanting to get his hands on Draper. His breezy openness might be a mask. Ulysses Smith? I didn't think so, although he alone showed moral outrage at Draper's greed leading to another man's suicide. Arthur Buckingham might bore someone to death, but I couldn't imagine anything beyond that. Rachel Minsky? Yes, I thought, remembering the impenetrable black pools that were her eyes. She probably had it in her to kill.

That left Cecilia Perkins, faithful secretary. Maybe she'd had an affair with Draper and things had gone sour, but I couldn't see her killing him, even in a moment of passion. Last of all, there was Draper's mythical partner. If he – or she – was real, that's where I'd put my money.

The truth was, just about anyone might be capable of murder, given the right circumstances. Even a nun or two

I'd known. Since I was making no progress in that direction, I turned toward the task that had brought me here.

An hour or so later, skimming particular columns and pages in the city's various newspapers, I'd unearthed information I thought might help me. Wildman's sister, Dorothy Tarkington, had gotten her name in the paper twice in the last six months for drunken driving. That suggested she might have gotten off a few other times because of her brother's pull. She'd also been photographed at a society shindig along with her husband. His name was Vern and he owned an auto dealership on North Main. I looked at my watch. Time to pay them a visit.

* * *

Dorothy Tarkington lived far enough from downtown for her address to be ritzy, but probably not as ritzy as she'd like, given the things she'd shouted the night I'd met her. A driveway on one side led to a three-car garage in back. I parked on the street instead. My breath made puffs in the air as I went up the walk. It was lunchtime, a highly improper time for someone to show up uninvited, but I figured women like Wildman's sister slept late and lunched late. With someone who'd waved a gun in my face and been falling-down drunk, I wasn't too concerned about social niceties.

A dark-skinned maid in a starched apron opened the door.

"Tell Mrs. Tarkington I've come to see her," I said offering my card.

She told me to step in and hurried upstairs. I heard voices, one of them raised. The maid hurried back.

"Miz Tarkington says she doesn't have time and would you please leave."

I doubted Dorothy Tarkington had said 'please'. I smiled.

"Perhaps she'll find a minute or two if you tell her she can talk to me or the cops."

The maid's eyes wearied with the dread of one who knew her own fate hinged on her employer's. She turned and started up again, but before she'd climbed half a dozen stairs, Dorothy herself came storming down.

"What the hell do you mean, the police? How dare you threaten me? Who the hell are you?"

"Hello, Mrs. Tarkington." I gave her a big smile. "How nice to see you again."

She came to a halt one step up from me, staring blankly. She pushed back a wave of blonde hair. The maid retreated.

Attempting nonchalance, Dorothy came down the last step and brushed past me.

"You were at my brother's." She spoke tersely, moving toward a room on the right. "If you're here after money – thinking of suing – the joke's on you."

She had some recollection what had happened, then. The state she'd been in, it surprised me. I followed her into a sitting room, cream walls enclosing royal blue upholstered pieces with modern lines.

"I'm not after money."

Dipping into a silver cigarette box, she lighted up and turned to face me, arms crossed defiantly.

"I get it now. The bastard's hired a private detective to spy on me."

"Wrong. It has nothing to do with you. I just want to ask you some questions."

"About what?" She tossed her head.

"Your brother."

She snorted. "You heard what I said the other night. You know what I think of him."

Dorothy looked better sober. Her makeup was fresh and her face was made interesting by a trace of her brother's self-certainty. I wondered how late in the day her good looks lasted.

"What I want to know is who else has differences with him? Who might have it in for him?"

"How would I know?" She waved a hand in disinterest. "Plenty of people. He acts like he's God Almighty."

"I think it has to do with a man named Harold Draper?"

"Who? I don't know anyone by that name."

She turned, all at once in search of an ashtray. The question had made her nervous.

"Harold Draper. He had some business dealings with your brother."

"I never heard of him. I don't know anything about my brother's business! He thinks I'm an idiot!" Her voice had grown shrill.

"Draper made a fool of him. And of some other men."

"Look, I'm busy–"

"What's going on? Juniemay came in saying...."

I waggled my fingers in friendly greeting. A scowling man halted halfway through the door.

"Hello, my name's Maggie Sullivan. You must be Vern."

For several seconds he didn't know what to say. I wondered briefly if he was somebody else, caught in the act of being cozy with Dorothy. But I knew who he was from the photograph in the newspaper. Wavy black hair, slender and stylishly dressed. He started toward me, trying to pull off a threatening look, which is easier when your shoulders aren't built by a tailor.

"How dare you push your way in here and bully my wife?"

"Vern–"

"She's not well."

"Oh, dry up, Vern. There's nothing wrong with me." Dorothy crushed her half-smoked cigarette with jerky movements. "She just had some questions about some man. Somebody she says did business with Ferris."

"Harold Draper," I supplied helpfully.

"I told her we'd – I'd never heard of him."

Vern gave her a glare.

"I don't recognize the name either. Now if you'll excuse us–"

"They had some financial dealings that didn't turn out very well."

"I'm the last person Ferris would discuss business with," Vern said sharply. "We don't care much for each other."

"Gee, I'll bet you sell a lot of cars when you turn on the charm like that," I said.

He reddened. Dorothy crossed her arms again and looked like she wanted to pace.

"Don't worry," I said. "I can see myself out."

One of them was lying to me.

Or both.

FOURTEEN

I'd learned a couple of things in the course of the morning. I just wasn't sure where they fit in this particular jigsaw puzzle. Lunchtime having come and gone, my stomach and brain ganged up to suggest I might think better if I went to the Arcade.

The soaring building occupied most of a city block smack in the center of town. Its grand glass dome let in light even on cloudy days like this one. Going to the Arcade meant you didn't have to wait for your food. At one end the ground floor was thick with stalls selling fresh fish and chops waiting for dinnertime skillets, but the center was populated by ones offering things that were ready to eat. Sausage rolls, cheeses and slices of ham were some that beckoned.

I went for liverwurst on a crusty roll and added a sweet pickle. When I'd settled on a bench and taken a couple of bites I started to think about my visit to Dorothy and Vern. He'd looked daggers at her when she made that slip about neither of them knowing Draper. It had raised the embarrassing question of how she could claim her husband wasn't acquainted with someone she denied even hearing of, and Vern realized it. They were hiding something. Either they were in cahoots or one was covering for the other.

Wildman had dismissed any suggestion that either of them could be connected to the swindle or to the ramming of his car. I wasn't so sure. I wanted to find out more about both of them. It reminded me I'd neglected to call Tilly Sweeny, the gossip columnist on Jenkins' paper.

Stretching my legs, I looked up past the shops and offices that ringed the second floor of the Arcade. I studied the turkeys decorating the base of each metal arm that supported the glass of the dome. Their tails were fanned and every time I saw them I wondered why the architect had chosen turkeys instead of eagles or falcons or maybe peacocks. I didn't have any answers there either.

Bringing thoughts and vision back to earth, I stopped midway through a chew.

Boike?

Yes, I was sure it was Lieutenant Freeze's underling that I'd just glimpsed. He'd turned away now, chatting with a butcher clear to the other side from where I sat. The blocky build was right, though. And I thought I recognized the suit. Something about his presence here, strolling along as if he had all the time in the world, made me wary.

Surely he wasn't following me. Mick Connelly had said Freeze trusted me, so why would he have one of his men keep tabs on me? The possibility that popped up in answer made my blood simmer. Could Freeze have a tail on me to find out who'd hired me?

"Your face is going to freeze like that, Mags. Better stop frowning."

The smell of potato chips hot from the fryer engulfed me. Jenkins slid onto the bench, already chomping on one from the paper cone in his hand. Ex-governor Cox's newsmill where he worked was out the door by the butcher section and across the street. I figured he was headed back from some assignment.

"Guy you wanted me to find out about is dead," he said.

"Yep."

"Bashed on the back of the head."

"Yep."

His eyes crept toward me a fraction while the rest of him stared ahead at the stands and the people.

"By person or persons unknown," he said.

"Nice try, Jenkins, but that's not how I hear it."

His breath of vexation assured me he'd heard the police were closing the case, and was hoping he knew something I didn't.

"So," I said stretching my legs and crossing my ankles. "You now owe me double. Once for not delivering the goods on Draper and once for Herman of Troy."

He winced. His wife's cousin had been even duller than I remembered when the four of us went out Saturday night. Worse still, toward the end of the evening, he'd attempted to hold my hand.

"In fact, you should owe me double for him alone."

Jenkins offered the cone of chips. I shook my head. I like my spuds mashed, or boiled in the jacket. He munched for a few seconds.

"You still interested in talking to Tilly Sweeny?" His voice was resigned.

"Yes, but I keep forgetting to call her."

"I could spare you that ordeal at least. I might still owe you, but it ought to earn me something on the account book. Tilly's company makes Cousin Herman look good in comparison. It may be beneath me, but I can sniff out society dirt as well as she can."

Behind the wire rims of his spectacles his eyes were earnest. With the light from the dome above us brightening his curls, all he lacked was a harp and some wings to make him the picture of innocence. Which was why I suddenly realized he was trying to fox me.

Jenkins' antennae were always alert for something that would land him a newsworthy photograph before the competition even caught wind of it. He knew as well as I did that Draper's death looked suspicious, and he had good instincts. He'd put two and two together and guessed, correctly, that my earlier interest in the gossip columnist somehow related to Draper.

This was going to be fun.

"I don't know," I said dubiously. "There may not be anything to it. It's just that on another matter I'm looking into, I've heard rumors the man it concerns might be having an affair with some socialite who parties more than she should."

"Doesn't that include all of them? I didn't think you did divorce work," Jenkins said, losing interest.

"It's not a divorce. It's a business matter. His partners are concerned it might be ... detrimental to their concerns."

"Detrimental? How big a business we talking?"

His interest was back. I gave him a coy smile. I loved Jenkins like a brother. Better than the one I'd had – and might still have somewhere. That didn't mean I had any qualms about putting one over on him. He'd been baiting a hook for me. Instead, with luck, he'd bite into mine.

"Not much to go on," he groused.

I was about to answer when a man with his nose in *The Saturday Evening Post* caught my eye. Boike. I'd been right, then.

"Mags? You okay?"

As Jenkins started to follow the line of my gaze I pressed my hand to my mid-section.

"Just some gas. Pardon me. What were you saying?"

"You need to give me more to go on. Kind of business, maybe?"

"I can't–"

"Come on, Mags. I can't help if I don't know *something*."

I couldn't play wide-eyed half as well as Jenkins could, so I shrugged.

"If I knew any more I could do it myself. All I've heard is she's a real boozer and her brother made millions in some sort of business."

"Gee, that narrows it down," he said in disgust. He glanced at his watch. "Have to go."

I gave him enough time to settle his camera. Boike was still reading.

"Then again, the men who're all in a tizzy thinking it could bring down their business could have it wrong. Maybe the guy they're worried about's just seeing some showgirl."

I caught the slight pause as Jenkins straightened a strap, and knew his ears had pricked. My bit of backpedaling, coupled with the vagueness of my information, would make him dig like crazy.

* * *

As soon as Jenkins disappeared toward Ludlow, I got up and sauntered toward the opposite entrance. After eight steps or so I did a basketball pivot too quickly for Boike to find cover. Pivoting again, I hooked my arm through his.

"Detective Boike. Fancy seeing you here. Enjoying yourself? Catching up on your reading?" He was red as a beet and attempting to free himself. "Relax. I won't tell your girlfriend how cozy we got." Releasing his arm, I stood arms akimbo and we eyed each other.

"That the best you can do when you're tailing somebody? A magazine?"

"I thought about putting on an apron and standing at one of the meat counters. I was afraid all that blood might make me faint."

I wondered if he was making a joke. He hadn't cracked a smile.

"Mind telling me why you're keeping tabs on me?"

Shifting uncomfortably, Boike looked over my head.

"Lieutenant didn't like it how that guy Draper ended up dead right after you started hunting him. He figured if it wasn't an accident, whoever was responsible might decide they wanted you out of the picture too."

"You're protection?" I wasn't sure I believed it.

He shrugged. "Just until he needs me on something else."

"Hey, I'm as fluttery as if he'd sent roses. Thanks all the same, but I manage fine on my own."

"Guess you do at that." He considered some. "One day your luck could run out."

"Luck!" I opened my mouth to argue, then thought better of it. There had been a time or two when it might have been mostly luck that saved my skin.

"I appreciate it – and I'm not saying that to be smart." I started to walk toward the Main Street entrance, with Boike in step. "I don't need a baby-sitter. Clients wouldn't go for it. If you or anyone on the force else tries to follow me, I'm going to spot you, and when I do, I'm going to give you a big, fat smooch – even if it's Freeze himself."

We stepped out into cold drizzle that by evening would turn into sleet. Boike looked indecisively from me to a skinny three-storey gingerbread building across the street. It was Market House, where the chief of police, the detective squad and the evidence boys were based.

"Yeah, okay." He didn't sound happy.

We crossed the street together and he disappeared into the mouth of the staircase into Market House. After I'd gone a couple of blocks I looked back to make sure he hadn't come out a side door. The damp in the air created the kind of cold that seeps through clothing. I was glad when I reached my own building, and looking forward to putting my toes on the radiator.

I unlocked my office and stepped through the door. I was reaching for the light switch when the door slammed shut behind me.

"Don't bother taking off your coat," said a voice. "We're going for a ride."

FIFTEEN

"Turn around slowly and don't make any sudden moves," the voice ordered.

I thought I recognized the voice. When I obeyed I saw I was right.

Rachel Minsky sat in one of the visitor chairs against the wall. Her legs were crossed. The top one swung angrily. On the other side of the door a sharp-featured man lounged casually back with one hand tucked inside his coat.

"I helped you," said Rachel. "Answered your questions. Told you things you didn't know. And this is the thanks I get? You sic the cops on me?"

"I didn't sic them on you. They had names. They had them when they dropped in on me." It was sort of a fine point that they hadn't had hers yet at that point. Just now I wasn't feeling very friendly toward Rachel. I tilted my head toward the guy on the wall. "You always travel with a bodyguard? Nice touch."

"Pearlie?" Her lips made their secretive line that suggested a smile. "He's my boyfriend."

"Gee, I didn't realize this was a social call. I'm flattered. Mind if I sit down for a minute? Catch my breath?"

"And take a gun out of a drawer? You'll have plenty of time to sit on that drive I mentioned."

She got to her feet. A fluffy fur coat draped her shoulders. It was nearly as dark as her hair, beaver maybe. She shrugged into it without taking her eyes off me.

Pearlie and I were measuring each other. He was all edges: thin face, slim build, narrow feet. He reminded me of a well-honed knife, and I figured he could do just as much damage.

"Pearlie will enjoy your company more if you let him take a peek in your purse. Loud noises startle him."

I offered it to him. "Be my guest."

A woman wouldn't settle for only one lipstick. I saw no reason to settle for only one gun. I kept my automatic in the car as a backup and the Smith & Wesson, which I liked better, at the office. It wasn't in a drawer, precisely because I'd planned against visits like this, but it wasn't where I could get to it, either, unless I sat down. Oddly, I wasn't especially worried just now. Something told me Rachel was keener to show off her power than she was to harm me.

"Be sure to lock up," she said, marching ahead of us like a countess. It irked me more than anything else that they'd picked my lock. "We took an opportunity to note the back stairs," she said turning toward it. "We'll go out that way."

The only other office we passed going that direction was a domestic employment firm that kept its door closed. Going the front way would have taken us past an accountant's place and the long glass window of a sock wholesaler, where my sort-of-friend Evelyn worked and her nosy mother-in-law noted every coming and going but wouldn't have batted an eyelash if I'd been murdered in front of her.

"I like going places lots more when I'm invited," I said as we reached my building's small lobby. "If I start to kick up a stink, somebody's sure to come to my aid."

"Rachel wouldn't like that," Pearlie said tightening his grip on my arm as the two of them marched me between them. It was the first time I'd heard him speak; the first chance I'd had to glimpse the dazzling teeth that apparently gave him his nickname.

'Rachel'? Jesus, maybe he really was her boyfriend.

I couldn't judge yet how likely it was someone would get hurt if I started yelling. Besides, I was curious. A few times over the years since I'd hung out my shingle I'd had tough guys drag me somewhere to work me over a little and give me a warning. This didn't have that feel. I let them put me into the big black Buick I'd noticed outside Minsky Builders. The lock on the back seat passenger side had been welded down. Rachel motioned me in and then slid in beside me. Pearlie went up front to drive.

That part was pretty much what I'd expected. Except for the welded lock.

* * *

It wasn't the sort of ride where you make small talk. They hadn't blindfolded me or knocked me out, so I'd been on worse rides. We went south and turned off Patterson, heading west across the river. Then we followed a paved road which after three or four miles turned into gravel. When the road petered out, a large open field stretched before us.

Pearlie stopped the Buick. He came back and opened the door for Rachel. He didn't offer a hand to help her out. Her air of bottled-up energy made me think she might find waiting on such niceties a waste of time. She looked back at me.

"Time to enjoy the view."

I got out slowly, trying to figure what this was about. The place was out of the way, but not isolated enough to rough someone up in mid-afternoon unless you were crazy. It occurred to me there was at least a hint of craziness, or something like it, in Rachel Minsky.

"This is where Draper was going to build his big project," she said when we'd walked a few yards. Two big factories. Warehouses. Supposedly."

She'd tucked her hands inside the pockets of the fur coat swaddling her. Her eyes were narrowed on our surroundings. She didn't say anything else.

Neither did I.

Neither did Pearlie.

For a good five minutes the three of us engaged in spirited non-conversation. I studied the bare land I saw. A section looked as though it might have been graded, ready for building. Then again, it might have been plowed. I was a city girl. I saw a barn in the distance.

"Well?" Rachel asked at last. "What strikes you about it?"

The only thing that came to mind was how far it would be for the workers. Five different trolley companies operated routes in Dayton, and I'd ridden every last route, either with my dad or during my first year in business when I hadn't yet scraped together enough to buy a used car. Unless they'd built it the last couple years, not one of those routes came out here.

"Going to be awfully rough on the men who work in the factories," I said. "Forty-five minutes to walk from the nearest trolley line with their lunch buckets, same at the end of the day when they're dead tired."

Rachel, her eyes closing, gave the same pleased little nod a teacher gives when a student answers a difficult question.

"Exactly. And before that, men building the whole thing would need to do the same toting their tools. I'm in the construction business. I know how to look at a site. I know what you have to consider to bid on a project, to estimate expenses. If you want good workers, on some jobs you need to cover some of their transportation.

"Draper had been vague on where Champion Works would be located. He gave an address, but when a street's not mapped, that's not much help. After I pressed him a couple of times, he finally brought me out to see it. Maybe afraid I was getting suspicious." Her chin raised. "He probably thought I'd have no idea what I was seeing."

"And when you did?" The wind had picked up. It was hard to keep my teeth from chattering.

"I asked how the workers would get here. He sat there and didn't say anything for a minute. Then he told me there was a trolley line. When I got back, I checked. There wasn't. I called him and told him I wanted my money back or I'd tell the other investors."

The wind that was chilling me had whipped colors into her cheeks. She turned to me with triumph glinting in her eyes.

"Let's get back in the car."

SIXTEEN

"We have to make a stop on the way back. Check on a job. Cooling my heels in your office put me behind schedule." Rachel gave me an accusing look.

"Gee, making appointments prevents a lot of problems like that."

She ignored me.

Her construction site was also southwest of the city, but in Van Buren Township. By the looks of its skeleton the building going up there was going to be four stories and decent size. Pearlie parked like before, only this time there were some pickups and one bigger truck to keep him company. There were also plenty of workmen braving what had now become a steady drizzle. Come the end of the day, they'd have less than a ten minute walk to the nearest trolley.

"Going to be offices," Rachel said with a nod. "Come on. You might learn a thing or two."

Pearlie closed the door after us, then got behind the wheel again where he opened a dime novel. Pearlie had a cushy job.

"Rain's kind of hard on a nice coat like that, isn't it?" I could see small beads of moisture attaching themselves to the tips of the fur.

Rachel slanted a look.

"Ever hear an animal complaining its hide shrank?"

What she thought I might learn watching the activity around me was anyone's guess. A man who seemed to be the boss came over and took off his cap and they conferred. Some kind of beams were arriving tomorrow. Something else was delayed. If the rain got worse he'd have to send the men home early.

Rachel moved on, with me trailing. She stopped to ask one of the workmen if his new baby had arrived. The wind bit in harder here than at the last place. I started to shiver again. Rachel said something to the foreman, who tossed down a plank. She clicked briskly along it to survey something he pointed out above her head. I waited and watched. It was clear she'd navigated muddy sites like this before. Her high-heeled shoes didn't waver, let alone veer off the plank, as she made her way back.

"You're cold," she observed, stepping off to join me on firmer surface not yet turned to goo by countless comings and goings.

I shrugged. "It's that kind of weather."

She turned, fixing onyx eyes on the building rising in steel and timber instead of on me.

"I don't lie. You needed to see that."

I let the lie part go for a minute and nodded. "You know what you're doing."

"Yes."

She was quiet awhile, letting it sink in or maybe just contemplating her building. She spoke abruptly.

"I've put in my appearance here – made sure everything's moving along and the boys are keeping their noses to the grindstone. Let's head back."

Her quickness of movement caught me off guard. I trotted a couple of steps to overtake her.

"Don't some of the workmen resent it, their wives darning a sweater the umpteenth time while you show up wearing furs?"

"I sign their paychecks. No reason I should freeze my bottom for them as well." She gave me the once over.

"I know a furrier who'd make you a good deal on something warmer than what you're wearing."

"This coat does just dandy."

She looked amused.

"You figure any of the other investors went to see that site of Draper's?" I asked when we were back in the car.

She shook her head. "It looked okay on paper. Three other lots in the area had been sold for business. Platted out. The thing is..." she turned to face me. "...no one had applied for building permits."

"You think those lots were swindles?"

"Probably not. Just this lousy Depression. But it made Draper's deal look less rosy; made me uneasy enough that I wanted to see it."

We rode in silence. I was glad to have time to think.

"Did Draper's partner know he'd taken you to see the site?" I asked at last.

Rachel shrugged, her expression suggesting her thoughts were elsewhere. "Probably."

"And you have no idea who that partner might have been?"

Now I had her attention.

"Same answer as last time – no," she said tartly. Her lips pursed and she regarded me with speculation. "But I know somebody who might be able to find out. If you're interested."

What was she up to? I couldn't figure it.

"Yeah," I said. "I am."

Pearlie pulled into a space another car was conveniently vacating in front of my building. He came around and opened the rear door. Rachel had gotten in first coming back from the building site, which maybe meant she'd displayed all the power she needed to, or maybe that she'd found out I didn't scare easily. When I'd stepped out, I leaned back in.

"Kind of hard to take you seriously when you say you don't lie. What about that goose chase you sent me on, telling me a nightclub owner who can't even keep his bills paid on time invested with Draper?"

"I already told you, I was testing you."

"What about Draper having a partner? Is that a lie too?"

"No." She was lighting a cigarette. She jutted her chin up and exhaled and grinned through the smoke. "But then if it was, that's what I'd say, isn't it?"

SEVENTEEN

I didn't trust Rachel Minsky much farther than I could spit. For what remained of the afternoon I thought about her claim that someone else had been in league with Draper. The more I considered it, the more it made sense. It would explain a couple of things, the main one being why someone might kill him once they found out I was trying to find him. The fact no one else had mentioned a partner was odd, but odd didn't necessarily mean unlikely.

I still was thinking about it when I came out of Mrs. Z's the next morning and found her overfed orange tomcat on the hood of my DeSoto, yowling and hissing. A stray dog so starved its ribs showed stood barking up at him. The cat excelled at escaping Mrs. Z's apartment and sinking his teeth into every passing female leg, so I was on the dog's side. If I got in the car and drove away, the cat would slide off after a yard or two, the pooch might get a good meal, and everyone at Mrs. Z's would dance a jig of joy.

Everyone but Mrs. Z. She'd cry her eyes out.

Muttering darkly, I trudged back up the walk.

"Oh, Margaret! Of course I'll get you a gunny sack," my landlady said when I went back inside and explained what I needed. "Bless your heart, you're the only one of the girls who seems to give a fig about my poor Butterball."

Jolene, whose job as a cigarette girl meant she had her days free, came down the stairs with a kerchief covering her blonde curls. A laundry bag under her arm indicated where she was headed.

"Something going on?" she asked watching Mrs. Z's hurried retreat toward the kitchen.

I told her.

Jolene leaned toward me, lowering her voice.

"I've got a better plan. Let's lift the dog up so he can make short work of that nasty puss."

* * *

By the time I got to the office, I was later than usual. A bandage hid a gouge inflicted by the furiously struggling Butterball, and I was trying hard to remember how crazy I'd been about the pet cats I'd had when I was a kid. On the bright side, no one was waiting to ambush me when I opened the door.

I went through my mail, relieved I could pay the phone bill that had arrived. I made a phone call or two. Finally I sat and considered the new paths opened to exploration if I embraced the idea someone might have assisted Draper in his swindle.

The place to start was narrowing in on who that might be. If it was someone I'd never heard of, any clever conclusions I reached would be futile. Therefore I'd stick to the theory it was one of the people I'd met.

Yesterday I'd made a list of all the people who might want to kill Draper. The idea of a partner would mean different motivation, though. Getting rid of Draper insured he couldn't break and reveal your part in things. It might also mean you could get all the money instead of a split.

Unfortunately, going in that direction added names to my list instead of shortening it. More people would kill for money than out of anger. That meant all the men Draper had swindled were once again possibilities, except

Ferris Wildman unless he'd hired me for his own twisted amusement, which I thought unlikely. It also meant adding Cecilia Perkins to the list of suspects. Who'd be better equipped to work with Draper than his own secretary, who already knew his habits and who, by her own admission, needed money?

Oddly enough, I was willing to eliminate Rachel Minsky this round. She might be capable of killing, but I didn't think she'd do it for money. She was proud of what she could do, and of making her way on her own terms. Moreover, I couldn't see her playing second fiddle to someone else.

I also had some new possibilities since this time yesterday.

First there was Wildman's sister, Dorothy. I couldn't see her killing someone, at least not when she was sober. I was fairly certain I didn't agree with her brother's assessment that she was a scatterbrain, but she probably didn't have patience enough to plan a murder. Given how often she apparently went on a toot, I couldn't see anyone trusting her to help pull off a swindle either. Or anything else demanding secrecy, for that matter. She'd recognized Draper's name, though. Her husband had been angry when her very denial made it obvious.

Which brought me to Vern, a dandy new candidate in my opinion. His concern for his wife yesterday had been a good deal less convincing than his irritation. Still, that could result from extricating her from countless scrapes through the years. Wildman had referred to him as a spendthrift, which if true meant he might not be particular how he came by money. Vern needed a closer look.

And maybe I should add James C. Hill to the list as well, though it seemed like a stretch. He seemed to revel in the status bestowed by being Wildman's adviser, and as fussy as he was, I couldn't see him trying anything as messy as bashing someone on the head. All the same, he understood the ins and outs of investment deals better than most. Maybe I'd start there; pay him a little visit. I needed some information he could give me anyway.

Rachel Minsky's implication that my coat wasn't up to snuff had rubbed me the wrong way. It was only a couple years old, and good wool even if it wasn't the finest. The coat did look drab, though, so that morning I'd decided to break out the sky blue muffler Billy's wife had knitted me for Christmas. Blending in was a virtue in my line of work, but I could always leave it behind when I didn't want to be noticed. Decked out in the scarf and a perky blue hat, I set out for the Hulman Building feeling just about as fashionable as a woman in fur.

* * *

"I'm sorry, Mr. Hill has a very busy schedule this morning," Hill's secretary reported dutifully as she replaced the phone with which she'd announced me. "He says he could possibly fit you in this afternoon if you'd care to leave a message telling him what it concerns."

"Perhaps you could ask him if he'd rather I called Mr. Wildman directly," I suggested.

She complied while staring at me as if I'd developed a case of rabies. She hung up hastily.

"This way."

Hill stood at his desk consulting his pocket watch as I entered.

"I can spare you five minutes. No more," he said crossly. "I'll do what I can to assist you with this ... quest of Mr. Wildman's, but please bear in mind I have other responsibilities which Mr. Wildman himself would tell you take priority. I assure you he wouldn't be pleased if you bothered him with your questions. There are proper channels for reaching men in his position. I am that channel."

The paperwork spread on his desk confirmed his busyness, but his pompousness grated on me. He hadn't invited me to sit down, so I did.

"Lovely day, isn't it?" I settled back, nodding at the cart holding tickertape loops that sat beside his desk. "Looks like you got your standards on time. And you need to report to Mr. Wildman by eleven, as I recall.

"Now here's how my channels work, Mr. Hill. I tell you what I want, and the sooner I get it, the sooner I'm out of your hair and you get back to those priorities."

He stared at me in disbelief.

"And since you're busy, I'll get right to the point," I continued. "I need the full names of everyone working in Mr. Wildman's household, when they started there, where they worked before and their home addresses if they live elsewhere. Also the names of anyone who left in the last two years. Organized as you are, I'm sure you have their employment records somewhere out there."

Hill sat down. His fingertips patted the edge of his desk, the only hint of his displeasure.

"Yes, of course. If you deem it important. I assure you, though, none of Mr. Wildman's household staff is capable of being this ... mythical partner if that's what this is about."

"All the same, I want it. I'm sure your secretary is a lightening fast typist."

He frowned. He gave me a sulky look. He called his secretary and conveyed the request.

"While we're waiting, since you don't think any of Mr. Wildman's household is a likely candidate, why not humor me and give me your thoughts on who would have been capable of running the swindle with Draper?" I said when he'd replaced the receiver.

"I consider it too ridiculous even to contemplate," he replied loftily. "Draper never worked with anyone. He'd had an unfortunate experience with someone letting him down where he worked before, taking credit for something he'd done. I believe it had left him somewhat distrustful."

"You knew a bit about him, then. You were friends? Apart from business."

"No, no. I'm afraid work leaves me little time for socializing. We enjoyed a cordial relationship when we wound up at the same meeting, luncheon, something like that. We made no effort to see each other apart from business."

"A past betrayal hardly seems like the thing a businessman would discuss in public."

"It was just a comment in passing. Perhaps in the lavatory. My only point in telling you was to debunk this idea about him having a partner. Who suggested that, if I may ask?"

I smiled without answering.

"What chance his partner could have been Vern Tarkington?" I asked.

"Tarkington! That oily little dolt? A person would be a fool to trust him in anything – especially anything requiring duplicity! He gambles, carouses, runs off at the mouth. He's nothing but a leech, getting everything handed to him – *everything!* – and still wanting more."

A startling savagery blazed in Hill's eyes for an instant. Then, recognizing his lapse in control, he pressed them closed briefly and cleared his throat.

"I do apologize. I have a low opinion of Mr. Tarkington. It may somewhat color my judgment, but no, I don't believe he could have been helping Draper."

Hill took out his watch again. I didn't think it was entirely a hint.

"Just a couple more questions. Can you remember who first mentioned Draper's deal?"

"Regrettably, no. I've thought about it numerous times."

"Do you attend parties with Mr. Wildman?"

He looked at me blankly.

"I ... banquets and other events sometimes, yes. Why?"

"I'm told Draper often talked to the wives."

"Did he? Yes, perhaps."

"Anyone in particular?"

His forehead wrinkled.

"Surely you're not suggesting–?"

"I'm not suggesting anything, just thinking one of them might be able to tell me more about him."

"I'm afraid I don't differentiate wives very well. I meet them, of course, but–" He spread his hands.

In other words, they didn't merit his attention. He glanced at the clock on the wall.

"If there's nothing else pressing, Miss Sullivan, I really do have a full schedule. Oh, and as regards the backgrounds of Mr. Wildman's domestic staff, you might wish to start with his chauffeur, Rogers. You'll find no mention of it in his file, but the man has served time in prison."

EIGHTEEN

Leaving James C. Hill, I was so deep in thought I didn't notice the elevator at the end of the hall arriving. Nor did I register someone stepping out of it until a friendly voice greeted me.

"Lovely scarf, Miss Sullivan. It brings out the blue of your eyes."

Looking up I saw Frank Keefe strolling toward me.

"Nice coat, Mr. Keefe. It brings out the silver of your tongue."

Keefe threw back his head and laughed. No denying he was a fine looking man, his dark hair windblown and his expensive gray topcoat open in a display of insouciance which none of the other men duped by Draper even approached.

"What brings you to these parts?" His gaze flicked over my shoulder toward the door that led to Hill and Wildman.

"Tried to talk to someone I'd heard might or might not have invested with Draper. He wasn't very forthcoming."

Keefe chuckled. "James C. Hill?" He pronounced the name with the same rounded importance Hill himself did. "He's like that."

"How about you?" I asked, not confirming it.

"Meeting with Hill. We're on a committee studying how that proposed speed change is likely to affect downtown businesses. Dull way to start a day. My spirits would improve considerably if you'd agree to dinner with me tonight."

"Thanks all the same. I can't."

He looked over my shoulder again.

"You're still looking at something to do with Draper, then? Even with him dead?"

I shrugged. "Just tying up loose ends. Speaking of which, you mentioned Draper talking to the wives at parties."

"There's no figuring people, is there? Do a good deed here, rob people blind there."

"Can you recall him talking to anyone in particular?"

Keefe pursed his lips.

"Lucinda Graham," he said suddenly. He gave a chuckle. "Skinny little woman, timid as a mouse. Most likely her husband scared any spirit she did have out of her. All bluster and bully. Have to say gatherings are nicer without him around."

"What happened to him?" My brain was perking up considerably.

"Big competitor bought him out. Made him a bigwig at their headquarters in Chicago." Keefe eyed me, his brain working too. "They didn't move out there 'til after Christmas, though, months after Draper took off. You're not thinking there's a connection, are you?"

I decided to dangle some bait.

"Who knows? I've heard rumors Draper had a partner."

"That's sure one devil of a loose end." He stretched an arm and checked his wristwatch. "Late again. James C. will be testy. I'd better go." He broke out his grin. "Sure you won't reconsider dinner?"

Resuming my course toward the elevator, I gave a wave with my bandaged hand.

"I already got one cat scratch today. Can't risk getting more from your other girlfriends."

His laugh was still echoing when I pressed the button. The elevator started up from somewhere below. As it arrived, just before the door began to open, Keefe's voice floated to me.

"You should wear your skirts shorter, Miss Sullivan. You've got terrific legs."

* * *

Had Keefe asked me out because he was an unapologetic skirt chaser or because he wanted to find out why I was still asking questions related to Draper? It was a coin toss. His claim of a meeting might be true. The city commission was considering reducing the speed limit to twenty-five in some areas. Then again, Keefe might simply be fast on his feet, particularly if he had something to hide. I mulled over such possibilities the whole time I drove to Wildman's place.

Rogers was waxing the long navy Cadillac when I found him. It was blustery for that sort of thing in the open, but he and the behemoth were both tucked comfortably safely inside a garage whose overhead doors suggested room for four cars. Working inside ensured the fresh shine didn't get spotted if it started to drizzle, but Rogers was probably glad enough for it since he was working in rolled up shirt sleeves. His back was toward me.

"Good morning, Rogers," I called before I got too close.

He looked around, giving a pleasant nod as he recognized me.

"Good morning, miss."

"How's that cheek you banged?"

"Good as new, thanks."

"Looks like the car is too." I indicated the front fender. Both it and the headlight looked fresh as a daisy, no sign that they'd ever received so much as a scratch.

"It is amazing," he said proudly. "Mr. Wildman had replacement parts flown in by aeroplane. We just got it back yesterday, late. I thought I should give it a polish before it was used again – take a good look at it just to make sure nothing was missed."

I nodded. It had been a gamble hoping to catch him here, given how often he must be out driving Wildman places. But I'd learned showing up without notice got more productive answers than giving people time to concoct stories.

"I guess it helps having a brother-in-law who can tell his mechanics to drop whatever they're working on and pitch in," I said.

Rogers looked around for a place to put the chamois he'd been using. Avoiding my eyes he wiped the tips of his fingers across the top of the canvas apron protecting his clothes.

"Mr. Wildman doesn't use his brother-in-law's facilities. I believe ... well, the car requires special expertise. And of course a large work bay."

His embarrassment was hard to miss. If he didn't want me to know there was family discord, I'd play along.

"Well, it's a beauty of a car," I said. "Why I actually strolled back to see you, though, is I'm trying to learn about anyone working in Mr. Wildman's house who quit in the last couple years. Especially anybody who might have been miffed."

Rogers frowned, comfortable meeting my gaze now.

"As far as I know, the last person to quit was the man I replaced, and he left because he was getting to an age where he got stiff waiting in the car day after day. His cousin had a chance to buy a taxi company that went bust. I think he – the man I replaced – went in as a partner."

"And when was that? When you came here?"

"Five years ago." He was curious now, and maybe a little bit wary.

"This has to do with Mr. Draper. Harold Draper."

"I'm afraid I don't know who you mean."

"He did some business with Mr. Wildman a while back. There were some problems."

His puzzlement seemed genuine. "I know very little about Mr. Wildman's business."

"Still, you drive him places; recognize some of the people he meets; maybe notice who some of them seem chummy with." I gave him a smile of encouragement. "People often notice things they don't even think about at the time."

He gave it some thought.

"You mentioned problems," he said.

"Yes."

"You think someone in this household might have contributed to those problems?"

"I think someone who had a good bit of contact with Mr. Wildman did. Someone who also knew Draper."

The chauffeur considered for a time, then shook his head.

"Sorry, nothing's coming to mind. I honestly can't put a face with that name, nor an office building either. I wish I could. Mr. Wildman's been ... very kind to me." He looked at his hands. His jaw worked once. "You should probably know ... I served time in prison. Mr. Wildman hired me in spite of it. He said everyone deserved a second chance. I pinch myself every morning at my good fortune."

Before I could comment, or form a question, one of the doors at the back of the house burst open and the little boy I'd seen the night Wildman's sister brandished the gun came racing out. He jumped down three steps at the edge of the terrace while a woman in a proper gray suit hurried after him calling at him to be careful.

Roger's eyes had lighted with anticipation. The boy ran toward him waving.

"If you need to know anything else – about me – could we talk later? I'm supposed to drive young Stuart and his governess to his music lesson."

I nodded agreement as the boy barreled toward us, filled with excitement.

"Is she good as new, Rogers?" He ran to the Cadillac.

"Good as new, Master Stuart. We'll be taking the Dodge today, though, since I still want to check a few things on The Duchess." He shrugged out of the apron and reached for his jacket. "Why don't you and your governess wait under the apple tree while I back out?"

The boy skipped obediently off. Smiling faintly, Rogers looked after him.

"If you do think of anything – not just about Draper, but anything odd in, say, the last six months – will you let me know?" I asked.

He nodded, but his thoughts were elsewhere. I went back outside.

Wildman's son trotted over. He'd looked like a normal kid running in to see Rogers. A gap in his teeth announced a new tooth soon to break through and he was a little bit bowlegged. But as he looked at me, his face was grave for its years.

"You were here the night Aunt Doro came with the gun. You're helping my father."

"That's right." I felt awkward. I wasn't sure how I should answer if he said more about his Aunt Doro.

"I love my father. Will you please make sure no one hurts him?"

My throat phlegmed up. "I'll do my best."

He blinked somberly.   His small head nodded approval.

"Father says that's what we should always try to do. Our best."

NINETEEN

Downtown, at the heel of it where I had my office, was worlds removed from the sort of existence Wildman and even his household staff enjoyed. I parked my car in a gravel parking lot. I ducked through the produce market to buy a couple of apples from one of the sellers braving the blustery day. They were sheepnose, with skin so dark it was almost black. There were tastier apples, but sheepnose ripened and got picked later than most, which meant they were crisper than others this time of year. I stuffed them into my purse and headed for a sandwich shop on a little street called Pine.

Usually I cut through an alley, and today was no exception. I'd only gone a half dozen steps when I heard a thump, something soft against metal, maybe. A sound I couldn't identify. Even alleys I wouldn't risk at night were generally safe in the daytime, but caution kicked in. I hadn't forgotten being roughed up and left in a ditch last year, or that Draper, although he'd drowned, had gotten a blow on the back of his head.

The sound had come from somewhere ahead, so turning my back to return to the street didn't seem like a great idea. Easing my hand toward the Smith & Wesson in my coat pocket, I moved forward a couple of steps. There were garbage cans halfway down. From the sandwich shop where I was heading, maybe, or a nearby bakery. Since I thought what I'd heard might have been something bumping metal, I moved toward the cans. As I got closer, I could see there was no one behind them. Two of the lids had been flung aside, though. Irritated to think I'd been spooked by a rat or a hungry cat, I leaned in for a peek.

There was just time enough to glimpse hair and a face as a figure surged up at me. I jerked back with fingers taking position on my still-hidden .38.

"Get out! I ain't doin' anything wrong," warned a hostile voice. A woman whose hair was just a shade or so lighter than mine stood nose-to-nose with me, shivering in a summer-thin dress patterned with small purple flowers. "I ain't hurtin' nothing – just lookin' for scraps nobody else wants. Ones I wouldn't have fed to the dog when I had a job."

She clutched a shriveled turnip top and what at best guess might be a string of dough in one raw-knuckled hand. Her nose and cheeks were red and chapped. The glob I thought was dough had black bits clinging to it. She'd brought her prizes up to her chin, ready to cram them into her mouth if I made a move.

"You scared the bejesus out of me, banging around in that can," I said. "There's a soup kitchen two blocks up."

"They're out." She eyed me with weary contempt. "Been to three this morning, and all of them run out."

I opened my purse. Her tongue darted to her chapped lips as I gave her the apples. She bobbed her head.

"Thank you kindly."

"Ditch whatever you found in that garbage can. It's likely to kill you."

"You think that's worse than starving?"

I turned away so she could bite into the apples. Before I'd put one foot forward I heard the first crunch behind me. I went back to the street with my shoulders hunched in spite of my coat, knowing full well she'd likely eat what she'd found in the garbage can too.

* * *

I wasn't very hungry after meeting the woman. Back in my office I warmed up and thought about how fortunate I was compared to some. It wasn't the first time.

After a bit I had some gin and began to go over the information I'd gleaned from my visits that morning.

Wildman had been at home when I left Rogers and went around to ring the bell at the front of the house. The butler told me his employer was on another long distance phone call. He conveyed my request and a few minutes later came back to report I had Wildman's permission to talk to the people who worked in his household.

None of them told me anything useful. No one recognized Draper's name, or appeared to, other than the butler. He thought he might remember the name from a phone call or two. Although he and the cook were more astute than the others, none of them seemed as alert as Rogers. Maybe that was what being behind bars did for you. Or what landed you there. The governess wasn't back from the music lesson by the time I left. I'd talk to her later.

All in all, the richest tidbits from the morning had to do with Hill and Keefe.

Hill had known Draper well enough to mention something about the dead man's past. He was digging his heels in awfully hard against the idea there could be a partner. He definitely didn't like Vern. And having previously told me nothing unless I asked him directly, he'd volunteered information he had no reason to think I'd find elsewhere about Rogers serving time.

Frank Keefe, underneath his blarney and charm, had been curious, maybe even suspicious. He'd given me a name I hadn't had before, Lucinda Graham – a woman who conveniently was now in another city. Since he was the same one who'd told me about Draper talking to wives in the first place, the whole thing could be an attempt to send me after a wild goose.

Puffing out frustration, I paced around my office a couple of times. Why had Hill told me about Rogers being in prison? Should I attribute that to conscientious, albeit unwilling, cooperation, or to Hill's love of superiority? And why would Keefe spin me a tale of bored wives entertained by the late Hal Draper?

I went out for some soup. Afterward I made phone calls to the previous places of employment listed by everyone working at Wildman's place. They all panned out. There was no previous address or recent work information for Rogers, but I knew why.

Somewhere along the way I remembered Draper's secretary mentioning calls and visits from angry men after he'd gone missing. I'd told her I'd stop in to see her again. This seemed like the perfect time for another chat.

TWENTY

People loosen up over tea, particularly when they need to lick something sweet off their fingers. On the way to Draper's office, I stopped and picked up a couple of elephant ears. They were big as a man's outspread hand, crispy and fragrant with cinnamon. I'd never known what it was to be hungry enough to eat garbage like the woman in the alley, but smelling the pastries set my mouth watering.

Four men got off the elevator when I got on. I didn't know any of them. The hallway on Draper's floor was quiet. As I neared his office, I heard a toneless, scarcely varying hum from inside. Pausing for a minute, I listened. If it was Cecilia Perkins, I hoped she didn't sing in a church choir.

"Oh, hello," she said in surprise when I'd knocked and she'd called to come in.

The hum had stopped. The edge of my eye caught someone else in the room. I looked around.

"That's Donnie," his mother said. "The woman I leave him with needed to see her eye doctor this afternoon, so he came to help me at work, didn't you, Donnie?"

He stared without answering. Based on his size he was nine or ten, his face flattened out with small features all in the middle.

"Hi," I said. My skills with kids could probably use a little work.

"Hello," answered the boy. The sound was distorted like he had a bad cold.

"I'm Maggie," I said.

He gave me a flickering smile. One hand clutched a pair of snub-nosed scissors. Strewn around him on the floor, where he sat with knees together and legs turned out, were pictures cut from an open Sears and Roebuck catalog.

"Donnie's working on his collection, aren't you, Donnie?" his mother explained.

He nodded vigorously.

His work was uneven at best, mostly haphazard shapes. Sometimes he'd managed to clip complete images. Other times, parts had been left behind. I swallowed a lump in my throat, thinking how hard it must be for Cecilia Perkins to sound that cheerful when her heart must ache.

"I thought you might be ready to have some tea," I said. "I brought treats to go with it. Okay if he has one? We can share." I showed her the contents of my sack.

"How awfully nice of you. He'll love it. Let me put the kettle on."

While she was turning the hotplate on, I went and knelt down by Donnie.

"Want one?" I asked offering him the elephant ears.

He looked from them to me.

"You'll need to hand it to him," his mother said over her shoulder.

When I did, his flat face beamed.

"Dank you."

He took it with the same hand that still held the scissors. As he began to maneuver the oversize pastry toward his mouth, he turned it awkwardly. The scissors tilted toward his eyes.

"Hey, it'll go easier without the scissors." I reached for them quickly. "Here, I'll take them."

Cecilia, who had started toward us with face going white, halted and sighed.

"Thanks," she said. "No matter how hard I try to think ahead, something always pops up."

"Looks like you and Donnie were both busy when I came in." I nodded at a stack of what looked like more than a dozen typed letters, interlaced with envelopes to accompany each, to the right of her typewriter. On the other side, the *Dayton Daily News* lay open to the job offerings. Beneath it I could see what looked like two other papers.

"After we talked yesterday, I decided I might as well use up all the stamps," she said wryly. "Today I've been applying everywhere – even a couple of places in Xenia. We have no family, so there's really no point in trying to remain in Dayton, I guess, apart from Mrs. Graves being so good with Donnie and my not wanting to move him out of the only place he's familiar with."

Her shoulders lifted in resignation. She turned away to get our tea.

On the other side of the room her son was taking small, careful bites of his elephant ear. His tongue made a circle around his lips after each one, collecting the crumbs. Occasionally he licked the top of the pastry as well.

I waited until Cecilia and I had sipped some tea and just about finished the elephant ear we were sharing.

"I got to thinking about something you told me yesterday."

She nodded, dusting her fingers over the torn piece of newspaper we'd used as plates. She waited expectantly.

"You said after Mr. Draper had been missing a couple of days, men began coming in and acting upset because they couldn't reach him."

"Yes."

"And some called as well? Ones you thought seemed irritated?"

"Yes. It's not that you don't get an occasional call from someone who's impatient, or curt, or even downright rude – a secretary does, I mean. But these were... different."

"Different how?"

She frowned. "Like they suspected something," she said slowly. "Or thought I was hiding something. The ones who came in hunting him especially."

"Any chance you might remember who some of them were?"

"Oh, yes. Of course." Her manner changed to that of a woman dealing matter-of-factly with things she understood. She opened a desk drawer and took out a leather bound notebook. "I keep – kept – a daily record. The phone calls are here." She opened another drawer.

"Not so nicely filed, I'm afraid," she apologized as she removed a cardboard box. "Since these would have gone on Mr. Draper's desk and been thrown away as he looked at them."

Placing one hand on the contents to keep them from shifting, she turned the box carefully upside down. Starting with the day Draper had disappeared, she read off the names of people who'd telephoned. I scribbled notes. Behind us, Donnie had resumed his toneless humming, punctuated by the slow snips of his scissors. We worked our way through two weeks worth, after which, Cecilia Perkins said, the people who called for her boss seemed more surprised at his sudden absence than upset.

"There was a little code I'd used for years," she said with a self-conscious laugh. "I put a little tick in the corner so Mr. Draper would be forewarned someone's feathers were ruffled."

I thought what a peach of a secretary she was. It brought to mind the one Rachel Minsky had, who seemed the exact opposite.

After that we went through the list of people who'd actually come in upset and looking for Draper. It wasn't as long. Cecilia had moved the newspapers with the job listings so she could put the book with their names where we could both see it.

Of the names she'd marked as being upset, only one was unfamiliar to me. A woman named Ingrid had called twice, scolding that Draper had missed his weekly sauna and massage.

"She called again later, too," Cecilia said with a laugh. "She said to tell Mr. Draper she was taking him off her regular schedule. Goodness! I'd hate to have her out of sorts and slamming me around on a massage table!"

Ulysses Smith, Charles Preston, Frank Keefe and the other two men who'd invested in Draper's phoney scheme all had telephoned. So had James C. Hill. Smith and one of the others had called a second time. Preston and Keefe had both called three times. There had been a few other upset callers who'd been noted on slips, but hadn't left names.

"All men?" I inquired.

"Yes, I think so. Ingrid has a somewhat low voice for a woman, but she also has quite a thick accent. And as you can see by the other messages, she's not shy about leaving her name."

I patted my finger up and down the edge of people who'd come in. Charles Preston, who had subsequently committed suicide. Frank Keefe ... then Keefe again.

"Keefe came in twice?" It fit the suggestion of scrappiness in his manner.

"He didn't give his name the second time – just in and out looking ready to spit nails. But I remembered him. He's very nice-looking." Her cheeks turned pink.

"And the one you listed as 'Scary'?"

"He wouldn't give his name – and he *was* scary. Oh, he didn't threaten or anything, but...." She shook her head wordlessly.

My interest quickened. "What did he look like?"

Small furrows appeared at the bridge of her nose as she thought.

"Do you know, I'm not sure I even noticed what color his hair was. Dark, I think. He wasn't particularly big or tall, and there was nothing rough about his clothes or the way he spoke. Only...." She shook her head again. "I can't explain. There was something about him. The way he just stood there, looking at me – looking *through* me – when I told him Mr. Draper appeared to have gone off without telling anyone where he was going."

She shivered.

I tried to fit the description to someone I'd met, but I couldn't. The name beneath it appeared to be a separate listing. I pointed.

"Vern Tarkington? Is that who you're talking about?"

"Oh no." Cecilia's mouth tightened. "That one was rude and obnoxious, but he wasn't scary. Demanded to see Mr. Draper. Yelled. Accused me of lying – all the time shaking his finger and ignoring me three times when I asked for his name."

"Then how did you know–?"

"He threw his matchbook on my desk. Right after he ripped a match out to light a cigarette. He said tell my boss 'if he tries to dodge Vern he'll be sorry.' Then he stormed out. The name on the matchbook was Vern Tarkington Autos. I was down in the dumps and it made me laugh seeing he sold cars since he'd used the word 'dodge'."

TWENTY-ONE

I don't care much for babies or kids either one, although plenty of people think I ought to settle down and have a passel.   Kids are smelly and sticky and not very interesting.   But today I'd met two who were just about opposites. I found myself thinking about them as I walked toward Finn's at the end of the day.

Little Stuart Wildman had everything a kid could want, except maybe enough love. The poor kid was scared something bad might happen to his father.   Donnie Perkins, with his clumsily cut out collection of pictures, didn't have much except love. He and his mother would likely end up on the street if she couldn't find work.

Draper's con had done more than fleece rich people who mostly could afford it. He'd hurt innocent people too. If he'd had a partner, that partner was just as guilty, and I meant to find whoever it was.

"Maggie, sweet Maggie. Come and give us a kiss," crooned Wee Willie Ryan patting the barstool beside him as the door to Finn's closed behind me and I shook off rain.

"I only see one of you, and I wouldn't kiss it on a bet." I slid onto the offered barstool. "If you buy me a pint, though, I might be persuaded not to tell your oldest why you had to wear a frilly apron for two weeks in Sister Mary-Patrick's class."

Finn and a couple of others along the bar pricked their ears with hopeful interest and started to chuckle.

"I wouldn't insult your standing as a successful businesswoman by buying," Willie responded, unruffled. We'd known each other forever.

"I would," someone else volunteered.

Behind the bar, Finn's wife shared a look with me and rolled her eyes. Finn grinned, flashing a front tooth that was mostly silver. He already was putting a perfect head on a Guinness which he knew very well I'd want on my own tab. I yakked with Willie while he finished his stout. He walked a mail route and had a wife he was crazy about, so he never stayed long. A stranger took his place, freeing me to turn my back to the bar and retreat into thought while the pub's familiar sounds coddled me like reading in bed on a Sunday morning.

The most interesting finding from my chat with Cecilia Perkins was that Vern had lied to me. Not that I was surprised. I'd suspected it yesterday when he barged in on my confab with Dorothy. Now, though, I had proof. Not only had he known Harold Draper, he'd gone to Draper's office. He'd been hot under the collar, too, by the sounds of it. Despite what Hill thought, Vern was looking better and better as a candidate for being Draper's partner.

Before I confronted him with the lie I wanted to think about it some more, see where it might lead me. When I'd returned to my office after my talk with Cecilia, I'd let it simmer. I'd busied myself making notes, running down information for a regular client, making a couple of calls to people I knew in hopes they might have or know of openings for a first-rate secretary. They didn't.

Now, as I watched tables fill up at Finn's, I found myself thinking of Vern again. Much as I wanted him to be Draper's partner, something didn't feel right. For one thing, he was too hot tempered. Too much of a loud-mouth, too. Based on the one time I'd met him, he seemed as much of a freeloader as Wildman and Hill both regarded him.

I was thinking about it when Seamus and Connelly burst through the door. They were shaking off rain and chattering like schoolboys, so caught up in conversation the rest of the world had ceased to exist.

"You look like a happy man, Seamus. Getting married, are you?" Finn teased.

Sixty, taciturn and afflicted with a bad knee, Seamus positively swaggered. His chest was puffed out and his shovel-shaped jaw gave a thrust that imparted a cocky air.

"Got me a Victrola," he announced proudly. "Mick and me like to stayed up 'til sunrise the last two nights listening to music, haven't we, Mick?"

Connelly wasn't floating as high in the clouds, but his nod was more than a little besotted. "Makes a man's spirits soar, I'll tell you that."

"Michael Coleman fiddling and a couple of lads playing jigs – those ones came with it, 'cause that was the deal we struck." Seamus' head bobbed, affirming his bargaining skills. "And I bought Patsy Tuohey doing some fine reels. Then last night, Mick made me a gift of a record – by a concertina player if you will."

I listened in fascination. I'd never heard Seamus string so many sentences together at one time."

"Patsy Tuohey, that old piper from Galway?" asked one of the listeners. "My cousin in New York wrote about hearing him play. Said it was the grandest thing he'd ever heard."

"First rate. I'll tell you, though, those jigs is awful nice too. How did that one go?" Closing his eyes in thought, he started to didle a tune: "DI-de-de di-de-de, DI-dl-de, di-did-dl...." His bony hands lifted and stiff leg and all he started to dance as Connelly chimed in on the wordless lilting.

The room had grown silent. A quiet old fellow they thought they knew had changed colors before them. Connelly's hand darted under his jacket and brought out a pennywhistle. He started to play the tune in question, each note sweet and precise. A few of the old-timers started to clap out the beat. Seamus grinned, but after a few more measures he gave out, heading toward the bar and a pint. He grinned sheepishly as he received congratulatory slaps on the back.

"Look there. Mick plays," Finn's wife said nudging her husband.

"Learns fast, too," Seamus bragged as Connelly put the whistle away. "Has two of those tunes we've been listening to down already."

"You should get out that fiddle of yours and play with him, Finn." Rose picked some glasses out of soapy water and started to rinse them.

"You fiddle, do you?" Connelly looked up with interest.

"Ah, the woman doesn't know what she's on about. Haven't touched it in years."

Half a dozen people were crowded around Seamus, most asking questions about his Victrola. Seamus was having a good time. Everyone in Finn's was having a good time.

I felt bad Billy had missed it.

* * *

After letting the mellowness at Finn's swirl around me awhile, I set out for my car. It was where I usually left it in a brick-paved lot near the produce market on Fifth. From the end of the work day until four in the morning or so when small farm trucks bound for the market and workers at coffee shops began to arrive, the lot was fairly empty. Tonight there were maybe eight or ten vehicles.

As I crossed the street to the lot, I heard footsteps behind me, faint but distinguishable. I looked casually back but saw no one. Odd. If someone else was headed this direction, I should have seen them.

Unless they didn't want to be seen.

My hands already were in my pockets because of the chill evening. Now the fingers of my right hand settled around the familiar contours of my Smith & Wesson. I slowed my steps imperceptibly, then all at once stopped.

The footsteps behind me stopped one step too late.

There was a light pole at Fifth and Patterson. Two other lights shone, not very brightly, on the backs of nearby buildings. Enough illumination reached the parking lot to walk without stumbling, but you couldn't see far, and the shadows surrounding the few cars remaining were deep.

"Is there some reason why you don't want to be seen?" I asked aloud.

Silence answered.

There were plenty of bums on the streets, but they didn't scare me. Mostly they were people out of work with nowhere to go, harmless in ones and twos unless they were crazy. Bums didn't shy away from making noise. Like the woman in the garbage can that afternoon, they kept clattering away, determined to claim whatever scrap of food or shelter they had their eyes on.

From the corner of my eye I caught movement. There. Parallel to me now, disappearing behind a car. I was sure I'd glimpsed the silhouette of a prominent chin, or a chin with a goatee. A prickling at the base of my neck confirmed it. I eased the gun out of my pocket.

"I have a .38," I said to the darkness. "I've used it a couple of times, and I don't miss."

If whoever was there had a gun, they might shoot first but at the distance, in the dark, they weren't likely to be very accurate. Chancing a quick look around to make sure no one was creeping up from another direction, I began to move toward my car. My keys were in my free hand.

"Last chance to come out from behind that car. Trolley's just about due. If I start shooting, they're bound to hear it and stop."

A shape broke free of the shadows and bolted away. The light on a nearby warehouse caught the merest flash of a fleeing man with jug ears. He sprinted toward the street. A car appeared out of nowhere and swerved to the curb. The man jumped in. They were gone in the blink of an eye – as fast as they would have been if the man had roughed me up or stuck a knife in me.

I got into my DeSoto and punched down the door locks. A pulse was racing in my throat.

I had no more doubts that Draper's partner was real.

TWENTY-TWO

Frank Keefe asked me out three times the following morning. If I hadn't already made him out for a skirt chaser who probably saw a turndown as a challenge, I might have been flattered.

The first time was shortly after I'd gotten in from dropping my weekly laundry bundle at Spotts' Cleaners. I'd been through the mail and was just commencing the inside pages of *The Journal* when the phone rang.

"Have dinner with me tonight," he said. "The Biltmore? Hotel Miami?"

"Thank you again, Mr. Keefe, but didn't I tell you no yesterday?"

"That was yesterday."

I smiled in spite of myself.

"You're a charmer," I acknowledged. "And I suspect it would be a lot of fun. But the answer's no for today, too."

I'd managed to skim my way through four more pages before the phone rang again.

"How about tomorrow, then? If the places I mentioned don't appeal, how about the Saville?"

This time I laughed. He was persistent, I'd give him that. Why was he showing this interest in me?

"It's not the places, and it's not the day of the week. I just make it a point not to mix business and pleasure."

"I thought you were just tying up loose ends."

Touché.

"I'm as loose as they come," he coaxed. "I might let you tie me up, too, but I'd need to think about that part."

I shook my head. Even by telephone, he was enjoying this sparring. So was I, as a matter of fact. What were the odds he had a wife and kiddies tucked up somewhere?

"Mr. Keefe, don't you have work to do?"

"Not as much as an honest man would," he said cheerfully.

"Find some. And thank you again."

I hung up. Surely that would be the end of it.

Five minutes later the phone rang again.

"How about just cocktails then? Today after work? You wouldn't risk being seen with a roué like me late at night."

"Mr. Keefe–"

"Don't think I don't find you completely tantalizing, Miss Sullivan – because I do. But a couple of things have occurred to me which you might find useful regarding... your current matter. Whether they are or not is hard to say, since I don't really know what you're looking for."

I leaned back in my chair. He'd met with Hill yesterday. Maybe he'd learned something. Or maybe he was up to something.

"Fine," I said. "How about Scott's?" It was on Second, not too far from either of our offices.

"Quarter past five?" Keefe asked.

"Okay."

"I'll look for your lovely blue scarf," he said.

* * *

Sitting and speculating what Keefe might tell me held some appeal. My plans for the morning were already laid out, though. They consisted of a tête-à-tête with Vern. I flipped through the rest of that morning's paper and was opening the drawer to get my purse when somebody knocked at the door. Before I could answer, an arm appeared waggling a sack which I knew by its aroma held donuts. Jenkins followed the arm.

"Thought you might be ready for sustenance," he said offering it. "That gruel you eat for breakfast can't fill you up much."

I bit off a nibble. It was warm and crumbly.

"*Daily News* paying its photographers to sit around taking donut breaks these days, are they?"

"Going to be running pictures of the Pope's funeral 'til hell freezes over," he sniffed. "Such a backlog of local ones I figure I can take half the shots I usually do the next few days and still be okay. Besides..." He paused dramatically. "I thought you should see I can find out about drunken socialites as well as any gossip harpy."

He looked smug. I enjoyed my donut.

"Nellie Thorndike, daughter of Chester, was discreetly escorted out of a bash at Hotel Miami," he began, counting off fingers.

I smiled as if tickled all the way to my toes.

"Europa Blaine's wrecked two cars, maybe three. Daddy gave her a bigger car – and her own chauffeur."

I smiled.

"Ferris Wildman's sister got so stink-o she took a swing at a cop. She might have good reason to stray, too, since hubby's a sponger and did time behind bars."

I frowned to keep my interest from showing. "Wildman," I said. "Who's that?"

He attempted a look of pity, reveling in my lack of knowledge.

"Probably the richest of the bunch."

"Blaine owns a railroad."

"So does Wildman, probably. Or part of one. He owns pieces of a lot of things."

"And all these women are playing hanky-panky with businessmen? Or maybe the same man?"

Jenkins' face fell. "Well, I don't know anything there–"

"In other words, the only thing you've brought me is donuts." I twirled a pencil between my fingers. "Tell you what, I have a line on a woman who might know something about the lady in question. She's moved to Chicago, though, so I need a phone number."

"Why would I be able to get it any better than you?"

"Because, my dear, they were socially prominent. Her name's Lucinda Graham."

"Ah."

"I'm sure your fête and fashion pages will want to carry a paragraph on them from time to time – Daytonians making a splash in the big city with their elegant dinner or whatever. Ergo, the gals who work on those pages have it. Get it and I just might cancel your debt."

I stood and collected my purse.

"Always delightful to see you, Jenkins, but I need to be somewhere."

* * *

Vern Tarkington's auto showroom was on North Main, at a prime location. He ought to be making a pretty penny. I turned into the lot, still shaking off a few drops of guilt over making Jenkins think the information he'd unearthed for me was useless. Most of it was, but what he'd turned up about Vern's being in prison was pure gold. I expected it to come in handy in the chat I was about to have with Wildman's brother-in-law.

As soon as I stepped through the door, a salesman came strolling me. He had his hands in his pocket and was shaped like an egg.

"Say, that's a dandy little DeSoto you drove up in," he smiled. "Couple years old? I'll bet you want to move up to something a little nicer – a little more stylish. Am I right?"

"Actually," I looked coyly down and fluttered my lashes, "I'm here to see Vern."

Only the briefest of pauses ensued before he adapted. His smile remained fixed in place.

"Of course." He gestured politely. "Vern's in his office."

Apparently I wasn't the first girl to come in hunting his boss.

A secretary or clerk of some sort sat at a desk in front of two partitioned-off rooms at one end of the showroom. The door to the one on the left was open and that room was empty. As the secretary looked up, I put my finger to my lips and raised my shoulders in girlish conspiracy.

"Shhh," I simpered. "I want to surprise him."

Before she could answer, I scooted past and opened the door to the right.

"Yoo-hoo, Vernie," I cooed. "Surprise, surprise!"

I closed the door. Vern had his chair tipped back and his feet on his desk. He was in his shirt sleeves, reading a magazine. His head snapped up. His feet came down.

"Just who are you and what–? I know you. You're that snoop who was at the house yesterday asking questions." He rose indignantly. "Get out before I throw you out!"

"Nice to see you, too, Vern." I pulled down the shade on a small window overlooking the showroom. I figured that probably wasn't uncommon when Vern had a female visitor.

"You lied to me yesterday, Vern. Since I was brought up to give even people I don't like a second chance, I'm here to offer you one. I thought you might prefer to talk without your wife around. If not I can invite her, and maybe her brother–"

"How dare you accuse me of lying!" Across his forehead beads of sweat now detracted from his carefully waved hair.

"Because you did."

Uninvited, I sat down in the chair in front of his desk and undid my coat.

"What'll it be, Vern? A cozy talk here, or include your wife?"

Vern gritted his teeth. He sat without grace.

"You came around asking if we knew somebody named Draper," he snapped. "We said we didn't. And we don't. Now leave."

I made a tsk-tsk sound.

"Now that upsets me, Vern, your lying to me again. You went to Draper's office. You tossed your matchbook down on his secretary's desk. The matchbook advertising this business."

He laughed harshly.

"Honey, I pass out hundreds to people. Or they pick them up when they come here looking at cars."

"His secretary remembers you. You threw it at her."

"So what? Okay, I went to see Draper. I was trying to sell him a car! I go to see lots of people."

"Is that the best you can do, Vern? Your were trying to sell him a car?"

"Believe whatever you want," he said belligerently. "It's the truth. Then rumors started that he'd swindled people. When I saw you there in the study, and you started grilling me like you'd grilled Dorothy, I knew what you'd think–"

"What would that be?"

"That I was mixed up in it. Dorothy's brother treats me like scum. He'd like nothing better than to connect me to Draper – frame me if he had to–"

"Quit lying, Vern. Draper's secretary jotted down every person who came in and what they wanted. When you slung that matchbook at her, you also told her to tell Draper 'he'll be sorry if he tries to dodge Vern'."

Vern saw he was cornered. He moved with surprising speed, springing up, rounding the desk, grabbing me by the shoulders. I'd anticipated the move and let his own momentum help. As he bent to yank me to my feet I threw my weight toward him instead of resisting. With a string of profanity he toppled back, losing his footing as he hit the desk. He landed sprawled on his elbows. His eyes glittered hate.

"For the record, Vern, you don't scare me much. Not with all your phony muscles parked on the coatrack."

I nodded toward his suit coat with its absurdly augmented shoulders. A snarl escaped him.

"Now level with me unless you want me to tell Dorothy's brother that you've done time in the pen." I was only guessing that he'd kept it from Wildman, but Vern's face went white. "Dorothy recognized Draper's name yesterday. How? And please don't tell me she sells cars too."

More beads of sweat had appeared on his forehead. Other places too. I could smell his fear.

"She'd – overheard her brother talking to someone. One day when she went there. It – they were talking about investing in some deal of Draper's."

He licked his lips. I was standing so close to his knees that he couldn't sit up without tangling with me, which for the moment he didn't seem inclined to try. He remained on his elbows, watching me warily.

"What else?" I prompted.

His eyes slid toward the door as if seeking deliverance. Or evaluating his chance of escape.

"I... I knew Doro's brother wouldn't let us borrow money from him. So I talked to the bank. I went to see

Draper to ask if he'd let me in on the deal. But he'd already taken off. That's all."

He licked his lips again. Somewhere along the way he was lying. If I squeezed him now he'd clam up. If I let it go, there was a decent chance nervousness and his anger at me would make him do something stupid. Vern wasn't dumb, but he wasn't half as clever as he probably thought himself.

"Muss your hair up, Vern."

"What?"

"Muss your hair up."

Reluctantly he raised a hand and halfway complied. By then I was at the door. Opening it wide enough for anyone interested to get a peek, I called back in my coquettish voice.

"Oh, Vern, you're such a kidder."

The clerk outside kept her eyes fixed assiduously on some paperwork. I leaned in and gave her a cheery wink anyway.

"Isn't he a kidder?"

TWENTY-THREE

I left Vern's showroom and drove down a block. Then I turned around and found a parking spot where I could sit and watch in case he came storming out in a hurry to tell somebody I'd been there. Our encounter hadn't done anything to change my opinion that Vern didn't have what it would have taken to be Draper's partner, but he knew something about the whole business that he wasn't telling me. After thirty minutes of sitting and watching, all I had was a fogged up windshield and cold toes. I drove back downtown and had a bowl of soup and a mug of coffee to warm up.

After that I paid a brief visit to Stuart Wildman's governess, who was pleasant and gracious but said she didn't know the first thing about his father's business associates. From there I headed for the address where Rogers the chauffeur rented a room. I'd gone half a dozen blocks when an alarm at the back of my brain began to go off. Had that old gray Chrysler I saw in the rearview mirror been behind me ever since I'd left Wildman's place? Had I glimpsed it even earlier than that? Maybe when I'd first set out from downtown?

Two intersections later I turned right. The Chrysler turned too. A few blocks later I doubled back.

This time the gray car continued in the direction it had been going. Maybe I'd been wrong about seeing it earlier. Nevertheless, my work had sharpened my awareness of cars and people. Sometimes survival depended on it. I couldn't shake off a wisp of suspicion.

Rogers' landlady sang his praises.

"I have two rooms I rent, both to men. It's just easier that way. It's been, oh, ten years now, ever since my husband died. I've had a few bad apples. Nothing terrible – just noisy or late paying rent. There's nary a problem like that with Mr. Rogers. He's a gem. Polite. Mannerly. Even offers to shovel my walk when it snows, but I pay a boy up the street for that." She leaned close, whispering, even though it was just the two of us in her white frame house. "Family needs the money."

I smiled and nodded. I'd told her I was collecting information about his habits for an insurance policy.

"I'd like it just fine if Mr. Rogers stayed forever," she said patting my arm. "Of course I'd be happy for him if he met a nice girl."

"I take it he doesn't have one?"

She sighed her answer. "A pity, but he doesn't go out much."

By the time I got back to my office, my ears were worn out. There was just enough time to read the late edition before leaving to meet Frank Keefe. At five o'clock I fluffed my hair and freshened my lipstick and set out, wondering whether the information he'd dangled as bait would turn out to be useful.

People were getting off work. It was a cheerful time of day. Trolleys chuffed along, swinging to the curb at stops to pick up passengers. Girls from the secretarial pool laughed and chattered together. Men turned up the collars of overcoats. At the corner of St. Clair and Second a knot of grim-faced matrons held signs denouncing women who held jobs needed by men with families.

Scott's was a pleasant, modest sort of establishment. It was too large and too far uptown to be exactly cozy, but the atmosphere was friendly. Business people went there for a drink after work. So did buyers from Rike's and Donenfeld's. I saw an architect I'd dated a year or two back. He was deep in conversation with a cute blonde.

I hung my coat and muffler on a rack near the door and threaded my way toward a table. There was no sign of Frank Keefe. It was still five minutes until our appointed time. When the waiter came over to take an order, I told him I was meeting someone.

Ten minutes later, Keefe still hadn't shown. At half past five, I concluded he wasn't likely to. My guess was he didn't have a long attention span when it came to women. He'd found a more receptive candidate than me for his charm. Or he'd forgotten about the appointment.

Since I'd been taking up a table and was in the mood for something, with or without Frank Keefe, I beckoned the waiter over and ordered a martini. When I'd finished it and nibbled the last of the olive, I headed back to the lot near my office where I parked my car. Lights had come on in store windows and people were lining up to catch trolleys. Temperatures were dropping. The damp cold penetrated clothing, causing newsboys to hunch their shoulders as they hawked their wares. I decided to cut through the alley that ran between St. Clair and Jefferson. It was warmer in the narrow space between buildings than it was on the street, and if I happened to meet the woman I'd seen digging through garbage cans, I'd give her a quarter so she could get a room for the night.

I was halfway to Third when I heard the engine behind me, only a sound at first, then growling with power as it gathered speed. I swung to step back out of the way, thinking the driver must not have a lick of sense to drive so fast in a space like this. The lights of a big car almost blinded me. In the split-second I saw it veer, I realized whoever was at the wheel intended to hit me.

There was nowhere to dodge; no time to run. As my . 38 cleared my pocket I fired. Ineffectually. I pumped two more shots at the tires. Heard a pop. Heard the squealing and sliding of rubber as the car fishtailed.

It was on top of me now. I heard a crash. Something hit me and tossed me into the air. I felt myself slide across metal and slam down hard. I was jerked, pulled, no longer sure what was happening as I was yanked back and forth. Something squeezed my neck, choking me.

TWENTY-FOUR

Lucidity came with blinding pain as my cheek scraped pavement. When the car hit me I'd been knocked off my feet. The long blue scarf wound around my neck had caught on something and I was being dragged along behind it. I clawed at the tightening loop of wool, then calmed enough to go against logic. Forcing a hand beneath the loop at my neck I fought panic. I shoved with all the strength I could muster. All at once I spun back like an unrolled carpet, free of the scarf and free of the car.

My forehead banged more times than I could count. I came to a stop face down, on my nose. Something thumped. I heard screaming. Then everything ebbed.

"Miss Sullivan? Miss Sullivan, can you hear me?"

The voice sounded distant, but I knew it came from close to my ear. With a groan I opened my eyes and tried to make out the figure kneeling beside me. When I did, it didn't make sense.

"Boike?" I squinted.

"Don't move." He touched my shoulder gingerly. "Lie still a minute. I'll be back as soon as I see what happened up there."

It took me a an interval of struggling through cobwebs before I recalled where I was and what had happened. When I did, I realized Boike had gone off toward where the car must have left the alley. I wanted to sit up, but right then it didn't seem like such a swell idea.

Every inch of me felt like the devil. I wiggled my fingers. They moved. I tried my arms. The left one caused me to jerk in my breath at the pain. Since it functioned, it didn't appear to be broken, though. I pressed my stomach, which turned out to be the only part of me not feeling the worse for wear. By the time I'd assured myself my legs were okay and I wasn't seeing double, I heard Boike returning.

"Couple of boys went for a stretcher," he said. "We'll get you to Miami Valley."

"No need," I said. "Everything's working. I wouldn't mind help getting up, though."

"You ought to get checked," he objected, but I was already struggling to sit.

"Some s.o.b. tried to run over me," I said thickly.

"Yeah, I saw. I'd been over at Ford Street checking something for the lieutenant. Saw you marching along. Minute you went into the alley a parked car lit out like a bat out of hell and turned in after you. Nobody takes off like that unless they mean trouble. I got there right when they spun and their back bumper clipped you. If it'd been the front of the car, you'd be a goner."

"Thought I was for a while. I shot out their tires."

"I figured. What'd you get snagged on?"

"No idea. You going to help me up or sit there jawing?"

With a breath of resignation he put a hand under my elbow, steadying me. I became aware of sirens. We were halfway between Market Street headquarters and the central police station, mostly called Ford Street. Still faintly disoriented, I looked around and saw a crowd at the end of the alley where I'd been headed.

"What's going on there?"

"Nothing you want to see."

"Yeah, I do."

Boike didn't know what else to do, so he let go of me. I hobbled along muttering words more than one nun had washed my mouth out for saying. One side of my cheek was scraped and bleeding, but I figured wiping it with the back of a grimy hand wasn't a good idea, and I'd lost my purse.

When I neared the end of the alley that opened on Third Street I saw police and a small knot of horrified onlookers out on the sidewalk. A few steps more and I saw a pair of thin legs jutting out from a cotton dress too thin for the weather. The soles of the shoes were worn through, stuffed with pasteboard and bound with rags. The dress had faded sprigs of purple.

The woman I'd seen scraping the last scraps from garbage cans lay stretched before me. She was alive, but not by much. One side of her face had been smashed to a pulp. Blood bubbled from the edge of her mouth. More seeped through the waist of her dress where there was a gaping tear.

"Black Mariah's coming for her," Boike said.

I nodded. Mariah was the backup ambulance, an old paddy wagon pressed into service when the new ambulance was in for repairs, which was most of the time. It was only coming from Ford Street, but the woman stretched before us probably wouldn't last the drive to the hospital.

She looked so cold lying there in her thin dress. I took off my coat and spread it over her. The coat was in pretty bad shape now. The sleeve on the side where my scarf had caught was ripped half off from bearing the brunt of my weight as I'd been dragged. Other spots were almost worn through from cushioning me. It was stained with oil and dirt and God-knew-what. The young patrolman squatting beside the woman eyed me curiously.

"You know her?" Boike asked, frowning.

"Not who she is. I saw her a block or so over yesterday scraping the bottom of garbage cans hunting something to eat. I gave her a couple of apples."

Boike took off his suit coat and draped it over my shoulders. I realized I was shaking, not so much from the cold as from what had happened. To me. To the woman.

"That bastard came shooting out of the alley and hit her, didn't he?" I said. "Drove on with no more thought than if he'd driven through dog droppings."

"She might have stepped into the alley," said Boike. "Garbage cans there, too. Let's get in a patrol car. It's warmer. Sure you want to leave your coat?" He cleared his throat. "It's not going to help her."

But I was remembering the woman's tone when she asked me if I thought dying of poison was any worse than starving to death. I hoped she felt the same way about dying quickly instead of freezing.

TWENTY-FIVE

I woke up cranky. Having a sprained shoulder, along with relentless stinging from a three-inch scrape on the shoulder blade, will do that to you. At least my sleep hadn't been troubled by the dreams of recent months in which I squeezed a trigger and a man fell dead. Instead I'd dreamed of headlights roaring toward me and a woman's broken body flying into the air.

Sliding my feet to the floor, I sat on the edge of the bed and waited while most of the muscles in my body objected. My recollections of what took place after I put my coat over the dying woman felt like remembering a picture show. Boike had maneuvered me to a patrol car and told the driver to take me to the hospital. The doc who patched me up had told me to keep the dressing on my shoulder dry for a couple of days. Boike and his boss had been waiting when I came out of the treatment area. They'd handed me my purse, which someone had retrieved, and asked more questions than I could handle. Finally, in a surge of gallantry, Freeze had told a patrolman to drop me off at Mrs. Z's. I'd had a quick soak — taking care to keep the dressing on my shoulder dry. Then I'd crawled into bed and pulled the covers over my head.

This morning, to add to my other miseries, my stomach growled and my head felt fuzzy. A cup of tea would help, and I knew Genevieve would be up. Getting into the bathroom when everyone was getting ready for work could be tricky, but the first time I peeked out it was vacant. By the time I'd washed my face I was moving more nimbly. I got my mug and knocked on Genevieve's door.

"Oh, my. You look the worse for wear," she said when she'd let me in.

"Yeah, but if you play Nurse Nightengale and give me some tea I'll be good as new."

Her eyebrow gave a cynical lift. Ginny didn't ask about my work and I didn't pry into her past. It was one of the reasons we got on. She went wordlessly to a small hotplate and filled my mug from the kettle it held. Mrs. Z had okayed the hotplate because Genevieve was older than the rest of us, and responsible. None of the other girls were to know she had it.

After we'd chatted a minute I went back to dress. Besides ruining my coat, getting dragged through the alley had shredded my skirt and destroyed the backs of my shoes. That left me with a work wardrobe of two pairs of shoes, one suit, one skirt, a sweater and several blouses, plus a dress that might be warm enough today if I had a coat.

I decided on the gray skirt, along with thick cotton stockings. They'd cover the bruises on both legs and a gauze pad on one that protected a weeping scrape. By the time I finished doing my hair and putting on lipstick, I was moving almost normally. For somebody twice my age.

On the bright side, Freeze had also returned my .38 when he came to the hospital. I felt almost chipper as I tucked it into my purse. There'd been times in the past when Freeze had kept it for several days while he sorted out my role in something.

Reluctantly I eased on the jacket from my remaining suit. It didn't look great with the gray skirt, but it was the best I could manage for warmth. I'd also ruined a hat in the alley, so I put on a sky blue Peter Pan number trimmed with a couple of long gray feathers. That part of my ensemble looked terrific.

* * *

"Miss Sullivan." The butler at Wildman's place was startled to see me. It was barely eight in the morning.

"Tell Mr. Wildman I need to see him," I said stepping in around him. "I don't care if he's in his pajamas. I don't care if he's on a phone call to Timbuktu. I want to see him. Now."

His eyes wavered toward the edge of a gauze strip which my hair didn't quite conceal. He gave a small bow.

"May I take your...." He stopped, realizing I didn't have a coat. "I'll tell him you're here."

In under a minute Wildman strode down the hall toward me.

"Miss Sullivan?" The words were clipped, displeased by my uninvited intrusion.

"Someone tried to kill me yesterday," I said bluntly.

His pupils flared. Only a couple of Tiffany lamps shed soft illumination in the oversized entry hall at this time of day, but I thought he lost color.

"You were right to come. We'll talk in the study." He turned on his heel.

By the time I'd followed him back to the room where we'd first met, the maid in the frilly apron was replenishing a silver coffee pot. The small side table held evidence I'd interrupted his breakfast. There were two cups, one of them unused.

"Coffee?" he asked.

"It would be very welcome."

He waited until the maid had departed, then walked tothe windows and stood looking out.

"If you wish to quit, I'll understand," he said. "I'll pay you in full. Whatever you deem fair."

I sipped coffee.

"Do you want me to quit?"

The fact he hadn't asked about my injuries indicated how shaken he was. Had he been behind what had happened, he would have slathered on innocent concern. Had he stayed the invincible tycoon that he was accustomed to being, he would have asked by rote as a business pleasantry. He continued to look out the window, hands locked behind his back.

"I don't want anyone to die because of me," he said at last. "Because of my – obsession, as James calls it." He turned. The piercing look was gone from his eyes. They looked tired. "Do you think I'm a fool, Miss Sullivan? To keep pursuing this?"

"In the beginning, yes. Now I think it involves someone with no conscience. Indifferent to how many innocent people they hurt. Someone who ought to be stopped."

His face relaxed. "Thank you. Do sit down. I haven't even asked about your injuries—"

"I'm okay. And I won't stay. I've got a cab waiting."

"I'll have Smith pay him. Rogers can take you–"

I held up a hand.

"Thanks, but no. I didn't come because I want to quit, or want more money. I came because if someone tried to kill me, they might take it into their head to kill you too. You may not care, may think it looks tougher to shrug it off, but your kid's scared to death of losing you. He stopped me on the way to his violin lesson the other day and asked would I keep you safe. That should count for something."

Wildman looked wordlessly at his hands.

"I started this for the wrong reasons. Vanity, I suppose. But now that I've stirred things up, I feel responsible. I'll take your words to heart – about being cautious. When we finish here, I'll arrange for Stuart and his governess to leave this afternoon. A vacation somewhere. So he's not in danger. But if you're willing, I would like you to see it through to the end."

"One condition: From here on, you're to tell no one what we discuss. No one. Not Rogers or your butler. Not Mr. Hill–"

"Surely you don't suspect James–"

"People let things slip. To a girlfriend, a buddy, somebody who doesn't even look like part of the picture. No one."

He hesitated, unaccustomed to ultimatums. Then he nodded.

"Could I hear about the attack on you, Miss Sullivan? You say you're okay, but you've clearly had injuries."

As briefly as I could I told him about the alley. Then I put my coffee cup down and he walked with me to the door. He took my hand.

"Stuart does quite well on his violin. I'll bear in mind what you told me about his concern."

* * *

With no coat, I didn't want to walk from McCrory's, so I had the cab drop me off at the coffee shop across the street from my place. It was small, and most of the working crowd had been and gone, leaving a single cake donut for me to have with my coffee. I wolfed it down in half a dozen bites and eyed a couple of raised ones, but they'd be like eating nothing at all.

I knew Wildman wouldn't object at the price of a coat and the other clothing I'd have to replace showing up on my expense account, along with my hospital bill for the previous night. That was down the road, though, and I needed a coat today. Rike's would probably have some swell sales, it being so late in the season. I'd have no problem putting one on credit there, either. But I didn't like buying things on credit, and had only done it a couple of times.

Still feeling glum about it, I left the coffee shop and immediately spotted Jenkins' halo of curls at the entrance of my building across the way.

"Mags! Are you okay?" he called loping toward me. We met in the middle of Patterson and he trotted beside me.

"One time in the whole time I've known you, you show up without food – and right when I need it," I grumbled.

"Have to get to an assignment. Already late." He opened the door to my building's small lobby. "Word is, somebody tried to run you down last night and damn near succeeded. True?"

Behind his specs his eyes were uncommonly serious. The concern embarrassed me

"Yeah, but they didn't."

"You still going to tell me this has to do with some pickled socialite?"

"My poking around may hve stirred something up," I acknowledged.

"You have a knack for that." His words were dry. Without missing a step he reversed course back toward the street. "Duty calls. I don't have that phone number yet, but I'll get it for you. Be careful, Mags."

TWENTY-SIX

Resigned to a couple of hours without even a paper to pass the time, I settled in at my desk. In an hour or two it would warm up some and I'd dash uptown as briskly as my scraped up leg and other injuries allowed to shop for a coat. Before I could even work up a good sulk about my situation, my phone rang.

"Rachel says you like people to make an appointment," a voice said.

"Pearlie?"

"Yeah, and I'm making one."

"Did you have a time in mind?"

"Ten minutes."

He rang off before I could say anything. I sat back with my brain on full alert.

Somehow I didn't think Pearlie had been promoted from so-called 'boyfriend' to secretary. Nor did I get the impression Rachel was likely to be part of this meeting. Coming fresh on the heels of how my previous day had ended, Pearlie's call made me plenty uneasy. I leaned back in my chair and let my fingers touch the reassuring curves of the .38 stowed in a holster tacked to the seat bottom.

On the other hand, if there was going to be anything sinister to Pearlie's visit or if he meant to harm me, why not show up without warning? I was still searching for an answer when there was a knock at the door.

"It's open."

Pearlie glided through and closed it behind him before I finished saying it.

"You're early," I said.

"Don't own a watch."

"Have a seat."

Ignoring the chair I offered he moved past me to lean on the back wall. Able to keep an eye on the door. Able to keep an eye on me. A window in easy reach if he needed a fast exit. It was the spot of choice for a gunney. It made me wonder why Rachel needed someone with his particular set of skills.

"You got plenty of guts, line of business you're in and no gun in your desk," he observed. "Figure you've got one stashed somewhere else. Thought you might take it the wrong way if I poked through your things that first time Rachel and I stopped by."

He gave a stray dog's grin. I waited. He took a cigarette out and scratched a match with his thumb to light it. The cigarette tilted up in his jaw, toward the ceiling. He crossed his arms. He was watching me closely.

"Rachel wants to know, you still interested in finding out about Draper's partner?"

"I am."

"Somebody you might want to meet then. Man you don't want to make an enemy of. Kind of touchy."

He reached over and cracked the window an inch. It let some of his smoke out, but it also let out some of the heat. I decided not to argue about it.

"What's the man's name?"

He regarded me around his upturned cigarette. So far he'd managed to talk without removing it from his mouth.

"Don't matter much unless you decide to meet him. Man's kinda what you might call reclusive."

"Reclusive?"

He grinned. His vocabulary skills had won my attention.

"He don't like people poking into his business. Especially cops. If you was to meet him and mention it to one of your pals, he'd take it real personal."

I felt myself sitting straighter, not so much on guard about Pearlie now as I was alert at the magnitude of what he was hinting. Before I could form a question, a flurry of knocking rattled my door. Pearlie never seemed to move. His crossed arms still looked relaxed and lazy. But somehow the fingers of one hand now rested just under the breast of his jacket.

"Who is it?" I asked.

The door swooped open as Frank Keefe entered. There was a foil box with a red bow under his arm.

"I am contrite beyond words," he began. "Please say you don't really believe I had anything to do with...." He noticed Pearlie.

Pearlie's cigarette still jutted up. It didn't seem to burn as fast as other people's cigarettes. But then Pearlie didn't seem to move as much as other people. He'd turned stillness into an art.

"Gee, the cops must have paid you a visit," I said to Keefe.

I'd felt a little bad about siccing them onto Keefe, but Freeze had peppered me with questions at the hospital. I hadn't mentioned my run-in with Vern because they'd beat a path from him straight to Wildman. Given how Keefe had pestered me to go out with him, though, and the fact he knew where I'd be at a fixed time a day and could have someone watching for me when I left, it had seemed smart to mention the whole deal.

"Uh... yes."

The sight of Pearlie had distracted him. Pearlie didn't help any, not even acknowledging him with a nod. I let the curiosity in Keefe's eyes go unanswered.

"Running late is a nasty habit of mine, I'm afraid. When I got there the bartender told me I'd just missed you

– all perfectly innocent, scout's honor!" He raised one hand in the boyish symbol as his charm began its faltering return. "When I heard how close you'd come to serious injury, I had twice the reason to apologize. Please accept this small peace offering."

With a flourish he presented the box of what I could see by the name on it were expensive chocolates. I like chocolates well enough, though I'd rather have a good piece of pie. But just as Keefe's interest yesterday had seemed excessive, so did his current contrition. It crossed my mind that if you meant somebody harm, chocolates would be a fine way to poison them.

"Thanks all the same, but you can keep them. Give them to your secretary, or one of your girlfriends."

Keefe was dumbstruck. Pearlie removed his cigarette and flicked some ash out the window. Keefe's eyes veered toward him, then as Pearlie resumed his crossed-arms stance, back to me. His mouth opened as understanding hit him.

"You think I *did* have something to do with what happened yesterday? You think there's something wrong with the chocolates? Here! I'll show you!" He yanked the ribbon, opening the box. "Pick one! Pick any one you want. I'll eat it!"

His wounded earnestness made it hard not to laugh. Frank Keefe was growing on me. When I made no move he plunked the box on my desk.

"Watch!" he said, squeezing his eyes closed and shooting his hand down to grab a chocolate. Still with his eyes closed, he started to chew. "See? Shall I eat another?"

My bruised ribs hurt from the amusement shaking them. I heard another knock at my door.

"Maggie Liz?" called Billy's voice.

I leaned back with a breath of frustration. "Come on in, Billy."

Pearlie straightened, his pretense of laziness fading, as Billy and Mick Connelly marched in wearing uniforms. Keefe quickly swallowed the last of his chocolate. The four men all took inventory of each other. My office had become a damned merry-go-round. I started to worry Pearlie would leave.

"They're sayin' at the station that somebody tried to run you over," Billy said planting his hands on his hips and eyeing me with concern that was fixing to boil over into a lecture.

"You know those flatfoots blow things out of proportion. Some nitwit was driving too fast and I stumbled getting out of his way. I'm right as rain. See?" I extended my arms.

Behind him Connelly already had taken in every pore and muscle of my body with a single glance. If Connelly hadn't heard details of the bruising I'd taken, he'd observed it in the way I was sitting; had analyzed faint variations in my posture and movement. As our gazes connected, I knew he wouldn't let on to Billy.

"And who are you two?" Billy finally noticed Keefe and Pearlie. Still too upset to give up being a mother hen, he favored them with equal glares.

Keefe recovered first. He kicked into full charm mode.

"Frank Keefe," he said flashing his smile and extending a hand. "And you must be Maggie's father."

"Godfather," Billy said stiffly.

Keefe and Connelly were eyeing each other like two dogs circling the same steak.

My phone rang. I picked it up thinking I sometimes spent an entire day in my office without hearing another voice.

"Have you remembered anything else about yesterday? Make of car, maybe?" asked Freeze.

"I appreciate it, but I've got an office full of people checking to make sure I'm okay."

He got the message.

"Call back when you can talk."

I hung up and planted my hands on my desk while I looked at the three men in front of it.

"I appreciate your concern. But I'm trying to run a business here. The gentleman by the window is the only one with an appointment."

Billy glowered, pursing his lips.

Connelly and Keefe eyed each other, neither willing to give ground.

I leaned forward.

"Out."

TWENTY-SEVEN

"The old guy arrested me once. I was sixteen, seventeen." With no observable movement, Pearlie had shifted enough he could look out the window. He watched for the trio who'd left my office a minute earlier to exit. "That redhaired cop the one you keep company with?" he asked.

"I don't keep company with anybody. Tell me about the man who knows about Draper's partner."

"May know."

"Okay, may know."

Somewhere along the line he'd removed the cigarette from his mouth. He pinched it out and flicked it through the narrow gap in the window. Closing the sash, he crossed his arms again and gave me a long look.

"He'd take it the wrong way if you was to have a weapon. One of his boys will pat you down before you meet him. Got any objection to that?"

"I'd be an idiot if I didn't – but I'll go along with it."

"Won't be meeting him at an office. Likely to be a junkyard, vacant lot next to a factory that's gone belly up – someplace like that."

I nodded.

"Have to go by yourself."

"I figured."

Pearlie left the wall where he'd been leaning. He moved toward the door.

"I'll give you a call around three, three-thirty. Let you know where to meet him."

"You said you'd tell me his name."

"Oh. Nico. It's Nico."

"He have a last name?"

"Not one you need to know." Pearlie gave his dog's grin. He started to turn toward the door. He paused. "I could maybe tag behind in another car if you wanted, park a couple of blocks away."

I didn't know what to make of the offer. For that matter I didn't know what to make of this whole gift of helpfulness. The terms he'd outlined for the meeting had been enough to stir the down at the nape of my neck. On the heels of yesterday's near miss, I'd have to be blind not to see it could be a trap.

"I'm a big girl. I'll manage. But thanks."

His lean face told me nothing. He opened the door.

"One more thing," I said. "What does Rachel expect in return?"

Pearlie shrugged.

"Rachel don't consult with me. I just do what she tells me."

* * *

After he'd gone I sat for an interval wondering about Rachel and Pearlie and the man named Nico. That he was some sort of crime boss seemed clear. Maybe he was part of the Cincinnati outfit that had tried to muscle in on Woody Beale a while back. Except something in the way Pearlie talked about him, coupled with Rachel saying she knew somebody who might be able to find out what I wanted to know, made me think the man I was going to meet had been around for some time.

There wasn't exactly a way I could check on it. Lacking a last name, or any hint of connection to some business or public office, I couldn't even wade through papers down at the library hoping to come across something. If I asked Jenkins or Connelly or Freeze what they knew about someone named Nico, they'd start sniffing even if I neglected to mention he was probably shady. Besides, I meant to halfway honor the promise I'd made about keeping my meeting with him confidential.

I returned the call from Freeze and had to wait for a couple of minutes.

"It was getting close to dark by then, but I think the car was black," I said when he came on. "I don't remember any snatch of color."

"That narrows it down," he said sourly.

"It mostly looks big when it's coming right at you." I closed my eyes and tried to remember my dreams. "It wasn't a teardrop, though. It was older, closer to square."

"That's something. Bullet headlights?"

"No. They stuck out."

All they had to do was check around for a black car, probably older than 1935, or '36, with a shattered right headlight and bashed in fender from hitting a woman.

* * *

I went upstairs to the loo. Gents was on my floor, ladies one up; same setup on the two floors below. I was back in the office, opening the window to check whether it was warm enough to head out for something to eat and a new coat, when my door got the knuckle treatment for the fourth time that morning.

"It's Rogers, Miss," the voice on the other side told me. He looked around with mild curiosity as he came in. He removed his chauffeur's cap.

"Mr. Wildman asked me to deliver this to you." He reached across the desk to hand me an envelope.

I expected it to contain a message from Wildman saying he'd had second thoughts about continuing. Instead I found a generous check with a note indicating he'd realized some of my clothes must have been ruined in yesterday's fracas.

When I finished, Rogers was watching me with an awkward expression.

"I ... was glad of an opportunity to see you," he said. "There's something I've been wondering if I should mention. It may not be important–"

"Why don't you sit down?" My interest was quickening.

He complied, although with obvious hesitation.

"When you were asking me questions the other day, you told me to think about anything odd that had happened. I don't know if this qualifies..."

"Rogers, you're smart. And if I had to pick one person I felt certain had Mr. Wildman's interests at heart, it would be you."

It startled him. He began to relax.

"It was late last summer. Possibly fall. I can't remember, exactly, but it was unpleasantly warm that night. I couldn't sleep. I'd been seeing a young lady–" He brushed a hand at the air, dismissing what he'd been starting to say about his own problems. "Anyway, I'd gone for a drive. Out toward Bellbrook ... do you know the area?"

"Not much out there."

"That's why I like it. The countryside. The peacefulness. Especially at night. When it's warm, with the windows down, you hear frogs ... owls.... Anyway. Four or five miles outside the city there's a place, a tavern. It's not exactly rough, but it's not a place you'd expect to see someone from Dayton. I've stopped there a few times – not in one of Mr. Wildman's cars, in my old clunker.

"Coming back that night, just after I passed it, I noticed a car in the ditch. The one Mrs. Tarkington drives."

His teeth scraped his lip, then scraped it again. This was uncomfortable for him.

"I knew Mr. Wildman would want me to stop. And she's a nice woman. When she's not drinking." He looked at me earnestly. "She's ... left her husband a few times. Stayed at the house. She gets dried out, and she's very pleasant. She adores her nephew. But it wasn't Mrs. Tarkington in the car that night. It was her husband."

He set his cap on the desk and looked squarely at me.

"I don't like him. It's why I hesitated coming to see you. For fear that my judgment is clouded. That because I don't like him, I'm making too much of it."

"Why don't you just tell me what happened. For the record, I don't like him much either, but I'm used to sifting through things and I know more about the problem."

He gave a wan smile.

"He was mad as hops. Asked if the old goat had me spying on him. Then he spun around, and I thought he meant to punch me, but drunk as he was it wouldn't have done much damage. He lost his footing and I had to catch him to keep him from falling. He started looking around, yelling was that little toady even helping himself to the limousine with the boss away – Mr. Wildman had gone to a meeting in Indianapolis. He kept raving, slurring, saying he knew the two of them met there, that he knew a lot of things, that he wanted his share."

"Then what happened?"

"He passed out and I put him in his car and drove him home."

TWENTY-EIGHT

By one o'clock my stomach was pleasantly full and I'd bought a terrific new coat I found on sale at Rike's. Several of the better places had marked theirs down to make room for spring things coming in. I'd looked at Thal's and Donenfeld's, but you couldn't find much better quality than the one I'd ended up with. It was gray like plenty of others, so it would blend in, but it was warmer and a cut above the one I'd had.

What sold me on it were the large pockets angling slightly down. As soon as I got back to the office, I tried them out. My Smith & Wesson fit easily into the right one. It came clear so smoothly Wyatt Earp would have been impressed.

I'd picked up the early edition of the *Daily News* as well as that morning's *Journal*. Both carried lengthy articles about what they were calling a hit-and-run, the line the brass at Market House headquarters were peddling. Both listed the victim as "a vagrant woman whose name was unknown". Such an unmarked end to a life bothered me. The *News* noted that the woman had died shortly after reaching the hospital, and that another pedestrian (that was me) had been "slightly injured" by the recklessly speeding car. There was a bordered box next to the story. It asked readers who might have seen a black car with non-streamlined headlights and a crumpled right fender to call the police.

At three twenty-five Pearlie called.

"You still want to do this?"

"I do."

He grunted and gave me an address.

"You know how to find it?"

"More or less."

"There's space between it and what's left of the building beside it for trucks to get through. In back's an area where they stored iron and such. Nico will be about halfway back. Him and another car."

"He's that scared of me, is he?"

"Nico don't take chances. And he don't like–"

"Smart mouths. Yeah, I'll remember."

"Park by the first car. One of the gentlemen in it will introduce you to Nico."

"When does this happen?"

"Four o'clock. They'll wait five, six minutes. You ain't there by then they'll be gone."

"Gee, think I should scoot?"

I hung up before he could answer. Half an hour. I was dealing with someone who didn't take chances all right. No time for me or anyone else to get to the rendezvous spot to check it out or to get an accomplice in place. I shivered, all too aware I could be walking into a trap.

But I already was hoofing it toward the elevator.

* * *

The address Pearlie had given me was in an industrial area a good way north of the river. The street had a salvage yard and some warehouses, two mid-sized factories that looked to be limping along and a couple more that had closed. One building of indeterminate use had burned to the ground, leaving only a wall and its corners. Per instructions I turned in between the burned-out wall and a warehouse that showed no signs of activity.

Ahead of me was an open area big enough for another factory. Iron girders rusted in one corner. Next to them was a stack of something covered by canvas. There were barrels and some sort of flatbed wagon, but mostly the place was empty. At the center of it sat a large gray Cadillac, not as big as Wildman's but fine enough.

A black Buick waited between me and the Cadillac. At sight of me four men got out, each standing behind the door he'd opened. I stopped forty feet away and killed the engine. I sat with my hands on top of the wheel.

In honor of the meeting, and mostly to show my motives were pure, I'd even put on gloves. It didn't seem to impress Nico's boys. While two of them started toward me, the other two got back in and drove the Buick around behind me. Nice manners seemed to dictate that a guest wouldn't check on them, so I didn't. I knew without looking that they'd blocked the drive I'd come through, cutting off any exit.

"You expected?" asked the man who opened my door. He had a scar on the side of his chin.

"Why, yes, I believe I am. My name's Maggie Sullivan. May I give you my card?"

Pearlie hadn't specified I couldn't get smart with the hired help.

In answer he motioned me out with a natty looking automatic. I complied, arms bent at the elbows to display my hands. Someone behind me patted my coat pockets.

"Undo your coat and turn around," the one with the scar directed. "Don't worry none. Pete's a gentleman."

Pete was middle-aged with a sour expression. He ran his hands over all the right places, looking bored by the process. At his nod, the one in charge spoke again.

"Okay. Come on."

The three of us walked to the Cadillac where a man who was leaning against it straightened and opened the rear door.

"Get in," said the man who sat inside.

He was short and squat with a soft look which I suspected might be deceptive. I wasn't eager to find out. His fleshy hands were folded on the ivory handle of a walking stick. I figured this was one of those don't-speak-until-spoken-to situations, so I waited.

"A private detective," he said, looking me over. "Not something I'd let a daughter of mine do. Uncouth."

I held my tongue. Could be he was testing me. He appeared to lose interest, turning his head to gaze out the front window.

"Maggie Sullivan. I'd heard about you before an acquaintance asked me to meet you. They say you're good. You're not as mannish as I expected."

There was a roundness to his cheeks and to the knees beneath his fine wool trousers, yet he wasn't fat. His black hair contained flecks of white. He mostly looked straight ahead as he talked to me.

"I understand you're interested in a man named Draper."

"I am."

"Can I ask why?"

"In the beginning, because someone hired me. Mr. Draper had conned him with a bogus business deal."

"What I hear is Draper made fools of several smart men with that scheme." The man beside me sounded amused.

"One took exception to it."

"The smart one." There was the sound of stirring spittle, which I took to be Nico chuckling. "Let somebody get away with duping you and a man looks weak."

Nico and my client were a lot alike, it appeared.

"As soon as I began asking questions, someone took exception to it," I said. "Then Draper ended up drowned."

"And last night someone tried to kill you, I'm told."

"Yes. In my occupation, letting somebody scare you off makes you look weak."

He nodded. I didn't care to contemplate whether Nico and I shared any similarities.

"I've been told Draper might have had a partner," I said. "But no one's confirming it and no one seems to have an idea who it could be."

He recrossed his hands on the walking stick. A few flakes of snow were sputtering down outside. He turned to look at me again.

"It would be a mistake to think you were weak, I expect. When you came to this meeting it must have crossed your mind I could be that partner."

"It did."

"You came anyhow."

"Yes."

The walking stick rocked back and forth. Maybe it was his personal Ouija board.

"I never met Draper. I had no business with him. I deal with a different clientele, you might say." His eyes were bright as they studied me. "I hear things. Maybe another time I'll know something that helps you. This time I can't."

Reaching across with his walking stick, he rapped on the window. My door opened.

"Thank you for seeing me," I said and got out.

The door closed. The man who had held it went around and got in the front. A driver I hadn't noticed was already behind the wheel. I turned, expecting the two who'd patted me down to be waiting, but they'd disappeared.

"Miss Sullivan."

Behind me, the Cadillac's rear window lowered. I stepped closer to hear.

"Maybe he's not dead."

"What?"

"Maybe the man you're looking for isn't dead." He started to crank the window up. "You're a most attractive woman, Miss Sullivan. I'd hate to see that change. Please don't mention this meeting."

Before I could speak an engine purred to life and the gray car glided away. The black Dodge guarding the entry doubled around behind the Cadillac and they drove off and I was alone.

TWENTY-NINE

After leaving the spot where I'd met Nico and his choirboys, I pulled over in front of the first respectable looking business I saw. I needed to let my brain catch up. My palms were damp, which didn't happen to me very often. I closed my eyes and took a couple of deep breaths. It irked me that I hadn't noticed the plate number on the car used by Pete and the guy with the scarred chin. Since I was sitting here with my hide intact and all my teeth, it was possibly a fair trade.

What in the name of St. Peter did Nico mean saying Draper might not be dead? He claimed not to know Draper – not to know anything about him. Maybe it was only a trick to throw me off. Except it was the sort of comment guaranteed to make me dig more. And if Nico was helping someone who didn't want me snooping, as private as our confab had been, why not get rid of me then and there with a bullet?

One of the keys to surviving in my line of work was thinking clearly. Right now I knew I wasn't.

"Maybe we should call it a day," I muttered to the DeSoto.

Instead, as I neared downtown, I decided to try and catch Freeze before he went home. If he ever did. I parked the car in the same place it had spent the night and walked to the office. To my surprise, Freeze picked up on the second ring.

"Anybody besides his secretary identify Draper's body?" My chair felt unusually friendly.

"No. His lawyer was out of town. Sister up in Cleveland was about to have a baby and couldn't travel. But the secretary had been with him a good while. Seemed pretty torn up. Why?"

"Just wondering if there could be anybody I'd overlooked. Grasping at straws, I guess. I don't suppose you've turned up anything on that car?"

"Had men checking garages all day. Nothing."

When I hung up Nico's voice filled my ears and all my bones went wobbly. I felt cold in spite of the radiator clanking away. All day I'd been running on anger and pride and determination not to be stopped. Suddenly everything in the past twenty-four hours caught up with me. The alley last evening. The terrifying sensation of being strangled and dragged at the same time. The dying woman. Getting into a car with a man whose hands rested on an ivory-topped walking stick.

I opened my bottom desk drawer and poured half a jigger of gin. My hands were trembling. A couple of sips of the gin helped, but if I had any more I'd keel over. I got up and emptied the rest in the pot that held the dead plant. When I made it back to the desk I propped my elbows on the familiar wood and supported my head. My last smidgen of energy had evaporated. I could no more get up and walk to my car than I could to the moon.

For a while I tried to negotiate with myself. A good night's sleep would put me back on my pins. My bed was an absolute pleasure palace with three pillows. I had a new Hemingway novel from the library, or a P.G. Wodehouse I'd received for Christmas if I wanted something sillier. I wished I could bounce back like Mickey Finn in the comics

It's possible I closed my eyes for a minute. At any rate, the soft rap on my door frame startled me. My hand shot under my chair at about the same instant I snapped to enough to see Connelly watching me with amusement.

"Jesus, Connelly! I could have drilled you."

When had he nudged my door open part way? How long had he stood there watching me?

"Rough day?" he asked.

I shook my hair back.

"I've had worse."

I wanted to grind the heels of my hands into my eyes to push back the weariness. I settled for flicking crossly at a curl that had stuck to the edge of the adhesive tape on my cheek. Connelly ambled in with his arms crossed, looking relaxed.

"I got off early. Seeing as how you got the roughing up you did yesterday – and remembering times when I was fool enough to put in a day after similar treatment – I wondered if you might like me to go bring your car to you, maybe drive you home?"

The impulse to refuse got lost somewhere between my brain and my tongue.

"I wouldn't mind it." I admitted.

"I'll need your keys."

"Right. You know where my car is?"

"Yep. Heard Freeze sent you home in a squad car, so I knew it sat out all night. I stopped by on the way and gave it a look over, made sure it hadn't been tampered with."

That possibility hadn't even occurred to me when I'd driven off to meet Nico. More proof that my mind wasn't hitting on all its cylinders.

"Thanks." I handed him the keys.

Connelly said to give him ten minutes and then come downstairs. By the time I made it, I realized he'd been a better judge than I was of how slowly I'd move. I'd just reached the door to the lobby when he pulled to the curb directly in front of me. He got out and came around to help me in.

"It's getting a mite slick," he advised. "Watch your step."

He took my arm. Snow was falling thickly, fluffy white flakes, yet somehow it didn't seem as cold now. I found myself leaning on the arm that supported me more than I wanted. My body wouldn't listen to me.

"Why don't you keep the car after you drop me," I offered as we set out. "Bring it back sometime this weekend."

"It's not much of a walk from your place to the trolley, and I like walking. Feeling the weather and that. Don't do near as much of it as I did back home."

There was a wistfulness in his voice which I'd never heard before. Not that Connelly and I had spent much time around each other, and when we had, we were usually sparring. He rubbed at the windshield, which was starting to fog.

"I heard details of what really happened yesterday in that alley. Don't think Billy got wind of it, though. Figured if I brought him by first thing this morning and he saw you were okay, he wouldn't have reason to poke around asking questions."

"Thanks. I appreciate it."

"How bad hurt are you?"

"Sprained shoulder and a couple of scrapes I could do without, but I'll live."

We drove for a minute.

"So, that dandy with the chocolates," he said. "You going out with him?"

I started to chuckle. "So that's what this is about."

"It's about exactly what I said it was when I made you the offer. I'm not one for playing games, Maggie *mavourneen*." He gave a small smile. "Don't mind admitting I'm a bit jealous, though."

I chuckled again, too weary to stop myself.

"He's someone I met on this case, and yes, he keeps asking me out. But he's not my type and I don't quite trust him."

His deep chuckle blended with mine. I'd partly turned and was leaning against the door of the car. Connelly reached out to rub the glass in front of him clear again. The streetlights we passed threw alternating bands of light and darkness across his face. It made looking at his strong profile like watching a picture show when the projector started to stutter. The small, enclosed space of the car even had the intimacy of a theater. I spoke to break free of the spell that was settling.

"What do you make of the Japs taking over that island out by the Philippines?"

"Can't be good. They seem as greedy to grab land as that puffed up Adolph Hitler."

"Think they'll try for the Philippines then?"

"I think they're right fools if they do. The Philippines are what, seven hundred some miles from the place they just took? Lots different from just rolling across a border. And America's not going to turn nancy like the Brits and the French."

I traced a finger through the fog on the window beside me. I felt glum and weary and taken care of in a way I hadn't been in a long time. Dangerous territory.

Forcing my eyes open I made myself focus on streets and turns until we reached Mrs. Z's. Windows along the street were cozy with lights. Here and there at the curb cars parked for the night or the weekend already were covered by a skiff of snow. Connelly gentled the DeSoto to a spot in front of Mrs. Z's and turned off the engine. Silence swirled through the darkened car, as inescapable as the snowflakes dancing against the windshield. There was no one around but the two of us.

"Beautiful."

"Yes, it is."

Connelly removed the ignition key and handed it to me. His fingers were supple, with traces of long-ago calluses on the middle sections. I opened my purse and dropped the keys in next to my Smith & Wesson. By the time I'd finished, Connelly had come around to open my door.

Without quite meaning to, I let him take my arm again. At this time of evening all the other girls were in, some of them primping for Friday dates. We didn't speak as we walked up the neatly swept concrete leading to Mrs. Z's front door. My new coat which did such a fine job of keeping out cold didn't keep out the thrum of energy which Connelly exuded. As we reached the porch and stopped at the door, I spoke quickly to preempt any awkward ideas he might be hatching.

"Thanks for bringing me home. And for not fussing over me the way Billy does. It drives me crazy."

"Sure, I know. You're invincible, tip to toes."

I thought maybe he was peeved, but when I glanced up, he was smiling. He took my hand between both of his and folded it, caressing it with his thumb. Time hung suspended while we looked at each other and snowflakes fell. Then his fingers squeezed mine.

"Take care of yourself, Maggie Sullivan."

THIRTY

The ride home with Connelly and the scene on the doorstep bothered me throughout the weekend. I'd felt safe. And cared for when I needed it most. And I'd liked it. I'd liked it too much.

I slept late on Saturday, then joined the other girls filtering into the kitchen. Saturday was the one day each week when Mrs. Z gave us the use of her toaster and teakettle. We all split the cost of a couple of loaves of bread plus coffee and tea and a stick of butter. Mrs. Z supplied cream and sugar. Sometimes somebody – usually Jolene, whose folks had a farm out near Xenia, or Esther and Constance, who had an aunt in town – shared a jar of homemade preserves. Today there was strawberry-rhubarb. Anticipation of its tart sweetness bathed my tongue with saliva at every bite.

Papers rustled as sections were passed back and forth. Today's front page news was that William O. Douglas, chairman of the SEC, was the top pick to replace retiring justice Brandeis on the Supreme Court. It generated nearly as much discussion as yesterday's mention of Ohio's own Senator Taft as a favorite for the 1940 Republican presidential candidate. Interest in both lagged well behind talk of last night's dates and sale ads with sketches of new spring fashions.

Amid the cozy companionship, I thought about killers. Had the same person who pushed Draper into the drink also tried to kill me? More likely whoever it was had hired others to do their dirty work.

"You won't *believe* who she was with!" Constance was saying dramatically.

If the driver of the black car in the alley had been paid to kill me, did he collect half price for missing me and killing somebody else?

The giddiness of the thought made me realize I needed more tea. Once I'd refilled my mug and my brain cleared, I thought more productively. The attempt on my life meant I was getting close enough to the truth that someone felt threatened. The knowledge dangled in front of me like a carrot, along with the two new leads I now had to follow.

First there was Rogers' account of Vern's drunken ramblings. Vern claimed someone – by the sounds of it, someone he knew – had meetings at an out-of-the-way beer joint. And he'd mumbled something about wanting his cut. The last part was particularly interesting since it jibed with what Cecilia Perkins had told me about him storming in and making a scene. It might also be one of the places where Vern had been less than truthful when I'd had him spread-eagled. He'd claimed then that he wanted in on Draper's investment, but wanting a cut – or maybe trying his hand at blackmail – seemed to fit him better.

The second new trail to emerge was Nico's parting firecracker hinting Draper might still be alive. Yesterday both brain and nerves had been overloaded by my meeting with him. Today I examined the possibility from all angles. I still hit the same conclusion. Nico would know very well a morsel like that would make me turn over rocks I hadn't looked under previously, along with quite a few that I had. If he'd told the truth about not knowing Draper or anything about him – and why should he lie? – then he must have heard something. Had someone seen Draper? Thought they'd seen Draper?

"I still say they should have picked an American actress! She's opposite *Clark Gable*!" The page in Jolene's hand cracked as she turned past it.

What else could lead someone to think a supposedly dead man was still alive? I tapped my teeth with a fingernail. As I cast about for reasons, the tapping slowed. Draper had done something. Or rather someone presumed to be Draper had done something. Now all I needed to do was figure out what.

* * *

Late Saturday I took the trolley downtown in time to find a pair of shoes to replace my ruined ones. On Sunday I went to dinner at Billy and Kate's. I had a standing invitation, and whenever I needed reminding what decent, normal life was like, or maybe just a tie to the past, I went. Unlike the other cops' wives who'd watched me grow up, Kate could be trusted not to serve me potential suitors along with her roast. The bonus was the best string beans I'd ever eaten and pies that were out of this world. Ordinarily Seamus was there, so his absence indicated the riff continued between him and Bill.

Monday I got an early start so I could stop by Wheeler's garage. Then I picked up the laundry I usually retrieved on my way home on Thursdays. By midmorning I'd caught up on papers, mail and other routine business. Something told me Rachel Minsky didn't start her day as early as other people, but it was late enough I chanced a call.

"Pearlie says somebody tried to run you over," she said when her officious male secretary put me through.

"Yeah, but they did sloppy work."

She chuckled.

"The gentleman I met on Friday, how much can I count on what he told me being true?"

There was silence at the end of the wire, but not because she didn't understand I meant Nico.

"I haven't had many dealings with him," she said carefully, "but from what I know of him, and have heard, it's sound as silver."

"And he's not someone who needs to bother lying."

"That too."

"Thanks."

"Was he useful?"

"I'm not sure." I'd asked all I needed to, but I found myself speaking again. "You interested in a drink after work?"

This time the silence was short, just enough to tell me I'd surprised her.

"Quarter to six?" she asked.

"Sure."

"Where?"

I couldn't quite picture her in Finn's.

"Hotel Miami?"

"I think I'll leave Pearlie elsewhere." She chuckled and hung up.

* * *

It was just about noon when I got to Vern's dealership. Three salesmen in suits were giving their spiels to potential customers who were all bundled in coats. One of the salesmen was Vern. I parked and moseyed toward one of the most expensive models near Vern.

"Be right with you...." he began, looking up. His sunny smile started to sag as he saw who it was.

"Just a few more questions about this number, Vern," I trilled, waving. I pointed to the glossy roadster where I'd stopped. It was far enough away that the customers wouldn't hear if Vern kept his voice down.

With a few words to the couple he'd been wooing, he hot-footed toward me.

"What the hell are you doing here?" he snarled under his breath

"Finding out why you tried to run me over on Thursday. Or hired someone to."

"I – don't know what you're talking about." His eyes shifted and the whites were expanding. I'd made him nervous. "I told you last time you came that you're not welcome here. Now you're going to clear out and not come back if you know what's good for you." He grabbed my shoulder.

"I don't think so, Vern."

The Smith & Wesson made its public debut from my new coat's pocket. Its tip nudged his belly about where his shirt met his trousers. His eyes traveled down. His tongue flitted out like maybe his mouth was dry. He managed a sneer.

"You wouldn't dare. Not here."

"Wouldn't I? I'm still pretty shaken up from that car coming at me, Vern. Not really thinking straight. Hysterical, even." The shiny roadster I'd pretended interest in was blocking the view of everyone else on the lot. So was Vern himself. Unless someone came up behind us, the gun was hidden. I kept at it. "You grabbed me ... you'd just admitted trying to kill me—"

"No! It wasn't me!" His voice went soprano.

"And I panicked–"

"I didn't know! He said he just wanted to scare–"

"Who, Vern?"

"I don't know! A-a voice on the phone."

"Quit lying. I know about the beer joint out toward Bellbrook. I know about you wanting a cut."

"Anything wrong, Vern?"

The other two salesmen were walking toward us. Vern hadn't kept his voice down.

"This creep won't cough up any money for our kid – that's what's wrong," I snapped.

The salesmen did an about-face. From the edge of my eye I saw a husband and wife who'd been looking at cars walk quickly back to their own. Vern's panic and rage had left him almost apoplectic.

"You're in this up to your ears, Vern. The swindle. A woman's death."

"No! All I did was give someone a phone number – that and drive a package down to Lebanon and leave it in a car!"

"Whose car?"

"I don't know."

"You chose one at random?"

"Of course not!"

He'd reddened, furious I was ridiculing him. Here's where he'd tell me he'd had a license plate number which he then threw away. I nudged his belly with the .38.

"I looked for a particular car. A maroon Ambassador. A straight-eight Speedstream" he said sullenly. "Probably the only one in the whole state."

He'd described such a flashy car he had to be making it up. Except he was sulking so much I believed him.

"What was the package?"

"A bag. Like a doctor carries. With a lock around it. I got a telephone call at home telling me it was on my doorstep. Where I was to take it. I drove to some roadside park this side of Lebanon. The luggage compartment on the Nash was unlocked. I put it in and turned the handle."

Vern smoothed his hair. He was recovering his wits.

"That's all I know. Now go away. And don't come back." He gave a smirk. "You can't pin anything on me, no matter what you think you know."

I returned the .38 to my pocket and leaned close enough to kiss him.

"I can still come up behind you some night when you're out catting around. So can the men who are paying you off. You're an inconvenience to them, Vern. You know too much."

THIRTY-ONE

Turning my back on Vern, I sauntered to my car and drove away. Two blocks from the dealership I pulled into a side street. Exactly as planned a gangly young kid hopped out of his jalopy to lope toward me. His name was Calvin and he was learning the mechanic's trade from Eli Wheeler.

The two of them took care of my car. Calvin was crazy for any excuse to drive it. Now and then we traded cars so I could follow someone who might recognize mine. When Calvin had to wait around to switch like he had this time, I tried to pay Eli for his helper's hours away from work, but mostly Eli wouldn't take it. When that happened, I took him half a ham or a chunk of the cheese that he liked.

Calvin flipped open one of the clean towels he and Eli always used to protect the seat of customers' cars, slid behind the wheel and drove away. From the time I got out to the time he got in took about ten seconds. I crossed the street and got into Calvin's well-worn vehicle, which despite its looks started as fast as a sleeping cat springs up for a bird. I let the clutch out and headed back toward Vern's place, circling a block to park where I had a view not only of anyone leaving the lot, but of cars coming out from behind the building. In back was likely to be where anyone working there parked.

I'd shaken Vern with what I knew, even though some of it had been guesses which his reactions confirmed. Right about now, I suspected he'd be running to someone for help. That might mean calling; it might mean heading out at any moment to meet someone. If he'd tried telephoning, chances were he got cut off fast. Either way he was likely to bolt.

When Calvin and I made arrangements, I'd transferred a pair of binoculars I kept in my car for stakeouts to the passenger seat of his car. Using them told me one of the salesmen who'd been on the front lot earlier was still there, buttering up what might even be the same customers. Vern and the other salesman were nowhere to be seen. Before I noticed anything further, a car shot out from behind the building. It wasn't the brown-and-tan number Vern had been driving the day I dropped in on his wife, and it wasn't the pretty champagne colored one she drove, but even Vern was smart enough to think of switching cars. As owner of the dealership he'd have his pick of plenty. The one I was watching was a navy blue Buick.

Of course it could be someone else. The other salesman giving potential buyers a test ride. A customer whose car had been in for repairs or an oil change. I started the engine without lowering the binoculars, but reflection from the windshield of the navy blue Buick made it impossible to tell who was inside. It had cut through the lot as if in a hurry, and it entered the street with the same sense of urgency. But then it crept along. It could be the uneven pace of a customer unfamiliar with the car's controls and wary of an accident. It was also a fine speed for someone watching to make sure they weren't followed.

When the Buick pulled into the parking lot of a furniture store a block up and came back, continuing past the dealership at the same slow speed, my confidence increased. I did a U-turn of my own and went maybe a little faster than I should have down a street parallel to the one the Buick was traveling. After a couple of blocks I cut over to Main in time to see the Buick passing. It was picking up speed, heading downtown by the looks of it. Keeping several cars between us, I followed.

Dark blue cars weren't as common as black ones, but they were common enough to make keeping track of one tricky. Fortunately new car dealers liked to deck their offerings out with the latest doodads, and the one Vern had picked – if I was right about it being Vern – had white sidewall tires.

As we reached the middle of town and the car I was following turned, I started to frown. Surely Vern wasn't headed where he appeared to be. But a block from the Hulman building he spotted a parking place and pulled over. It was Vern all right. He got out as I passed.

"Lots of luck," I said under my breath as I started to look for a parking place of my own. Did he really expect any help from the brother-in-law he'd helped swindle?

*   *   *

The closest spot I could find for Calvin's jalopy was a block and a half away on a side street. As I came around to the sidewalk, a reflection in the window of the menswear store I'd parked beside caught my eye. Four or five spaces behind me, another car was pulling in. Absent minded female that I was, I turned to peek back into my car for something. The performance took just long enough to give me a look at the old gray car that had just parked. Coming back from Wildman's the afternoon before someone tried to kill me there'd been an old gray car trailing behind me.

I moseyed on in the direction I'd started, pausing occasionally and pretending to window shop while I thought. If the car down the street was following me, whoever was in it had seen me switch cars with Calvin. That meant they'd been following me from the time I left Mrs. Z's.

I'd had it up to my teeth with sprains and scrapes and cars that tried to run me over. I'd had my fill of figures skulking after me in dark parking lots.

At a nice-sized shoe store I pretended interest in the contents of a window set at right angles to the door. It gave me a look at a guy who'd stopped as if studying something in the store I'd just passed. I couldn't tell much except that he had a VanDyke beard. The chin on the figure following me in the parking lot had stuck out a lot, and he'd had jug ears. The man I was watching stood sideways, so I couldn't tell on the ears. He was dressed on the rough side with a brown cap pulled low over his eyes and a short jacket.

When I moved on and stopped again, he stopped too. I crossed the street. So did he. Four doors up there was a narrow lane between buildings. I figured that was where he'd make his move, if he meant to make one here in the middle of town at midday.

Sure enough, at the store just before the lane he closed the gap between us and grabbed for my arm. Aided by the shop window showing his every move, I pivoted out of reach and rammed my knee against the back of his, throwing him off balance. As if lovey-dovey, I hooked my arm through his so he couldn't get to the gun I felt under his jacket. It would also leave us unnoticed by passers-by. My free hand caught his pinkie. I shoved him against the store front.

"I don't like being followed. Understand?"

I bent the finger a little to get his attention. I saw his teeth grit. He was three or four inches taller than me, and there were muscles in the arm I held. His nose had a bump in the middle from being broken somewhere in the past. Ah, yes. He had jug ears.

He started to struggle, so I bent his finger some more.

"Who sent you?"

He called me a name that wasn't nice.

"Whatever they're paying you isn't enough for the grief you're going to get from me if you don't lay off."

His lips stretched in a snarl.

"You think I'm scared of a broad? You're nothing but a smart mouth."

Surprise had given me the upper hand, but I could feel him bunching to break free.

"You learn slow," I said.

I jammed his finger back as hard as I could and heard his bone snap. He howled, curling over.

"Terrible indigestion. Hits him out of nowhere," I told two passing women who'd stopped in their tracks.

As I walked away, my new pal's fumbling move toward his gun gave way to his need to cradle his hand against him. He wasn't going to be in a good mood if we met again. My own mood was considerably improved since he wouldn't be able to hold a gun too well or punch too well for a while.

THIRTY-TWO

"Don't know any garage that would do what you're asking about – fix up a car from a hit-and-run and not let on to the police." Eli Wheeler looked properly scandalized.

"Now and again – mostly back when times were really bad, before Mr. Roosevelt – I've heard rumors about places that took cars apart. Sold the parts. Didn't ask whether you owned the car. But helping to hide hitting someone...." He shook his head at the wickedness of it.

I was pretty near stuffed with humble pie. Confronting the guy who'd been following me had caused me to lose Vern. Not much time had elapsed. Ten minutes? Fifteen? Still, by the time I'd walked on toward the spot where Vern's car had been parked, it was gone. Now Eli Wheeler, who knew more mechanics and local garages than just about anyone else in the area, had proved a dead end where I'd hoped against hope for information.

"It was a long shot," I acknowledged. "So's this. Do you happen to know who drives a maroon Ambassador, Speedstream model, straight-eight? I'd settle for who sells them."

"Umm-um!" Eli's eyes glowed with appreciation. "Not around here. You hear that, Calvin? She wants to know does anybody around here have a Nash Ambassador Speedstream in that reddish ... what do you call it? Maroon."

"Holy smokes." Calvin grinned. He'd just come in from bringing my car out for me and parking his jalopy. "Don't think I've even seen an Ambassador. Not a new one, anyway." He looked quizzically at his boss from the door of the little shack they used as an office.

"Probably need to go to Cincinnati to buy something like that," Eli said rubbing his chin.

Muffling a sigh I pushed off from the desk I'd been leaning against.

"I was afraid of that. Any dealers you know who might have a picture? One I could borrow just for a couple of days?"

Eli made another pass at his chin. "Let me see what I can do."

* * *

It was late and my set-tos with Vern and the guy following me had used up my energy. I stopped on the way back from Eli's for a fried egg sandwich. I took a swing past Vern's house, but the only car in sight was his wife's. When I got to the office I called his dealership.

"This is Shirley," I said with a giggle. "Is Vern there?"

"He's in the showroom. Just a minute, please," said a long-suffering voice.

I thanked her and quietly broke the connection when I heard her step away from the phone. At least I knew where he was for the moment. Maybe I'd missed him meeting someone after he got away from me, and maybe I hadn't. With other possibilities waiting to be checked I couldn't sit watching Vern full time, hoping he'd lead somewhere.

Most of the afternoon dribbled away with me making phone calls to Wildman's home and his office, but he was out and Rogers was driving him. My question for

Wildman could wait, but I was impatient to talk to Rogers. In between calls I thought about what would make Nico tell me Draper could still be alive, and what had been in the bag Vern delivered to Lebanon.

Could it be that Draper was living in Lebanon, driving a fancy car purchased with the fruits of his swindle? That didn't make sense. If you stole that kind of money you'd go farther than thirty or forty miles before you started flashing it. And you wouldn't try to disappear in a small town.

Maybe it was Draper's partner. Could he live in Lebanon, or maybe have relatives there?

The question of the red car niggled at me, so I called Draper's office.

"How many cars did Mr. Draper own?" I asked Cecilia after we'd chatted a minute.

"Only one, as far as I know."

"Which was?"

"A tan Buick."

Tan, not black. And not remotely maroon. A dead end.

At a quarter past four Eli called.

"I should have that picture you wanted first thing in the morning," he said.

"Eli, if I didn't think your wife might object, I'd give you a big smooch."

He chuckled.

"Calvin's not married, and I expect he'd like that just fine. I could count it toward his pay for the week. You may want to give him a smooch anyways. He thinks he may know of a couple of bad apples who'd do the sort of work on cars you were asking about."

THIRTY-THREE

I was standing up with my compact out, freshening my lipstick to meet Rachel Minsky, when somebody knocked. It was Billy. His white hair was ruffled from the walk down from Ford Street after his shift ended.

"Have a date, have you?" he asked as I snapped the compact closed. It was gold-tone with pretty scrollwork on the top. He and eamus had given it to me a couple of years before on my birthday.

"Not exactly. Just meeting someone."

"Oh." He sounded disappointed. "I was fixing to buy you a pint."

He wandered aimlessly over and studied my Julienne diploma. I started to get the picture.

"I expect Seamus would be glad to have you buy him a pint."

"He's still sore at me." Billy looked at his toes. "Guess I never realized how much he missed hearing music from home. Anyway, him and Mick are thick as thieves now."

"You and Seamus are a whole lot thicker. I expect he feels as bad about how things are between you as you do," I said softly. "Why not give him some kind of peace offering? Let him know you want to be friends again?"

"Wouldn't know what to get him."

Billy could be as stubborn as a mule. Which was maybe insulting the mule.

"How about a record? I expect that would mean a whole lot."

"Wouldn't know what kind to get."

I gave a gargle of frustration.

"You were partners a long time, besides being friends. You know Seamus better than anyone. If you put your mind to it, I'll bet you remember somebody he mentioned hearing, or someone he read about coming to play in Boston or Chicago. If he doesn't like what you pick, the store will let him take it back."

Billy was silent, which gave me some hope he was thinking about it. I retrieved my coat from the coat rack and let him hold it for me as I slipped it on.

"Now," I said tucking my arm through his and patting his hand, "if you promise to give Kate a nice kiss when you get home, I'll let you walk me as far as your trolley stop."

* * *

Rachel was at a table with a Gibson in front of her when I reached the lounge of the Hotel Miami. It was a fancy place where tiny lamps topped little round tables dressed in starched linen I apologized for being five minutes late, and in light of what had followed my last martini, I ordered an old fashioned.

While I waited for it to arrive, Rachel fitted a cigarette into its gold holder. She snapped the flintwheel on a tortoiseshell lighter that fit in the palm of her hand. Her eyes took note of my slight shift backward. As she exhaled, she added turning her head to the move I'd seen her execute in her office: jutting her jaw to the side to blow smoke from the corner of her mouth.

"Not many women invite me for drinks," she said. "Or anything else, come to think of it."

"That could have something to do with Pearlie. He has a certain air about him."

"'A certain air.' He'd like that. Mind if I tell him?"

"You might also tell him he makes a better impression than other practitioners of his, ah, profession that I met last week. Definitely a better vocabulary."

I had a feeling she was struggling to control her lips.

"He's decided he wants to write crime stories. Thinks he can do a better job than the ones in *Black Mask*."

My old fashioned was arriving. I raised the glass.

"To Pearlie and his literary career," I said somberly.

Rachel doubled over and her shoulders started to shake. She waved smoke away, choking on pent-up laughter. It set me off too. The departing waiter threw us a jaundiced look suggesting behavior like ours was inappropriate in such a nice place. Rachel's cigarette smouldered untouched in an ashtray. When we'd laughed ourselves out, she dabbed at her eyes with a cut-work hanky.

"Jesus that felt good. It's been a pig pile of a day," she said.

"A pig pile couple of days as far as I'm concerned."

We both sipped our drinks. I ate a maraschino cherry from my toothpick.

"So," I said. "Why are you helping me?"

"Maybe I'm not." Her dark eyes glimmered.

"And maybe you are. Why?"

She got another cigarette going. Cupped her elbow with her free hand. Blew some smoke.

"Pearlie's a first-rate 'boyfriend'. That's no guarantee there aren't some better."

I thought maybe I knew what she was getting at, but I wanted to make sure.

"And?"

Her jaw released smoke.

"It has occurred to me Draper's partner might think I know who he is."

I nodded.

"As to why I told you there was a partner in the first place...." She looked away, across the civilized islands where people talked in muted voices and ice cubes clinked against glass. She shrugged with unhidden irritation. "Who knows? All those questions you asked, but you never asked me about a partner. It hit me that maybe none of the country club schmoozers you'd talked to had told you – possibly didn't even know. I saw a chance to twist their noses. Show I knew something they didn't. Even scores some for what they probably said about me."

Her expression dared me to deny it.

"One did refer to you as impertinent."

"I'm surprised it wasn't a whole lot worse."

"Another one thinks you're a hot little number."

Her lips formed their secretive line.

"That sounds like Frank Keefe. He thinks anything under thirty that wears a skirt is a hot little number." She glanced at my legs and grinned. "He tell you that you should be modeling hoisery?"

"Just that I ought to wear my shirts shorter."

She gave a throaty chuckle.

"He does turn a good line. It's different assets he admires on me."

I sipped some old fashioned. Across the rim of the glass I saw a familiar face enter the lounge. James C. Hill. His prim air and devotion to efficiency made it hard to imagine him stopping off to enjoy a drink. He sat down by himself. I didn't think he'd seen us.

"Frank and I went out a couple of times," Rachel was saying. She shrugged in answer to a question I hadn't asked. "Some men are curious about Jewish women."

"Does he even bother pretending he's not a Lothario?" I wondered if Hill was meeting someone.

"No. It's what makes him fun. And lots more interesting than the nice Jewish bankers and lawyers usually pushed on me as marriage fodder."

So she got that too.

"But maybe not as interesting as Pearlie," I observed.

She chuckled again. "I have occasionally wondered what Pearlie would be like...."

A lift of her eyebrow finished the sentence. Hard not to grin.

I asked her if Keefe, or anyone else she knew of, drove a maroon Ambassador. She said no. I asked her how far she thought Keefe could be trusted, apart from amorous escapades. She said she didn't think he'd go for murder if that's what I was wondering. Hill had ordered a drink, but he either downed it quickly or left it mostly untouched since he soon got up to leave.

Halfway across the room a brief hesitation in his step told me he'd spotted us. His eyes went from me to the woman across from me and back again. Rachel noted the direction of my gaze and looked. Hill came toward us.

"Miss Minsky, how nice to see you," he said with a stiff smile. He nodded to me with no hint of recognition.

"An unexpected surprise, Mr. Hill." Something in Rachel's tone caused Hill to move on without further pleasantries. "I expect you'd met that little toad," she said, watching him. "Works for one of the men Draper fleeced."

"I don't appear to have made much impression on him."

Rachel snorted. "James C. Hill is sweet on himself. Thinks he's superior to most of the human race."

For once I was inclined to be charitable toward him. Hill was big on correctness; prided himself on doing things right. He'd probably been unsure if acknowledging me would reveal who'd hired me.

"I went out with him once too," Rachel said.

"With Hill?" I couldn't believe it.

"I was curious. He's not nearly as much fun as Frank Keefe. Lively as a post." She glanced at her rose gold wristwatch. "I have to be going."

"One more thing. Who told you about Draper's partner?"

Her eyes narrowed as if in thought.

"I think it was Draper himself. It could have been Frank. No, I'm pretty sure it was Draper. When I told him I wanted my money back. Something about he'd have to check with his partner."

She scooped her lighter into her handbag and stood. We said good-by. She moved toward the door at a brisk clip. I got up too.

My opinion of Rachel Minsky was changing some. I was starting to like her.

I still didn't trust her.

THIRTY-FOUR

A pretty little stand in the hall held Mrs. Z's telephone. We girls were allowed to use it to make and receive short calls. In the daytime most of the calls were for Mrs. Z, so she answered. From five to ten in the evening, when all calls had to stop, someone was usually coming or going and picked it up. They'd come up and get whoever was wanted or leave a note under your door if you weren't there.

There was a note under my door when I got in. It was from Rogers. I'd left a message with his landlady in addition to the one at Wildman's place, and he'd called back to let me know he'd be in all evening.

"I need your help on something," I said when he answered. "Can you get me a photograph, or it may take a couple of them, of everybody who comes to Mr. Wildman's house on a regular basis? Not ones who make deliveries; the ones who stick around. Work there, come to small dinner parties. That kind of thing."

He was silent.

"I could ask Mr. Wildman, but he's got enough on his mind–"

"No, I'm sure I can get what you need. I was just thinking. Do you ... want one that includes Mr. and Mrs. Tarkington?"

"Them in particular."

"He has a photographer come and take a big picture of everyone at the household Christmas party. The

Tarkingtons come. And Mr. Hill, of course. And there used to be a cousin, but he died just over a year ago. Everyone gets a copy."

"That sounds perfect."

"When you asked, I was trying to think if I knew where mine is. If I can't put hands on it, I'm sure Miss Fisher will let me borrow hers. I won't tell her why."

He agreed to drop it off first thing in the morning. Since I was heading for Wheeler's garage first thing and didn't know when I'd get in, I asked him to leave it with Evelyn at Simpson's Socks.

"Not with the older woman, though," I cautioned. "She'd feed me to wolves if she could. She'd be likely to throw it out and tell me she never got it."

He laughed and hung up.

The tangle of weeds and briars I'd been picking my way through on the Draper case was finally yielding two fairly distinct paths. If one of them didn't lead anywhere, I was confident the other would.

* * *

Wheeler's opened at half-past seven so customers could drop their cars off for servicing on their way to work. It was busy that morning. A good twenty minutes elapsed before Eli, followed by Calvin, had a chance to get back to the little office where I was waiting.

Eli had offered me coffee from his Thermos and I hadn't said no. I'd sipped it while I looked at the picture of a Nash Ambassador he'd borrowed for me. The page was the size of a magazine page and the drawing filled about half of it, so detailed that it almost looked like a photograph.

"I promised the fellow I borrowed it from you'd take real good care of it," Eli said.

"And I will. Thanks a million."

"He doesn't sell Ambassadors, but he orders other things so they send him the ads. Not the color you asked about, though."

"It's perfect, Eli. Even has a little picture of it in maroon here at the bottom."

I switched my attention to Calvin. He blushed and looked down.

"It never even occurred to me Calvin might know a place like the one you were asking about," Eli said. "But then I got to telling him later, and he.... You go on and tell her about it, Calvin."

The kid's Adam's apple worked a couple of times. His head raised bashfully.

"I've never seen the place or anything. Just heard about it from this fellow I ran around with some a couple years back. He liked talking cars and that. Wanted to build one like my jalopy. He said he'd heard of a place up on Milburn – around Lamont or someplace like that – where maybe he could get some cheap parts. Said his cousin had told him these brothers had a garage there, that the oldest one had done time for assault but all three were tough nuts – didn't think much of cops and wouldn't give them the time of day."

Eli made a tsking sound. I felt my breath quickening. Calvin tugged at his ear.

"Anyways, his cousin told him you could get parts there cheap, if you didn't ask where they came from." Excitement at what he was telling made Calvin forget to be shy. "The cousin claimed those men with the garage had fixed up the car of a city councilman involved in a hit-and-run. Did it so fast the councilman never even got looked at. Said they'd do just about any sort of dirty work for a price."

I let out a whistle. A car was pulling up outside, but Eli said he'd get it.

"Sounds like the place I'm looking for," I said. "You know the name of those brothers?"

Calvin rubbed his head.

"I think maybe it was Kirkland ... Curtis ... something like that. You're not fixing to go there, are you, Miss Sullivan? They sound like real bad apples."

"I know a couple of gentlemen who'd be glad to check it out for me," I said with a wink. It was true, if I asked, which I didn't intend to do just yet. "This friend of yours, where can I find him?"

Calvin shook his head that he didn't know.

"Night he told me that was the last time I went out with him. It made me think maybe he wasn't the sort I ought to be mixed up with," he said stoutly. "I'd seen him smoke, and he'd let on a couple of times as how he'd had beer."

Calvin was some sort of protestant and didn't believe in drinking, which seemed to me like a pretty strong argument against being one. From what he'd heard, the fellow who'd told him about the garage wasn't around any more.

"Calvin, you are a gem," I said handing him four bits.

"Hey, no," he protested. "I don't want anything."

"Yeah, but those ribs of yours could use about a dozen milkshakes."

* * *

Some details remained before I could follow the trail of Vern leaving a bag in a swank car he claimed he'd never seen before. Meanwhile, there was the question of what could make someone suggest a dead man might still be alive. After thinking it over a good deal, I came up with what could be an answer. What I lacked was anything to support my idea, so after I let Izzy serve me my oatmeal, I headed to see Cecilia Perkins.

"Oh, hello," she said, looking up with a smile as I entered.

She'd been crying, not before I came in, but maybe the night before or that morning. Red still rimmed her eyes.

"No luck on the job front?" I asked as I noticed envelopes neatly opened on the desk in front of her.

Cecilia shrugged.

"Two said I should check back in a couple of weeks, that my qualifications were wonderful and they'd keep my letter on file." She fought to keep the bitterness from her voice. "What can I do for you?"

"Is Mr. Draper's bank account still open?"

Her cheeks flushed.

"Yes, but I haven't written any more checks–"

"That's not what I was getting at. I was wondering if all the checks written to it had cleared."

"Oh." She bit her lip. "I-I'm awfully sorry. I don't know why ... you've been so nice...." She drew a breath and closed her eyes momentarily, gathering control. "I should have said that as far as I know the account's still open. I believe all the checks have cleared, though it was a bit fuzzy on one. You'd need to ask Mr. Draper's lawyer."

"Galen Miller."

"Yes. He's taken charge of settling the financial things that need to be settled. He said he'd let me know when the account was closed, just in case any late bills came in."

My pulse had quickened a little at mention of a "fuzzy" check. I was pretty sure Galen Miller would tell me the status on that, but I couldn't count on getting much more from him.

"What was the date on that last check you wrote?"

Cecilia blushed again, but only faintly.

"Somewhere around the first of the month. Let me check." She opened a desk drawer and took out a ledger. "Here it is." She pointed.

The sixth. A good week before Draper turned up dead, with no entries after it. Apparently it wasn't activity in Draper's bank account that suggested he might be among the living.

"Did Mr. Draper have any other bank accounts?" I asked slowly.

"Savings, I should think, since he made quite a lot of money. And I believe he had a personal account as well." A frown formed between her eyebrows. "Why?"

"Someone said something odd, but maybe I misunderstood. Were his others accounts at the same bank?"

Her blonde head shook. "I don't know."

Galen Miller would probably also be willing to tell me about the other accounts.

"I hate to be a pest," I said, "but could you give me the telephone number of that place where Draper got the massages? I've got a friend with a bad shoulder. Also, I'd like to borrow a photograph of Mr. Draper if you have one."

Cecilia flipped through a long leather address book.

"If you ever learn what Ingrid is like, I'd love a report," she said as she slid me the phone number. Her smile faltered. "Of course I won't be here. Let me get that photograph."

I had a feeling she was fighting tears as she hopped up and fled through the door to what had been Draper's office. It gave me a chance to peek at the ledger she'd left out. Sure enough, peeking from under the back page were two more blank checks Draper had signed and left with her. In Cecilia's position they must be a strong temptation, but one I felt sure she'd resist. Jotting down

Draper's bank account number in case I needed it, I went to join her.

"Are you after a good likeness of him?" she asked frowning at a framed eight-by-ten she'd removed from the wall. "Something to jog someone's memory on what he looked like?"

"Something like that," I agreed.

"There's this." She handed me the photo from the wall. "But I think.... Let me look...."

She checked in a cabinet, then lifted a cardboard box from the floor to look through that. Meanwhile I took the opportunity to flip through Draper's appointment book, going back to the last day he'd come to work.

"I think this one's better, don't you? Or there's this one." She handed me two more eight-by-tens framed in walnut.

The one from the wall was of Draper getting some award from the head of the Chamber of Commerce. Too much camera flash had partly washed out their faces. Both of the other pictures were good, though. They showed Draper and some other men hobnobbing at what looked like a banquet. There were women in the background. Faces there were indistinct, but I thought one might be Rachel Minsky with someone I couldn't see clearly.

"I recognize Mr. Keefe and Mr. Smith," I said, studying the main group, "but who's the other man?"

Cecilia peered over my shoulder.

"That's Mr. Preston, poor man. He ... died shortly after Mr. Draper disappeared."

She knew he'd killed himself. I wondered if she suspected why.

The remaining photograph showed the same men applauding. Smith was missing, though, and Frank Keefe was looking away.

"I'll take this one," I said, indicating the foursome.

As Cecilia turned, I took a final look at the page I'd turned to in Draper's appointment book. On the day before he disappeared, the last appointment listed had been with Rachel Minsky.

THIRTY-FIVE

"A very nice man in a chauffer's livery left something for you," Evelyn smiled when I stuck my head through the door at Simpson's Socks. She was pretty in an old-fashioned way, with dark hair rolled at the top of her head. Reaching under the counter, she slid me a paper-wrapped photograph the size of the one I was carrying.

"We are *not* your personal delivery service!" snapped the older woman reading a newspaper at the other end of the long counter. Her only expression was sour, and Evelyn had the misfortune to be her daughter-in-law.

"You know, Maxine," I said leaning in confidentially. "For someone who wears such flirty underpants, you're not very friendly."

She began to puff like Vesuvius. "I do *not*— How dare you!"

I gave a departing wave to Evelyn, who was holding her sides to keep in laughter.

A sealed, unmarked envelope had been shoved under my door. I tossed it onto my desk and unwrapped the picture from Rogers. As expected, it was a dandy professional job. It showed Wildman and his son, Dorothy and Vern, all the members of Wildman's staff. I set it and the one from Draper's office aside to use in the afternoon.

Then I called Galen Miller.

"I have just five minutes between clients," he said when he came on. "How may I help you, Miss Sullivan?"

"You're settling the late Harold Draper's affairs."

"That's correct."

"And his bank account is still open?"

"As is customary for an interval until it's determined there are no outstanding claims."

Did I remember that from when my dad died? That part of my life was blurry. I'd been nineteen, on my own, drained by the final weeks of his illness.

"It's a bit of a moot point," Miller was saying. "Even my own fee won't be forthcoming until his house is sold."

"He drained both accounts when he left town? Business and personal?"

Miller hesitated. "You might owe me a favor or two."

"Fair enough."

"He left enough in the business account to cover two checks he wrote to his secretary, for salary, and matters that might be outstanding. He closed the other the day he left town."

"Were the checks to his secretary the last ones written on his account?"

"Yes."

"Savings? Safety deposit box?"

"Don't push your luck, Miss Sullivan. Tell whoever you're making these inquiries for there's not enough left for a fly to dine on."

I opened the envelope next. Inside was a sheet of paper with the handwritten note PAID IN FULL. A string of numbers followed. To anyone else it would look like a simple receipt. Except FULL was underlined several times and I recognized Jenkins' writing. Just now, though, I wasn't as interested in the Chicago phone number he'd dug up for me as I was some things closer to home.

* * *

I decided to take a chance on calling Freeze directly, and was somewhat surprised when he took my call.

"It has been suggested to me that Draper might still be alive," I said.

"No. Impossible. The body was in good shape. Two people identified him."

"What I'm wondering, though, is if anything might have happened since his demise – something signed or sold or activity in his bank account – that could make someone think that."

"And how do you suppose we'd go about tracking down something like that?" he asked impatiently.

"Gee, I don't know, but then I'm just a helpless female, not even a real cop. I thought you smart boys with your big brains might come up with something."

I hung up. It spared him the heartbreak of not getting an answer when he asked me who'd told me Draper might still be kicking.

Calling Freeze had been mostly courtesy, although I'm a sucker for playing a long shot. With no idea whether he'd poke around or not, I reached for a notepad and got out my phone book, propped my feet on the desk and settled in to do just that.

Draper's bank accounts, at least the ones his lawyer and secretary knew about, were at Winters. I was wondering if he'd also had one somewhere else. Squirreling away a substantial amount of money you wanted to hide wasn't something it would be wise to do in a small bank, given how many had failed in the last decade. It also might attract too much notice in such an establishment. Therefore, I began with the bigger banks, or at least the ones I knew. Armed with the unsharpened pencil that fit the holes of a telephone dial, thereby sparing my nail polish, I dialed the first.

"This is Laura Draper Jackson," I said, putting the tiniest tremor in my voice. "My brother Harold died last week and I - I need to close out his bank account. Whom do I need to talk to, please?"

I was asked to wait, and after a minute a respectfully muted male voice came on offering condolences.

"I'm afraid you'll need to come in."

"Oh dear. Yes, of course." I sniffed as if trying to hold back tears. "Could you just check ... see if perhaps it's already been done? His lawyer may have said something ... I - I can't remember. I've been so upset...."

He checked and returned with more apologies to say they had no record of ever having an account in the name Harold Draper."

"Oh. Could I ... maybe I got the bank wrong. I'm so sorry. You've been so kind."

I repeated my performance half a dozen times with similar results. Maybe I was barking up the wrong tree. Maybe Draper, if he'd even had a second account, had it under a different name. I tapped my teeth, flirting with the thought of calling Rachel Minsky and asking if she knew where Draper did his banking. Having seen her name and the spot where it fell in Draper's appointment calendar, that might not be wise. After stretching my legs with a trip up the stairs to the loo, I went back to work.

It took me five more tries.

"I'm so sorry about your brother," said the voice that came on. "I'll get the paperwork ready to make it as easy as possible when you come in. I know it's a difficult time for you. Don't forget you'll need to bring your key for the safety deposit box."

My excitement soared.

"Thank you," I murmured. "I'll have to take the train from Troy, so it will be after lunch."

We said polite good-byes and I did a little dance around my desk to work off the burst of energy I suddenly felt. Then I picked up the phone and called a second-hand store called The Good Neighbor. Plenty of people needed second-hand clothes, and the quality there was better than some. Things that weren't in such good shape the store gave away free to people who needed them.

"Is Clarice there?" I asked.

She was the white-haired doll who'd started the place. It took several minutes before she came on.

"It's Maggie Sullivan," I said. "I need to buy a funeral hat, something with plenty of veiling. Can you fix me up?"

"I'm sure we have several. Shall I put them aside?"

"Just a couple. I need to borrow a black outfit, too."

"It's not a real bereavement, then?" She'd picked up on the 'borrow'. "I won't offer condolences, then."

I'd helped her out a couple of times when she wanted to find out who was pinching merchandise out of the storage room. She returned the favor when I needed some kind of get-up to make me hard to recognize.

"And the outfit ... maybe on the matronly side?"

Clarice chuckled. "My dear, it taxes my imagination trying to picture you as matronly."

* * *

The layers of black veil on the hat I got from Clarice were so thick I didn't risk driving in it. I'd pinned my hair up in a prim twist which the hat covered. Clad in a boxy black suit a good five inches longer than I usually wore, I arrived at the bank thinking even Billy and Seamus wouldn't recognize me. Mr. Hayworth, the man I'd spoken to on the phone, met me with such kind words I felt guilty over at least the bereavement part of my charade. He was a stoop-shouldered man with thinning hair. He ushered me into a small office and offered me a glass of water, which I declined.

"These are the records for his checking account ... and his savings," he said, handing me two lined sheets with neat figures and initials of the bank clerk who had made each entry. "You'll want to give them a look-over, I expect, before you sign the form I've attached to each. As you can see, your brother wasn't a very frequent user of his accounts."

"No.... No, he preferred to, ah, use cash whenever possible."

Reading was all but impossible through the black veil. I had to tilt my head back to see underneath. What the sheets revealed was worth the effort. Draper had opened both accounts seven months ago, no doubt laying the groundwork for his swindle. The checking account had never had much in it. Thirty dollars in the beginning. The checks made out had all been to "cash". Small amounts. Sporadic. Just enough activity to keep anyone from getting suspicious. There'd been two cash deposits, one for ten dollars and the other for twenty. Assuming this was the same Draper, the checking account was a red herring.

The savings account was a good deal more interesting. A series of deposits in the fall had brought it to nearly two thousand dollars. He'd drawn out most of it Friday before last, possibly the day before he died.

"Ah, here's Mr. Charles to take you back to the deposit boxes. If you'd like to get out your key...?"

Mr. Charles was younger, with bifocals. His nod could have been either greeting or apology. He awaited instructions with a deference suggesting he held a position several steps below that of Mr. Hayworth. I pressed one corner of my hanky to my lips and started to sniff.

"Oh, I-I'm so sorry. I looked everywhere, and I couldn't find ... I know Hal told me once where it was...."

Hayworth shifted uncomfortably.

"I'm afraid we can't release the contents of the box unless you have the key."

"But what if I *never* find it?" I wailed, trying to squeeze out a few tears.

"It's how we ensure security—"

"Couldn't I just have a *peek*? All I really care about is making sure Grandpa Fulton's Union Army discharge papers are inside. He fought at Gettysburg, you know. Aunt Josephine's in such a tizzy – great-aunt, really – fretting the family will never see them again, now that Hal's died. But my brother was very responsible! He told me himself that he'd put them in his bank box. Only Aunt Jo's so worked up we're afraid she'll keel over – what with her age and her weak heart...."

Hayworth was squirming. The other banker bent close to murmur to him. I dithered on.

"If I could just reassure her I'd *seen* the papers...."

Dabbing my eyes (no small feat what with needing to get under the veil without lifting it) I watched Hayworth draw back as if startled. A spate of whispering back-and-forth ensued. He swallowed.

"If she has a spell, everyone will blame me," I whimpered.

"Mrs. Jackson—"

"They care more about those papers than they did about poor Hal—"

"Mrs. Jackson, please!" Hayworth puffed out a long breath. He passed a hand over his mouth. "This is ... most irregular. Highly irregular. Nonetheless, I - I think you should hear what Mr. Charles just told me."

THIRTY-SIX

Hayworth cleared his throat, then cleared it again.

"I'm not sure this will ease your distress. In fact, I fear.... In any case, it seems only fair. The whole business is ... well, it's odd, really. Please do remember that telling you this is highly unusual, since contents of safety deposit boxes are confidential–"

"Oh, I am so grateful!" I gushed. If I didn't interrupt, I was afraid he'd never get to the point.

"Yes, well, the fact is Mr. Charles – inadvertently – has information about the contents of your brother's safety deposit box.

Forgetting he probably couldn't make out any expression through my veil, I looked expectantly at the younger banker. He straightened his spectacles.

"You see, ma'am, I took your brother back to get into the box the last time he was here. I'm generally the one who takes people back for them, and watches them put their key in, and gets their signature. Unless I'm off for the day or we get unusually busy, in which case another man helps."

Did they give all bankers lessons in circumlocution? My borrowed get-up was getting uncomfortably hot.

"I don't ordinarily remember names, not with so many customers, but I recall Mr. Draper. There are two small rooms where we put people so they can sit and open their box to put things in or take them out in privacy. Your brother wasn't in his a minute before he came storming out and grabbed my arm. He asked what we were trying to pull – the damned box was empty."

Mr. Charles grew pink at the edge of his ears.

"I do apologize," he said, with a nervous glance at Hayworth, "but those were his exact words. I could see it was true. The deposit box was dangling open in one hand."

"Oh, dear!" A dozen thoughts elbowed each other for my attention.

"Forgive me for asking," Charles continued, "but was your brother, um, upset at the time of his death? Preoccupied? Perhaps not himself?"

"Really, Ethan! I hardly think–" began Hayworth.

"Why, yes," I interrupted quickly. "How clever and - and kind you are to have noticed. He'd been jilted. By a girl he was hoping to marry. I think - I think he wasn't sleeping. Why do you ask?"

Mr. Charles gestured uncomfortably with a card he was carrying on top of the metal box.

"He'd been in just a few days earlier. He must have emptied it then and not even remembered."

I went utterly still.

"And that last time he came in was when again?"

He consulted the card in his hand. "Wednesday. Last Wednesday."

Three days *after* Draper was fished from the river.

* * *

I sat in my car several minutes, sorting my thoughts. Someone had come in after Draper was dead, with the key to his safety deposit box and the skill to duplicate his signature well enough to gain access. Of equal interest was the previous time the box had been accessed: the day before Draper took his last swim. He'd come in almost the minute the bank opened. It had been an occasion when the other clerk rather than Mr. Charles took customers back.

To wiggle out of signing anything, I'd manufactured a fresh flood of tears and fled with a mumbled apology, saying perhaps I should come back when I wasn't so upset. I did allow maybe my brother had taken great-grandpa's papers to Cousin Charlotte. With luck that would keep the two bankers from getting worked up.

Now I knew that Draper had kept secret accounts at a second bank. That he'd taken out most of his savings and emptied his safety deposit box a day before he was killed. That somebody who didn't know the accounts were depleted had come in pretending to be him. I took off the black hat and ran my hands through my hair.

Before I returned my mourning weeds to Clarice, I wanted to put them to use a few more times. First I drove to the house Draper owned. I tried the neighbor on the right first, again introducing myself as Draper's sister.

"Hal mentioned a friend of his who drove a reddish car," I said. "An Ambassador, I think he said. The car, not the man. But I simply can't remember his name. Do you happen to know?"

The neighbor looked like she'd just gotten back from having her hair done. It was glossy and smooth and she kept patting it from time to time.

"I'm afraid we didn't know Mr. Draper that well. He was extra man at the Thortons' dinner parties a few times, always very pleasant. But I can't recall seeing a car that looked even remotely red. They're mostly black and gray, aren't they? My husband's quite crazy for cars. I'm sure he would have talked about it if he'd seen something like that."

I said that reminded me I was supposed to look at the tires on the one in Hal's garage. It was on her side of Draper's house, and it gave me an excuse to peek without fear of arousing suspicion. Mercifully it had a window on one side, so I didn't have to resort to picking the lock on the overhead door. I peered inside and saw the tan Buick Cecilia had told me about.

No one answered at the house on the left. I tried two places across the street. One of them was a middle-aged woman who said she simply didn't know what they'd do now when they needed someone to pair a single woman at dinner. Neither she nor the other woman I talked to had seen a car resembling the ambassador.

That left Ingrid, the masseuse with the formidable phone presence. Sometimes people kept lockers at places where they took saunas and such. I didn't expect to find wads of cash from Draper's secret bank accounts, but I might find something.

The place was in the basement of a tailor's shop on Wilkinson. That made it convenient for men like Draper to duck out for steam and back pounding whenever it suited them. A sign above the door said simply Sauna and Swedish Massage. I went down the concrete stairs and stepped inside.

A bent-over guy with a walrus mustache bigger than all the rest of him looked up.

"You not selling, *ja*?" he said, surveying my black ensemble.

"Not selling," I agreed. "I was hoping to speak with Ingrid."

He surveyed me some more and sniffed with decision.

"She gives massage now. Five minutes more. You wait." He pointed to a hard-looking wooden chair.

It was as hard as it looked. The man with the walrus eyed me to make sure I wouldn't swipe anything. Moving like a man half his age, he disappeared through a door in the corner. Two identical wooden desks placed end-to-end formed a sort of counter. They were light wood, smooth but not glossy, and once you got past the idea they weren't finished, they weren't bad to look at. The room had a Spartan feel, but there wasn't a smudge or particle of dirt in evidence. Someone had painted the telephone a deep, bright blue. It was the only thing that might pass for decoration.

The walrus man returned and settled onto what I now realized was a stool behind his desk. A few minutes later a woman in a narrow white duster came out. A brief exchange in a foreign language sent the man out again. She turned to me.

"I am Ingrid," she said, advancing.

As I rose, I saw she was probably five-foot-ten and built like a wrestler. I decided not to offer my hand in case I wanted to use it in the next day or so. Her blonde hair formed a braid on top of her head. The stolidness of her expression would have discouraged even Frank Keefe.

"I'm Harold Draper's sister," I said. "I'm here to collect his things. And - and to thank you. He told me once that a massage from you made the whole week go better."

Ingrid blinked.

"Sister." She surveyed me. "Someone has died?"

"Yes."

"Is him? Mr. Draper?"

"Um, yes." The paper had run half a column or so on the body pulled out of the river. It had mentioned Draper's name, but the story hadn't been prominent. Ingrid clearly hadn't read it.

She bowed her head.

"I am sorry," she said. "Please wait."

She turned and disappeared back through the door in the corner. Moments later she reappeared. In her hand was a leather satchel.

"He was moving, I think? He had missed his massage for some weeks when he came and left it."

She handed it to me. The weight pulled my arm down. The bag itself locked. Another lock circled the handles.

"Yes. Moving," I repeated.

I felt lightheaded.

I hadn't come here expecting to find a bag full of cash, but I was afraid I just might have.

THIRTY-SEVEN

I felt jumpy all the way to my car and twice as jumpy once I got in. Although I was disguised, I'd realized standing in Ingrid's place with the bag in my arms that my car wasn't.

In an absent sort of way, I'd kept an eye out for anyone following me when I set out this morning. I'd been so revved up when I left the bank that I couldn't recall checking since. Whether or not the bag I shoved onto the floor of my car contained money, I was fairly certain it held the contents of Draper's safety deposit box. I didn't want to walk anywhere with it – not into The Good Neighbor store, not to my office. I wasn't that keen on driving around with it, either.

The solution that came to mind made it prudent to hide evidence of my widow's weeds. Keeping my eyes peeled around me, I took off the black hat and jacket. I unpinned my hair and shook it out like I usually wore it. I couldn't do anything about the dowdy black skirt. I slapped on some lipstick and headed a couple of blocks to Market House.

Finding a parking space right in front of police headquarters was less than zero, but on the building's north side there was a huge sliding door. Aware I was about to get myself in hot water, I pulled up in front of it and leaned on my horn. It took another blast ... another ... and another.... The sliding door opened halfway and a cop in uniform stormed out. An older guy.

"What the hell do you think – ah, jeez. It's the Sullivan kid. You doing okay after the business you took in that alley?"

"Yeah, I'm good." Half the department must know details. Fine, as long as Seamus and Billy didn't.

"Clear out before both our heads roll. You know there's no stopping here."

"I've got something for Freeze – bag of evidence in a homicide. Not sure what's in it, but maybe money enough to pay the salaries of the whole department. Didn't want to chance walking around with it. Someone's been following me."

He thought half a second.

"Okay, drive inside." He opened the door enough to accommodate me as he spoke. "Mind you pull to the side. You know where to find Freeze?"

I parked the DeSoto as close as I could to the wall and jumped out. Staring at me from the center of the garage was the massive steel-plated Cadillac used by the Flying Squad. If a bank was robbed, an alarm sounded here and members of the squad came tearing down and into the car, which would already have its motor running. Machine guns, shotguns, tear gas and more were lined up inside it.

Fortunately, no banks were robbed as I made my way up the stairs.

"Is Boike or the lieutenant in?" I asked when I reached Freeze's section.

"Boike is, don't know about Freeze."

I nodded and found him. Boike looked up as I dropped the bag on his desk.

"Draper had secret accounts at another bank," I announced. "He cleaned them both out the day before he died. Happens that same day he asked to leave this at a place where he got Swedish massages. He told the owner he'd be back for it. I'm guessing it may hold a good bit of cash."

I gave him a few particulars, mainly addresses.

"Hey, wait!" he said as I started to leave.

"I'm parked where I shouldn't be. You don't want me getting a ticket, do you, Boike? I've got to be somewhere. Tell Freeze if he has questions I'll fill him in later."

"At least tell me how you happen to have this."

I smiled from the doorway.

"A woman who looked like she was in mourning with a veil on her face handed it to me."

* * *

By the time I drove toward Bellbrook the afternoon was more than half gone. I'd returned my borrowed outfit to The Good Neighbor shop, followed by a stop at my office. There I'd dashed off some notes about what I'd learned at the bank and from Ingrid, with names and addresses. I'd put them into an envelope addressed to Wildman, and that envelope in another one to a post office box I keep. If anything happened to me at this point, Wildman would still get a decent account of what I'd learned.

The last thing I'd done was retrieve the photographs borrowed from Cecilia Perkins and Rogers. I removed them from their nice frames and put them in cardboard ones that protected them but were easier to haul around without breaking glass.

The drive from downtown to Bellbrook took half an hour, maybe longer. It was country roads most of the way, so I couldn't fly along at thirty-five like I did on the highway. That was fine with me since it was the first chance I'd had to sit and think through the considerable number of things I'd learned that afternoon. How did they fit with what I already knew, and what did it all tell me?

First there were the brief facts I'd shared with Boike. Friday before last, one day after Wildman had hired me, Draper had surfaced long enough to clear out his clandestine bank accounts. That same day, he'd left a bag with Ingrid. He'd told her he'd return for it.

Unfortunately for Draper, on the next day, Saturday, someone had hit him over the head and pushed him into the river. Several days after that, someone posing as him had opened his safety deposit box and thrown a fit upon finding it empty.

It had been the real Draper at Ingrid's. After she'd handed me the bag, while I was still standing there, stunned, she'd told me awkwardly that he was a good man. When she'd scolded him about costing her money by missing appointments, he'd apologized and insisted on paying her for them, she said. He'd told her he wanted to get back on her schedule.

What the hell had he been up to? Deflecting suspicion by indicating he meant to stay around, surely. But why reappear once you'd disappeared? And why hadn't he taken whatever was in the safety deposit box in the first place? I didn't have any answers by the time I saw the place I was looking for up ahead.

It was a simple wood-sided building, painted brown. There was nothing fancy about it, but it wasn't run down, either. Parked next to it were two pickup trucks and a car that looked like it might belong to a salesman. I pulled up beside them.

The place got right to the point with its advertising. A painted sign three times the width of the door it hung above said simply BEER. I'd switched to my blue hat and had on the new shoes I'd bought Saturday. They had stacked heels, stylish but sturdy enough for trotting around the way I did in the course of my work, and laced at the instep. What with the shoes and the hat and the progress

I'd made that afternoon, I felt positively chipper as I went inside.

A man whose features were sliding off of his face stood behind the bar. He greeted me pleasantly.

"Nice location you've got here," I said.

He nodded. "Get you something to drink?"

"A beer sounds good. Dark, if you have it."

While he moved to get it, I had a look around. Three men in workmen's garb were playing poker for matchsticks in the corner. Two others sat at a table sipping beer. A guy in a suit leaned on the opposite end of the bar with his chin on his hand. The walls were smooth, varnished knotty pine decorated with signs advertising Budweiser and Pabst Blue Ribbon and Lucky Strike. You wouldn't expect excitement here, but it wasn't a place where you'd worry about trouble either. A good part of their business probably came from people who were just passing through.

The beer I got was closer to amber than dark, something from the Olt Brothers. I paid for it and took a swig. It was okay.

"You selling?" the bartender asked, nodding at the big manilla envelope I'd placed on the bar beside me. The photographs were inside it.

"Buying, maybe." I slid six bits toward him.

He studied the room.

"Information?"

I nodded.

"Man's cheating on you, he's not too bright."

I laughed. "It's not like that."

I handed him one of my cards. He read it and the features on his face slid even lower.

"Nothing to make any trouble," I reassured. "I'm just trying to locate a couple of people who might have come in here."

He considered a minute. Another man, this one in shirt sleeves with a suit jacket over his arm, came in. His eyes made a sweep of the room. He came to the bar and ordered a whiskey which he took to a table. His manner was more alert than that of the other occupants, but that could be nothing more than being in a new place. I kept an eye on him anyway.

"You want me to look at pictures or something? Is that all?" asked the bartender as he came back from serving the new arrival.

"That's it."

He took the quarters. I removed the two photographs and turned them so we both could see. At the other end of the bar the guy in the suit had looked up with interest.

"Let me know if you recognize any of these gents." I watched the bartender's eyes. They didn't hesitate much. Neither did his finger.

"Sure, that one's been in." He pointed at Draper. His finger moved on. "That one too. Came in several times, both of them. Usually sat together. Haven't been in for a while, though."

I let out a long breath.

THIRTY-EIGHT

I knew who Draper's partner was now. What I needed was proof. After waiting outside the roadhouse for five minutes to see if anyone came out who might be following me, I started the engine and pointed the DeSoto back toward town.

The sad-faced bartender hadn't been able to tell me much more about the two men meeting there. Things were starting to jell, though. Except that I was ending up with more questions than answers. Why had Draper vanished while his partner remained? And once Draper had taken off, why had he come back? To get whatever had been in the safety deposit box, apparently. But why hadn't he taken it in the first place?

There was also the nasty little question of who had killed Draper.

I knew who Draper's partner was, but was that individual capable of murder? Maybe when you operated at the level of big time investment and big time swindles, you hired goons to do your dirty work.

Several people in this little drama knew goons.

* * *

The time for calling Ferris Wildman wasn't ideal by the time I got back. At this time of day he usually met with his manager. After what I'd learned, though, I wanted to make doubly certain he stayed safe these next few days. I propped my feet on the desk and pulled the phone over and dialed.

"Miss Sullivan. Do you have something to report?" he asked when he came on.

"I know who Draper's partner was, and I may have found part of the money, but I need you to act irritated from here on out like I'm not making progress. Did you send Stuart away?"

"Yes."

"Don't leave your house tomorrow – not for anything, not with anyone."

"I really–"

"Please. Plead illness if you have to."

Some seconds elapsed. When he spoke his voice was stoney.

"As you wish."

"I need to go to Lebanon tomorrow to see if I can learn one more thing. I should have plenty to tell you when I get back. Could I stop by sometime in the evening?"

"Nine o'clock?"

"Fine."

"You are not meeting my expectations." He hung up.

I hoped he was playacting.

The envelope with the phone number Jenks had left for me caught my eye. I looked at the clock. Chicago was an hour earlier. Chances were good I could reach Lucinda Graham before her husband got home, which was what I wanted.

It took a while to get through.

"My name's Sullivan, and I'm calling from Dayton about a friend of hers," I told the butler who answered. "I won't keep her a minute."

I wondered whether she'd take a call from a stranger with such a vague explanation. Judging from what I'd been told about her shyness, I thought she might.

Several minutes elapsed before a soft voice answered.

"Hello? This is Lucinda Graham speaking."

Soft and lovely and soothing, the voice matched Cecilia Perkins' description.

"Mrs. Graham, my name's Maggie Sullivan, and I hope I'm not inconveniencing you. I'm tying up some things related to the death of Harold Draper."

At the other end of the line, I heard her breath catch.

"When?" Her voice broke on the question. She hadn't known.

"A little over a week ago. I'm sor–"

My apology died as the receiver went down on a heart-broken sob.

Sometimes succeeding makes you feel like a heel. This was one of those times. I'd learned something that might help explain why Draper had done what he did. It looked like he'd had an affair with Lucinda Graham – and it had meant something to her.

* * *

I figured I'd earned some fun. I headed to Finn's to collect. There was a great story I could tell about Wee Willie Ryan trying to tie a firecracker onto a cat's tail. Wee Willie hadn't been able to pick his nose for a week. Once his ma finished with him, he hadn't been able to sit down, either.

As soon as I opened the door, the friendliness of the place gathered me into its arms. This time of year, no matter how often Finn mopped the hardwood floor, there was almost always a gray puddle right inside the door from people stamping off slush. I stepped around it. When I looked up I came to a dead stop. There was Connelly, watching me from the place where he stood near the back of the bar.

My thoughts has been so tied up on the Draper business, and I'd been in such fine spirits, I'd forgotten how unsettled the night he'd driven me home had left me. My taste buds were set on a proper beer, though, and Finn's had been my place a long time before Connelly happened along. I wasn't about to cede territory, so taking a breath to steady myself, I walked slowly back and sat down next to him.

Finn's tended to fill from the front. Several stools separated us from other customers. Connelly gave up leaning on the bar to slide onto the stool beside me. We didn't speak.

Connelly ducked his head to the full pint before him and took a sip, tilting the glass.

"Put out over me seeing you home, are you?" he said with amusement. "Here I thought you might be thawing a little."

I felt the force of his presence.

"I wasn't myself the other night. Don't make anything of it."

"You lecturing me or yourself?"

Down the bar Finn held a clean glass aloft and looked a question. I nodded. Finn drew my Guinness and set it aside to settle enough to top it for the perfect thickness of foam.

"There's nothing wrong with having feelings, Maggie. With making a chink or two in that wall."

But I'd seen too much of my dad's feelings – love, adoration, pain as he tried to please my mother and got back scathing indifference. I shook my head.

"You don't understand."

"You're right, but it won't deter me."

Memory of standing on the porch with him at Mrs. Z's pushed through despite my efforts.

"You fight dirty, Connelly."

He swiveled and leaned on his elbow, so close our breaths mingled. His voice was soft.

"I fight any way I can win, Maggie *mavourneen*. And I don't give up easy. When I was eleven, men came to the house and killed my brother while my mother begged for his life and the little ones screamed. I vowed to get the men responsible. Took me ten years."

"Jesus, Connelly–"

His head gave a shake, cutting me off. "Idiot thing to tell a woman. Sorry. I'll speak no more on it. All I meant to say is, I know how to wait. And I'll keep trying to win you 'til barley grows diamonds."

He turned and began to banter with Finn, who was bringing my Guinness.

My mouth was so dry I could hardly swallow. I'd just learned more about Connelly than all the rest I knew about him put together. More than anyone else here knew, likely. He was that self-contained. He'd come to manhood in bloody times, and had left Ireland only a few years ago, when he was already closing on thirty. He'd still been there when Michael Collins was killed.

I took another drink and saw him watching me from the edge of his eyes. I nodded. To indicate ... I wasn't sure what. Acceptance. Agreement that if his brother's death were mentioned again, it would be his doing.

As he opened his mouth to speak, cheery voices erupted at the front of the bar. Here came Billy and Seamus, arm and arm, their faces ready to split with grins.

"And here he gives me this record," Seamus was saying. "And it's not my birthday or anything!"

"Women give each other blankets and rattles and such when they have a new baby," Billy said proudly. "Figured I should do something like that for my oldest chum."

I rolled my eyes, unable to stifle a groan. Next to me Connelly chuckled, raking a hand through his hair as he gave me a sideways glance.

"Looks like the spring thaw came early," he said.

"And none too soon." I lifted my glass. "I was starting to think of finding a gunny sack big enough to hold them both." I slid from my stool. "Think I'll move to a table."

"Was that an invitation, then?"

I hadn't meant it as such, but I shrugged.

"Since when do you need one?"

Tables weren't as popular at Finn's, at least not on a weekday. We sat down. Connelly tossed his uniform hat on the chair beside him.

Back at the bar Seamus was saying proudly, "... when we've finished our pints, we're going to go have a listen."

"Glad they've made up," Connelly said. "They were miserable."

"Yeah."

I could feel him watching me as I watched the two old friends. Something had shifted between us, and I didn't like the tilt. It was time to restore balance.

"You ever hear of some brothers named something like Kirkland or Curtis? Run a dodgy garage? Sell car parts cheap, maybe make repairs with no questions asked?"

Connelly tipped back in his chair and started to chuckle.

"Safe ground, is it? Or did you come here tonight to pump me? Their name's Kirkmann. It came up early when we started hunting the car from that hit-and-run."

"You checked their place, then?"

"The boys in Auto Recovery did. It's up on Milburn. Legitimate repairs up front, good-sized bay in the back with a separate entrance is how I hear it."

"No sign of a banged up black car either place?"

"Nope."

He hadn't told me where it was. I drank some Guinness. Mouth slightly ajar, I trailed one finger slowly along my lip to wipe it as Connelly's eyes followed the motion.

"What about a maroon Ambassador? Anyone mention seeing something like that?"

"Maroon. No. That is, I'm not familiar with that make of car. It have something to do with the hit-and-run?"

"Maybe with Draper. I thought those brothers might be doing the dirty work for his partner. But from what you've said, I can check them off my list," I said brightly. "If you hear anything about a maroon car, will you let me know?"

"Sure. You leaving?"

I was gathering my purse.

"Long drive ahead of me tomorrow. See you later."

Seamus and Billy had vanished. Wee Willie hadn't come in. I waved good-by to some of the regulars on my way out.

Then I scampered, in hopes Connelly would go for the bait I'd just tossed him.

THIRTY-NINE

A few minutes after I'd trotted over to the parking lot and brought my car around to where I had a good view, Connelly came out of the pub. He swung along with a stride more at home on country roads than city streets. It brought to mind rolling green hills and sheep and thatched roof cottages ... and the violence he'd spoken of almost casually a short while ago. I pushed those images out of my mind and concentrated.

Since Connelly didn't own a car, I knew he'd have to borrow one if he did what I expected him to. Sure enough, after a block or so he crossed the street and opened the door to an old sedan. Its make was indeterminate. I strained to make out the license number as it went past.

He'd be quick to recognize my DeSoto if I got close. That was okay, because by the looks of things so far, I knew where I could pick him up next. Connelly was smart and he learned fast, but I'd grown up in Dayton, and I'd driven a lot of neighborhoods since I'd hung out my shingle. I knew where traffic lights were. I knew shortcuts. I cut north until I hit Milburn and followed it into an area where factories squatted alongside houses of hard-working Poles, Hungarians and Lithuanians. Just south of Leonhard I pulled up next to a small machine shop and doused my lights.

If I didn't get any results from tomorrow's trip, I knew I might want to take a look around the Kirkmann brothers' establishment. Unfortunately, Calvin hadn't been very clear on its location. Neither had Connelly when I'd raised the subject. Then, sitting across the table from him, I'd recognized an opportunity.

Asking questions about the garage itself would make him suspicious. Bringing up the maroon car might tempt him to check the garage. If the car was there, he'd tell Freeze of the possible connection, and possibly get a small feather in his cap. A nice feather for someone who wanted to work his way to detective. My plan was to sit and wait and let Connelly lead me to the right building.

I rolled my side window down an inch to keep the windshield from fogging. It let in the smell of the Kay & Ess paint and varnish factory on Kiser. Until a few years ago Maxwell automobiles were still being built not far from here, but a new subsidiary of Chrysler had taken over that space ... and here, unless I missed my guess, came Connelly.

Only one other car had passed since I'd parked. It was going on eight and the streets around me were black as pitch. Sitting had let my eyes adjust. As this car rolled by, I was able to make out that it was the one I'd expected. If it went all the way to Lamar, I'd have to put on my lights and risk being seen. Instead, it stopped half a dozen buildings away from where I sat.

Connelly waited five minutes, long enough to observe any movement around him. Long enough for anyone who'd noticed him to come out and check. Finally he opened the car door just enough to ease out, keeping his head below the roof of the car. He waited again before moving, the same way I did in such situations. The way my dad had taught me in childhood games, never guessing I'd put his lessons to real use someday.

When Connelly moved, he blended into the shadows so well it was hard to follow his progress. For an instant I thought I'd lost him and I swore. Then I saw a figure gliding toward the side of a building. It disappeared for so long I fidgeted. To the back, I presumed. The streets around were silent, except for the slam of a door and the protest of a cat being put out. At last Connelly reappeared, moving briskly now.

I waited until he pulled away from the curb and did a U-turn. Then I put my lights on and swung out, stopping where he'd have to go around me. His engine pitch changed, as though he meant to outrun any potential trouble. As he got close enough to realize who it was, he stomped on the brake.

We were window to window. I cranked mine down first.

"Find anything of interest?" I asked cheerily.

His jaw was set as hard as the brake.

"No – but maybe you should check for yourself, since you apparently don't trust me enough to ask me along. Or do you just have such a swelled head you can't even admit you might like company?"

With a grinding of gears he drove off before I could answer.

* * *

McCrory's had barely opened when I showed up for breakfast. The rest of the store was still roped off against early birds who wanted to shop. I was eager to get on the road. Although I had a map, I'd never gone to Lebanon before, and I wasn't sure how long it would take. It looked like somewhere around thirty-five miles, so maybe an hour and fifteen minutes, or even more. In my impatience I scalded my tongue on my coffee.

By being out and about this early, I was hoping I could catch Jenkins before he set out for his first assignment. I'd left a couple messages yesterday, but I'd been out so much his chances of reaching me when he called back were slim. As I was crossing Ludlow, he came barreling out of the newspaper building's front door.

"Hey, Mags," he called as I waved. We fell into step. He was between feedings, poor lamb.

"What's the best route to Lebanon?"

"Scenic or speed?"

"Speed."

"State route, then. The national's better in places, but it swings west so far you lose time cutting back over. Speed limit's thirty-five on both, so there's nothing to even out the extra distance."

"It entered my mind I might risk forty if I took the US route."

"Adds lots of time if you get a ticket. Or blow a gasket."

It sounded like the voice of experience. Jenkins and Ione had driven to Lebanon several times. He stopped to button his coat collar. The temperature was heading down.

"It's the middle of the week. Why are you going to Lebanon?"

"My reputation is growing," I said grandly.

"Your reputation for being a pain in the backside?"

Ahead of us a traffic light changed. Jenkins broke into a trot. I headed back toward my office to pick up items necessary for my trip.

* * *

I'd already logged more miles working for Ferris Wildman than I usually did on a case. By the end of today I'd easily triple it. When I wrapped things up, it might be smart to take my car in so Eli could look it over to see if it needed grease or hoses or anything.

Once out of Dayton proper there was the city of Oakwood, and after that Van Buren Township, which was building up. From there it was about ten miles to a town called Centerville, which wasn't much more than a crossroads lined with old stone houses. I'd been that far a couple of times. I'd even driven it once when some of us from Mrs. Z's had gotten the notion to have a picnic. When the stone houses disappeared in my rearview mirror, though, I was in unknown territory.

The fields opening out on either side were probably pretty in spring and summer. Right now they were desolate. Here and there I saw a farm house set back up a lane, and occasionally some cows or horses. I began to conjugate Latin verbs to pass the time. I thought about Seamus and his new record player. The world felt right again now that he and Billy had made up.

A couple of wide spots not even big enough to be villages came and went. It was as lonely an area as I'd ever seen. When I'd been driving about an hour, I started to keep my eyes peeled for the pull-off with picnic tables Vern had described. I saw it ten minutes later, a small roadside park that looked like it might have been put up by some kind-hearted farmer. There were three tables under a big tree that would give nice shade when it had leaves. The only other features were a can for trash and a weathered one-hole privy.

Apparently Vern sometimes told the truth.

I pulled off to look.

FORTY

Lebanon was bigger than I'd expected. Besides the route I'd come in on, which in town became Broadway, there were at least eight intersecting streets. When I reached what I thought was the center of town and circled a few blocks to park, I saw there were also streets parallel to the main one. The business district, the important part, I could manage, though I might have sore feet by the time I finished.

The center of things was a four-story brick hotel called The Golden Lamb. I'd heard it was the oldest hotel in the state. Mark Twain and Abraham Lincoln and bigwigs like that had supposedly stayed there. So had Jenkins and Ione. They'd driven down and spent the night to celebrate one of Ione's magazine sales. She said the creaky bedsprings had cramped their style some but the food in the dining room was first-rate. I picked up the envelope with my assorted pictures and started my rounds.

Banks, shoe stores, grocery. Dress shops, cafes, appliance repair places, dry goods. Every place I passed, my routine was the same:

"I'm trying to locate a man who has an inheritance coming. He may live around here, or come to visit. Do you recognize anyone in these photographs...? Maybe you've seen the car he drives...."

By the time I'd worked my way down one side of the main drag and reached the hotel, I had absolutely nothing to show for my efforts. Maybe Vern had lied after all.

Maybe he knew about the place with the picnic tables from catting around. But sometimes you have to trust instinct. Instinct told me there really was a maroon car. Since nobody seemed familiar with it in Dayton, if Vern had left something in it, the car almost certainly had come through here.

I fortified myself with coffee and pie in the hotel, gawking at beams that made me feel like I was sitting in an earlier century. I'd worked my way through half the stores on the remaining side of the street before I got my first crumb of encouragement.

"I think I saw that car. I'm pretty sure I did," said a barber who was whisking out the chair of a departing customer when I came in. His eyes lingered hungrily on the picture I'd borrowed from Eli. "Reddish, anyway, and fancy. I tell you, if I was a millionaire, I'd spend it on cars."

The other barber in the shop cast up his eyes and continued clipping away at the back of a customer's hair.

"Yeah, I'm pretty certain that's the one I saw," said the one I was talking to. "Just once or twice, though. It's sure not from around here."

My pulse had quickened.

"You saw it more than once?"

He tugged at his ear and squinted.

"Yes, it had to be. Once when I was standing here working and saw it pass. Another time I saw it parked somewhere. If it's the same car."

He couldn't remember where it was parked or when he'd seen it, and he didn't recognize anyone in the photographs. Still, it was more than enough to keep me going.

At a bakery at the end of the street where I'd started, I got lucky again. They did a good trade, and I had to wait while sacks were filled with rolls and cinnamon bread and cream horns and cookies. Jealous of the aromas, my stomach set up a clamor for lunch. Finally one of the two women working behind the counter was free. She gave me a smile.

"What may I get you?"

"Half a dozen of those sugar cookies," I said pointing. It seemed only fair. "And I'd like to know if you've ever seen a car like this."

She finished filling a sack and slid it toward me. Standing on tiptoe to lean closer, she glanced at the picture of the Ambassador. Another smile curved her lips.

"Oh, yes. That looks just like that lovely car that Miss Myr—"

"You better wait until Mr. Harris gets here," cut in the other clerk as she counted out change to a customer. "He's the one who saw it. And he might not take it too kindly, us talking about a customer."

"You know who drives it, then?"

"No...." The dark-haired woman helping me dropped her eyes. She was fairly young.

The departing customer went out the door. For the moment it was just the three of us. I struggled to curtail my growing frustration.

"Look, this won't make trouble for anyone. It has to do with a matter up in Dayton." I waved vaguely. "The person driving this car could come into a good deal of money." Not honestly, but that was another matter. "But I need to find out who it is."

The clerk who'd been helping me shook her head.

"I'm sorry. She's right. It's Mr. Harris, the owner, you need to talk to. He'll be in at one-thirty."

FORTY-ONE

It was almost one anyway. I had some lunch. I thought about my meeting with Ferris Wildman tonight, and the numerous things I had to tell him. I thought how I hadn't expected Connelly to get as sore as he had over what I'd pulled. What I tried not to think about was how the day was slipping away and what it would be like if I had to drive back on that empty road in the dark.

At half-past-one I returned to the bakery.

The dark-haired woman I'd spoken to was filling an order. Replacing the other clerk was a very tall woman who was ringing a sale on the cash register. A man in a bow tie leaned on the counter, making sympathetic sounds to a customer who had a tied-up pie box waiting before her. The tall woman closed the cash drawer and came over.

"What could I get for you?"

"I'm actually here to talk to Mr. Harris." I nodded.

"About that car? Mary said you'd been in." She glanced down the counter. "He's going to be tied up a while with that one. She'll talk your ear off." Her manner was cordial, but her lips pursed uneasily. "Is Myrtle in some sort of hot water over the car? The man who was driving it said it was just a little dent. At least that's what she told us."

Like that, I had information enough to work with.

"Myrtle doesn't own the maroon car, then?"

The tall woman gave a startled laugh.

"Good heaven no! She still drives the blunderbuss she's had for ages. Only a few steps up from a Model-T."

"The man who was driving the car is the only I'm interested in. There's a good chance he's mixed up in something shady."

"Oh!" The man in the bow tie was still busy. She hesitated. "Look, maybe I could help you. I'm Julia Harris. I was here that afternoon same as Pop, and saw it and listened to Myrtle. Why don't we sat down." Nodding at a wire table with two chairs in front of the counter, she untied her apron and came around.

I introduced myself and gave her a card. She had soft blue eyes and a pretty face.

"I suppose I should look at the picture you showed Mary rather than make assumptions," she said. When I took it out of the envelope she nodded and touched one of the smaller pictures at the bottom. "Yes. That color. And it parked right there, where we could see." She gestured toward the window, then gave a small sigh. "The truth is, we hoped at the time that Myrtle might get a ticket. Or better still, lose her license. She's an awful driver."

"Myrtle hit the red car?" Like Julia, I didn't want to make assumptions.

"When she was pulling out, yes. Maybe going too fast; Myrtle tends to be in a bit of a hurry. Poor thing, she jumped out – or as close as a woman who must be sixty, at least, comes to jumping – and covered her mouth. Then she ran around and looked at the damage and wrung her hands. Pop was just starting out to see about it and calm her down when the man who owned the red car came back."

"What happened then?"

Julia shrugged. "Myrtle caught his sleeve and took him around to the street side to look. A customer came in, so I didn't see the rest of it. The next time I looked up, the red car was gone."

The woman with the pie box finally was leaving. Julia's father, who'd eyed us a few times, ambled over. Introductions were made. Since Julia now seemed keen on helping, I let her do the telling about why I was interested in the car. It dispelled any reluctance on his part, but he wasn't able to add much to what she'd already told me.

"No, I can't say where he'd come from. I'd just opened the door, starting out to help Myrtle when I noticed him. He came from that direction, though." He pointed. "And he wasn't running like you'd think he would if he'd been crossing the street and seen it happen. I'd guess he might have come from around the corner."

"There are stores there," Julia put in.

"Could you describe him? Notice anything he did?"

Mr. Harris shook his head in apology.

"A customer with a baby buggy and a little hellion who needs hanging onto came up from the other way right about then, and the kid was jumping around the way he usually does and I held the door for them. I didn't really notice the fellow, to tell you the truth."

"He must have driven away not long after," said Julia. She turned and asked Mary, the dark-haired clerk, who was free now. Mary agreed.

"That little pest Tommy was still in the store when Miss Myrtle came in saying she was such a bundle of nerves she needed to sit down. I know that. And the car was gone."

The car had made a bigger impression than the driver. None of them could recall a single thing about him. Showing the photographs proved futile. They gave me Myrtle's address, and Julia gave me directions as another wave of customers began to arrive.

"I hope I didn't make her sound silly," she added as she rose and started to tie on her apron. "She's a lovely woman; gave piano lessons to half the children in town, including me. But she's a horror behind the wheel."

I crossed my fingers that she was a horror with a good memory.

* * *

Myrtle's last name was Bell. She lived just a few blocks north of downtown on a street of houses that looked like they dated back a century or so. They were modest but well built with nice yards. Myrtle's was a little brick cottage.

I didn't see a car in front, and the shed to the side that probably had been a stable once had an open front. Nobody answered when I knocked on the door.

"Myrtle's not home," called a woman who'd come out to sweep the steps next door – a common nosy neighbor tactic.

I moseyed over. "Do you have any idea when she'll be back? I drove down from Dayton to see her."

The interest in her eyes suggested she might be sharing the tidbit of news as soon as she went inside.

"Four o'clock," she said firmly.

I gritted my teeth.

"She goes to some women's meeting at church from two to four every Wednesday," the neighbor was saying. "Gads around like gas was free. Of course when her husband was still alive, she didn't get to go much, he was such a sourpuss. Now she's gallivanting all the time."

Church meetings didn't sound much like gallivanting to me, but I thanked her and said I'd be back around four.

* * *

Chaffing at the long delay, I went back downtown and talked to people who worked in shops around the corner from the bakery. None of them had seen a maroon car. A few had heard something about Myrtle Bell denting someone's fender, but none of them had any idea who the other driver was. At a quarter of four I went back to her place to wait.

Shortly after the hour an old but shiny Ford turned onto the street at an angle that took it close to the center before the driver corrected. In my rearview mirror I watched it drive more or less straight. As it came closer I saw the white-haired driver was peering through the steering wheel, her hands above her ears. The car nosed eagerly toward the curb where it stopped with a bounce. Glad I'd been forewarned about Myrtle's driving and parked in front of the house just beyond hers, I watched her climb out. It engendered a certain amount of sympathy for her driving.

Myrtle Bell was short, partly by stature and partly because of a humped back that reduced her height by a good ten inches and put her head an equal distance in front of her shoulders. She was a pretty little woman, though, with a peppy manner. I was fairly certain the pink of her lips had come from a tube, which in a woman her age probably caused tongues to wag.

"Mrs. Bell?" I asked, getting out of my car and starting toward her.

"Yes?" She peered up at me brightly.

"I'm Maggie Sullivan. I came down from Dayton. I'd like to ask you a question or two about the man with the reddish car you parked behind in front of the bakery a while back."

"Oh! Oh, dear!" She clutched her purse and a brown canvas tote to her chest, worried and fluttering. "Is it about insurance? The man said it was such a *tiny* dent I shouldn't worry!"

"It's not–"

"I offered to pay, but he said–"

"Mrs. Bell, it's not about bumping the car. It's the man himself who's in trouble."

It took her a minute to switch gears. "In trouble? What do you mean?"

The way she had to cock her head to look up gave me the odd sensation of talking to a bird. I lowered my voice and stepped closer, suspecting she'd find the hint of secrecy thrilling.

"I'm afraid he may have stolen some money."

"Stolen! Oh, my!" Her eyes were bright. "I don't know what I can tell you. He seemed so nice.... Would you mind if we went inside? I've been away all afternoon and I'm a bit tired."

FORTY-THREE

Myrtle offered to make us some tea. One of the first things I'd learned as a gumshoe was that if I showed up asking questions and someone offered me tea, accepting was usually a good idea. The preparations were familiar. They made whoever I wanted to talk to feel more in charge, which relaxed them. Myrtle didn't strike me as part of that minority who wanted the time to concoct a lie.

While she fussed in the kitchen, I had a chance to learn about her from her surroundings. One corner of her living room held an upright piano with a metronome and stacks of sheet music. A kid's cap next to the piano bench suggested she still gave lessons. On the wall, a framed photograph with an oval mat showed her and her husband on their wedding day. She'd been taller then.

When her bent little shape appeared with a tray, I hurried to help. I said she had a fine piano. She beamed. She still gave lessons, though not to as many students, she volunteered. Finally we got down to business.

"I want to make sure I'm asking about the right man," I said. "Can you tell me what he looked like?"

"Oh dear." She thought. "I don't remember much. He wasn't burly. My brothers were both burly." After some more thought, she sighed. "He had nice hands. I do remember that. They were so well tended I wondered if he might be a musician. I didn't ask him, of course."

"Dark? Fair? Bald?"

She tittered. "Not bald. Fair, I think. I'm not certain. I was so upset."

"Do you think you could pick him out in a photograph?"

She brightened. "What a nice idea! Why, yes."

I opened my envelope and took out the pictures. First I showed her the car, which she agreed was the one in question. Then I showed her the two photographs.

"Let me have a better look, dear. My eyes aren't what they used to be." Peering intently, she brought first one, then the other to within a hand's length of her nose. She began to nod. "Yes, that's him. Right there."

She tapped the same image as the bartender had yesterday.

They'd both identified James C. Hill.

* * *

Myrtle Bell might not make the most reliable of witnesses. I began to suspect her poor driving was the result of poor eyesight. The old doll needed glasses. Still, she'd shown no uncertainty at all in picking out Hill as the driver of the expensive car, a car he couldn't likely afford on his salary. If he'd been driving a car that belonged to somebody else, it was doubtful he'd have been sanguine about the dent. On the other hand, if he owned it and was up to no good, he'd want to attract as little attention as possible.

As I left Lebanon, I evaluated the implications of what I'd learned there. I'd connected Hill to the car, and I'd placed both him and the car in Lebanon. Vern had described the car and admitting to leaving a package in it just outside Lebanon. He'd also admitted to knowing that Draper and someone else met at a roadhouse. The bartender at that roadhouse had picked out Hill and Draper as the ones who met there. Yes, I had the proof I needed.

Vern would roll in an instant if the cops squeezed him. On Hill, on Draper, on whoever had been hired to run me over but killed somebody else instead. My guess was Wildman wouldn't lift a finger to help his leech of a brother-in-law. He'd show even less sympathy toward the trusted manager who'd helped bilk him, and was possibly behind the whole scheme. As soon as I'd laid it all out for Wildman, it would be time to bring in the cops.

I frowned at the road ahead of me. The leaden gray sky had the look of snow. Getting away from Myrtle had taken some doing, especially since I still had a couple of questions I wanted to ask her. In the end, it had been almost five when I left her house, and she hadn't had anything else useful to add.

By the time I passed the deserted roadside park, the light was fading. A few cars passed going south. Those I glimpsed ahead of me disappeared, one by one, the last turning onto a gravel crossroad. The ones I could see in my rearview mirror slipped away too. As I crested a hill, a big cattle truck swung out of a farm lane. My body tensed remembering the truck that had rammed Wildman's Cadillac with me inside it. There was no one else on the road. Just the two of us. The big truck rumbled along, not far behind me. And then, all at once, it turned off onto what must have been nothing more than a track, maybe some shortcut used by locals, or leading to a barn somewhere. My breath eased out. I began to relax.

Ten minutes later, in the middle of nowhere, I heard a thump, soft at first, but repeating louder and harder. The DeSoto started to shimmy. I pulled to the side of the road.

Swearing a blue streak I got out and circled the car. I saw the bad news I expected. Stalking back to the luggage compartment, I opened it to start the long process of changing a flat tire.

FORTY-THREE

Reason told me I was probably safer out here in the middle of cow pastures than I was in the city. Farms didn't grow thugs the way cities did. Nonetheless, given all that had happened on this case and how isolated I was, the first thing I did was get back in the car and retrieve the Smith & Wesson from my purse.

Changing a tire was a miserable task in any weather. The fact it was getting cold enough to see my breath didn't improve my mood. Nor did thoughts of how much more this was going to delay me. Nor the knowledge it would be full dark soon, with unfamiliar road ahead. I put my new coat in the back seat. Using the car to curtain me in case another vehicle happened along, I pulled off my skirt and got into the overalls I kept in the trunk for dirty work. I'd tossed the shoes ruined in the alley into the trunk for a similar purpose, never guessing I'd use them this soon. All the while, my .38 rested reassuringly on the running board.

I looked around for a rock to put under the back wheel with the good tire to keep it from rolling. The only one I could see wasn't quite as big as I wanted, but it would have to do. I got out the parts of the jack and used one to pry off the hubcap. Preliminaries out of the way, I put the jack together, slid it into place and set to work.

Halfway through, a car that was headed toward Lebanon pulled off on the other side of the road. A guy in a suit and topcoat came over.

"Flat tire, huh?" He seemed somewhat nonplused, either at my overalls or the .38 I'd picked up.

"Want me to call somebody to come finish changing it? I think there's a place in Lebanon stays open 'til eight. I'd help you myself, but I've got to get to a lodge dinner honoring my father-in-law. There'll be family fireworks like you wouldn't believe if I'm late."

I did a fast estimate. I could be done before help even got here.

"Thanks anyway. I'm doing okay."

I bent to it again, feeling more isolated than ever when the sound of the other car faded. It was full dark now, the only visible light a pinprick so far away I couldn't even guess the distance. A frail old fellow in a pickup stopped and apologized three times that he couldn't help.

"I've got a bad ticker. Doctor's real firm about me not lifting and such."

I thanked him and told him I was just about finished. Forty-five minutes or thereabouts after I'd started, I was. The sprained shoulder I'd forgotten about all day was screaming about the mistreatment it had gotten working the jack. I got back into the car, shivering so my teeth were rattling.

When I reached Centerville, the desire to stop for a whiskey almost overwhelmed me. Instead, I swallowed a couple of aspirin, dry, to calm my shoulder. I wanted a sharp mind when I had my meeting with Wildman. He was going to have questions aplenty. Maybe he'd offer me some of that nice whiskey of his. Mostly I wanted to be back in familiar surroundings before I chanced stopping again.

* * *

In Van Buren Township there was a place that served great chili. I pulled in and had a bowl. When I'd finished, I flirted with the idea of swinging by Mrs. Z's to change into warmer clothes and clean up better than I'd been able to in a ladies washroom. It was getting close to eight o'clock, though. I wanted to type up some notes before I saw Wildman.

This time of night there were parking spaces in front of my building. I was glad to save some energy. No one parked after I did, so I got out my key for the front door and went inside. The two Negro girls who cleaned were just starting on my floor. I told them they could skip my office since I'd been out all day and wanted to work.

"Um-um. You movin' stiff," clucked Sophia.

I grinned. "Think maybe I'll take boxing lessons. Toughen me up."

They laughed. They worked hard and were plenty smart. Not many of the other people who worked here ever saw them. I always gave them some money at Christmastime because that seemed right.

In my office I turned up the radiator, cranked a carbon set into my Remington, and started to type. I'd been at it half an hour or better and was almost finished when the telephone at my elbow started to jangle. Instinctively I reached for my gun. Who would expect to find me here at this hour? Unless they'd been watching.

My eyes flew to the door and then to the windows. The phone beside me repeated its summons. In my lap my hand wrapped comfortably around the contours of my .38. I answered the phone.

"Miss Sullivan? Miss Sullivan, is that you?"

The woman's voice on the other end sounded terrified.

"Yes, it is."

"This is Juniemay, Miz Tarkington's maid. Come help her, please! She's in a terrible state – all beat up and scared. They took that no-good man of hers. She's scared they'll come back, and that they're going to hurt her brother!"

FORTY-FOUR

"Who was it that came there?" I asked sharply.

"I don't know," said the voice on the phone. "I wasn't here, and she's not making much sense. She said there was three of them."

"Call Mr. Wildman–"

"I tried. The line's busy."

Wildman and his calls coming in at all hours about business, I thought in frustration.

"Keep trying. When you get through, tell them to keep their doors locked. Mr. Wildman's expecting me pretty soon, but I'll come to your place first. I'll flash my lights long and short when I pull in. Understand?"

"Yes, ma'am."

As soon as I hung up I tried Wildman. Still busy. I shrugged into my coat. Snatching the carbon set out of the platen, I peeled off the top sheet. On slow days I addressed and stamped a few envelopes to my post office box for when minutes counted. This qualified. I shoved the notes I'd typed into the envelope and my .38 into my pocket, grabbed some extra bullets and ran down the hall. As I was licking the envelope I spotted Sophia wringing a mop out.

"Put this in your pocket and mail it somewhere when you leave tonight, will you?"

She nodded.

In the DeSoto, with engine purring, I took a minute to think. Could this be a setup? Not likely. If someone wanted to lure me into a trap, they wouldn't have a Negro maid call me. They'd use a gun to the temple to get Dorothy or Wildman himself to make the call.

I drove furiously. A knot in my gut told me Hill and the men he'd hired had decided the game was up. They wouldn't care what they did from here on out. They were cutting their losses. And as Hill liked to say, tying up loose ends.

Vern was one of those loose ends. He knew too much. His worthless hide wouldn't merit a second's worry, save that he was my best way of connecting Hill to Draper. My greater concern was Dorothy's belief that the men who'd taken him meant to do something to Wildman. She was probably drunk. Maybe she'd misunderstood.

* * *

As soon as I got a look at Dorothy Tarkington, the certainty I had to act, and fast, intensified. She'd been slapped around hard. Her lip was split and bruises already were forming on her fair skin. Crouched on an ottoman, she held a china coffee cup that threatened to chip its saucer from her shaking. Her eyes had a glazed look as she lifted a tear-stained face and stared at me without recognition.

"She's not drunk," said Juniemay flatly. Going to her employer's side, she stroked her blonde hair. "She was all tied up in the coat closet with a gag in her mouth. I wouldn't of found her except for her thumping the door. Couldn't get no sense at all from her for the longest time. When I finally did, that's when I called you. She'd tossed that card you left last time into the wastebasket, but I'd fished it out and stuck it in a drawer in the kitchen."

"Did you reach Mr. Wildman?"

"No, ma'am. Line's still busy."

"Come on. We'll sort out the rest of this over there."

"No!" Dorothy spoke for the first time. "No, I can't." She started to weep. "He thinks I'm an idiot, anyway ... and this ... it's all–"

"Do you want to keep on being an idiot, or do you want to help him? If you stick around and those men come back, they'll use you to get at him. Is that what you want?"

She blinked. The glazed look receded. She pressed the heel of her hand to her forehead. "Oh, God!"

"Do you have a gun?"

"A gun? I ... Vern does. Up in the bedside table."

"I'll get it." Juniemay set off at a run.

"Juniemay said there were three men. What did they look like?"

She pressed her forehead again. "Big. One was. The others ... I don't know. They had flour sacks over their heads, with holes cut to breathe. I think Vern knew them. He ... then two of them grabbed him and tied his hands. That's when I started to scream. I threw a sofa cushion. One had a gun. And the other one slapped me so hard I fell over. And then they tied me up...." She started to sob.

I patted her shoulder awkwardly. Juniemay returned with an automatic. I checked and saw it was loaded.

"Come on," I said. "We'll all go in my car."

For the first time that evening, Juniemay's eyes widened nervously. "I can't–"

"Please, Juniemay! I need you!" Dorothy clung to her arm like a drowning woman. "Don't leave me!"

The maid looked at me in appeal.

"She needs you," I stressed. "You can ride in the back seat. Let's get a move on."

*　*　*

"What made you think Vern knew them?" I asked as we moved through the streets as fast as I dared.

"He didn't seem scared at first. Just mad at seeing them," Dorothy said.

I'd already learned that Juniemay went to her sister's place every Wednesday. She was usually there until half-past ten but her sister hadn't been feeling well, so she'd come home early.

"And what made you think they might do something to your brother?"

Dorothy was silent. When I glanced over, tears were sliding down her face. She struggled to speak.

"One of them said ... 'Wildman's got plenty of ready cash he can cough up. We may need her to convince him.'" Her voice broke. "It's my fault. I don't know what Vern's mixed up in, but I know it wouldn't have happened if I hadn't told him about hearing my brother and that insufferable manager of his talking about some big opportunity." She started to sob.

"I don't care what happens to Vern! I wish I'd left him a long time ago. Ferris makes me so mad, but if anything – if anything–"

"It's not because you told Vern about overhearing that conversation," I said sharply. "It's because of Hill."

That brought her up short. "Hill? What—?"

"He and a man named Draper cooked up a big-time swindle. Your brother was one of their pigeons. Vern's greed got him nosing around and he caught wind of it. He threatened to blow the whistle unless he got a cut.

"Your brother hired me to find out who was behind the swindle, and knowing I was getting close, Hill's decided to run.

"I don't know what he intends to try with your brother. But I know you need to walk into that house and be a help for once. Plenty of people think you're pretty fine when you're not drinking, and your nephew's crazy about you."

I turned into Wildman's drive.

"Dorothy, you stay down until I make sure everything's all right inside. Juniemay, you watch for my wave."

FORTY-FIVE

What I found in Wildman's house was chaos.

"There were three of them," Rogers said. He'd met me at the door wielding a crowbar.

The men he was talking about had forced their way in half an hour earlier, about when I was getting Juniemay's frantic phone call. The butler had seen only Vern when he opened the door, and he hadn't realized there was a gun in Vern's back. Then the others pushed in and bashed the butler over the head. He lay on the floor of the study where we all had gathered save for the cook, who to the surprise of all kept a gun in the pantry and was guarding the back door.

The butler's still-bleeding head was on a cushion. He'd been unconscious until shortly before I arrived, but he was brushing aside suggestions he needed a doctor.

"But don't even think of trying to get up," ordered Dorothy. "You may be concussed."

To my surprise, she hadn't gone to pieces at the news the intruders had taken her brother. She was, in fact, taking a stab at being in charge, though she looked frequently to make sure Juniemay hadn't left her. The household staff seemed to welcome her hand in things.

"Did the men wear flour sack masks?" I was sure they must be the ones who'd snatched Vern.

The maid in the frilly apron nodded. She was the only one who'd gotten a look at them, except for the butler in the seconds before they'd knocked him out. She was wringing the edge of the apron between her hands. Its frills were limp.

"I think maybe there was another man outside, too. After they used Mr. Vern to get in, one of them shoved him outside. That's when I saw his hands were tied. Somebody grabbed onto him."

I stopped my restless pacing. Four men made sense. Two captives, two men guarding each. That way they could use two cars, make sure their struggling captives couldn't conspire together. Four also added up to Hill and the Kirkmann brothers.

"Should I bring some tea?" The maid's sudden question suggested her need to return to things she understood.

Dorothy, who knelt by the butler, patting his hand, looked up and managed a smile.

"What a good idea. Juniemay can help you."

The maid eyed the black girl nervously, but she nodded.

"One more thing," I said to the maid. "Did you happen to notice if one of the men who came here had a bandaged finger?"

"Yes! His pinkie."

"Good. I know where to look first."

I slid into my coat. The household had been in too much turmoil for anyone to think of taking it.

"Should we call the police?" asked Rogers. It was a stroke of good luck he'd stayed late to see about a faulty connection one of the cars had developed late in the day. He instinctively gave the direction the others needed. Dorothy had left the room but was probably still within hearing distance. He lowered his voice. "Those men said not to or they'd kill Mr. Wildman."

I hesitated, not sure yet what Hill's game was. Maybe he only wanted Wildman as insurance, until he got away. Yet Dorothy had told me one of the man had said her brother had plenty of cash. Hill was in a position to know how much and where. Maybe he meant to force Wildman to get it, greedy little viper.

Hill was an amateur, albeit a smart one. Amateurs panicked. Having the cops burst in probably wasn't a good idea. At least not until I had a better sense of what was happening.

I did some quick time calculations. Spotting a notepad on top of the little mahogany secretary, I wrote a street name and the words *Kirkmann bros*.

"Give me one hour," I said. "If I haven't called you by then, tell the police to check here."

By then I'd either have things straightened out, or be uncommonly glad to see them.

* * *

Frost stretched skeletal fingers across the windows of houses I passed, hiding things. It gripped my thoughts as I left Wildman's place. I went north toward downtown, past hobos huddling around a fire they'd scratched together, through streets where traffic was sparse at this time of night at midweek. Time pressed at my back. Time and memories of the last time I'd faced men with guns. I hoped nobody had to die this time.

I drove as fast as I dared without attracting notice. I thought about Connelly and was glad he wasn't working nights any more. If I couldn't pull something off to free Wildman, things were going to get messy.

Finally I crossed the Little Miami, and not long after cut over to Milburn. The little houses scattered between the factories and tool and die places were already dark. Only a couple of beer joints showed signs of life.

I slowed considerably, knowing this hard-working, hard-drinking neighborhood might not be the friendliest to a woman out on her own at night. I didn't have time to deal with interference if I could avoid it. The smidgen of guilt I'd felt over tricking Connelly dissipated as I pulled to a stop in front of a welding shop just beyond the building he'd entered last night.

As I was waiting for my eyes to adjust, I heard a scream that raised the hairs on my neck. A man's scream. Terrified.

No time to delay. I reached for the car door. Four-to-one weren't very good odds, even if Hill wasn't armed, which I was counting on. An extra gun might turn out to be handy. I took the automatic from under my seat and left the Smith & Wesson in my coat pocket.

Opening the car door, I ran to the rear of the car and ducked down and waited. No movement. No sign of anyone coming in my direction. I took a couple of breaths and sprinted for the corner of the Kirkmann brothers' garage. Then I listened for sounds outside. There weren't any. Just a penetrating cold. Slowly I began to work my way down the side of the building. Connelly had mentioned a back entrance.

Stop. Listen. Stop. Listen. My eyes strained against shadows. At the corner I paused and peered around cautiously. There it was. A door. I moved again. From inside I caught the murmur of voices.

I put my foot forward carefully, feeling to make sure I didn't hit a discarded can or crumpled up paper which would announce my presence. As I began to shift my weight, an arm like the trunk of a tree caught me from behind, and the automatic was wrenched from my fingers.

"Going somewhere, girlie?"

FORTY-SIX

I tried to kick the big gorilla who'd grabbed me where I could do some damage, but he was tall as well as strong. He shifted me under one arm like a sack of feed. The back of a hand that now held my automatic smacked against my windpipe. What would have been a yell for help collapsed in a choking, agonized gasp for air.

Before I'd recovered from the blow to my throat, Brutus carried me through the door I'd seen and dumped me not very gently onto a brick floor.

"Lookit what I found."

He walked over to stand between two other roughly dressed men.

I pushed up with effort. I was getting tired of this particular bunch of goons inflicting bruises on me. It filled me with more lip than common sense.

"Gee, you must be the charming Kirkmann brothers. I've heard so much about you. Mind if I get up?"

I didn't wait for an answer. I got to my feet and brushed myself off. The back room of the garage was about what I'd expected: Parts stacked here and there. A disassembled car. Just inside the large double door I'd been hauled through, two new cars, one Vern's, looked as if they were poised to be driven away. Behind me a wall separated this room from the repair shop seen from the street. I stood more or less in the center of things, getting my bearings in light cast by a few bare bulbs.

A guy whose pinkie was splinted and bandaged stood directly in front of me and maybe eleven feet away. The giant who'd carried me in was to his right. On the end a boy of no more than sixteen stared at me, slack-jawed. They all had guns and the guns were pointed at me. The one with the bundled up pinkie wasn't likely to be as fast or as accurate as usual.

"You!" he hissed as he got a look at me.

"Took this away from her." The one I'd dubbed Brutus flourished my automatic and slid it across the floor toward the kid. "Ronnie, put that away."

I hooked my thumbs in my pockets and swayed my knees like a playground flirt. Cool as a cucumber. Wondering what in hades I was going to do.

"If you boys are smart, you'll run while you can. A cop was sniffing around here last night. I saw him come out just when I was getting ready to stop and have a look-see myself."

"She's lying, you idiots!"

At last I looked at James C. Hill, hoping I'd bruised his pride by not immediately making him the center of attention. He had a gun too. By the way he held it, he wasn't used to using one, but Ferris Wildman sat in front of him and Hill was keeping the gun too close to Wildman's head for me to take chances.

Wildman was tied to a chair. Vern, similarly restrained, sat next to him. Vern had a gag in his mouth. It had probably followed the scream I'd heard.

"Mr. Hill, you look immaculate as ever," I said. "Hair not even mussed. But then you didn't have a sack on your head like the hired help, did you?"

He started.

"And in case you're thinking of getting money from Mr. Wildman by threatening to kill his sister – she's not tied up any more. She's at his house, safe, boosting everybody's spirits and pulling things back into order."

"How did–? Tie her up," he snapped at the one with the broken finger, who gave an unpleasant grin.

"I don't think so."

The .38 slid smoothly out of my pocket, halting the thug in his tracks. It took them all a minute to absorb. Meanwhile I searched desperately for some way to pull off a miracle. A yard and a half to my left were some tires. If I could reach them, lean against one somehow, start it rolling.... I took a sidling step.

"Oh, and for all Mrs. Tarkington cares, you can go ahead and kill Vern. She plans to leave him anyway."

Vern squealed through his gag.

"Can't I trust you on anything?" Hill asked crossly. He started to round on his cronies, remembering me just as my finger began to move on the trigger. He swung back, keeping his gun aimed at Wildman's head. Smug superiority had replaced the deference he'd worn as Wildman's right hand man. His eyes dared me to try anything.

"Gus and me had the blonde tied up fine," the giant said angrily. "Put her in a closet just like you said. The dame's lying!"

"Mrs. Tarkington threw a pillow at you. That's when you beat her." I heard Wildman suck in breath.

The best chance I had at the moment was keeping the foursome off balance, spooking them with knowledge I shouldn't have. It still wouldn't take long until one of them figured out odds were on their side, at which point I would run out of time. I took another sideways step.

"Stay where you are!" Brutus warned. He worried me more than Gus with his busted pinkie, and a lot more than the kid, who'd let his gun hang down against his leg and looked like he might not be all there.

Hill and his captives were too far away from the Kirkmann brothers. I needed to make him turn my way, get his gun away from Wildman's head.

"I've got more witnesses than I need to prove you're a swindler, Hill – and that you killed Draper. Witnesses who saw the two of you meeting ... who know you own the maroon Ambassador where Vern left a locked bag."

"Already sold." He smiled loftily. "Regrettable. I liked the car. Once that dithering old woman drew attention to it, I had no choice. As to the bag, I'm afraid it held only clean socks for the weekend hidey-hole I'd just rented in Cincinnati."

"Vern didn't know what the bag contained, of course."

"Of course. I needed to keep his mouth shut while I planned a tidier exit than Draper had made. I paid him and gave him a meaningless chore. The only useful thing he's done is put me in touch with these gentlemen."

The two nearest Kirkmanns had been exchanging looks. The one with the gift-wrapped pinkie tightened his grip on his gun like he meant to try something. I shifted my aim just enough to discourage him.

"You really want to tangle with me again?"

"Go on. If she attempts to shoot you, I'll kill Wildman," Hill said.

"Yeah, but I'll have killed Nine Fingers here, which means his brother will kill you."

I wasn't sure family loyalty ran that deep in the Kirkmann clan, but Hill would be even less certain.

"Crime's not as tidy as business, is it, Mr. Hill? I also have witnesses at the bank where you passed yourself off as Draper several days after he died."

"So what?"

I ignored him and spoke to the Kirkmanns.

"He's going to jail for a nice long time. You boys will too if you stick around."

"I don't wanna go to jail!" whined the kid.

"Smart boy, Ronnie. Jail's nasty."

I heard what I hoped was a gun clatter to the ground. Ronnie took off.

"How many times are you going to let her outsmart you?" Hill demanded. "A cheap little know-it-all like her?"

I caught just enough of Brutus' expression to guess he didn't like being scolded.

Time to switch tactics. Stop needling Hill with what he'd done wrong. Let him wallow in showing he was smarter than me.

"For a long time I couldn't figure why Draper would take you in as a partner. You threatened to expose his affair with Lucinda Graham if he didn't, didn't you?"

"The scheme was *my* idea. All of it!" Hill corrected. "But yes, I had photographs taken of him and that - that scrawny little plucked chicken. He'd have done anything to save her good name. Oh, he liked the scheme well enough once he saw how much money we made. But the fool panicked when that bungler Vern saw us together and threatened to blab. He took off. We could have made half again what we did."

One shot. One clear shot was all I needed. One when Hill was shifted enough for me to take care of him without his reflex killing Wildman. What happened after that would be immaterial.

I started to take another step sideways. Hill brought his gun closer to Wildman's head.

"Stay where you are!"

"Why even bother with Draper if the swindle was your idea?"

"Because he had the contacts." Bitterness clung to each word. "I was just Ferris Wildman's lapdog. Allowed to eat at the country club table with rich men because he might want a statistic coughed up, or something I'd read in a journal. Pretending delight at the size of my Christmas bonus while I saw him give that much *every month* to an irresponsible freeloader who does nothing!"

Contempt boiling over, he spoke to Wildman now.

"Did you really suppose I'd ask ransom for you like some common thug? *I had you brought here because I want you to know who made a fool of you.* I want you to sit there every second of every minute you have left and *know*!"

Hate had started to gleam in his eyes. The arm that held the gun was straightening. I needed to derail him fast.

"How did you get Draper back?"

"What?"

"How did you get him back? How did you know where he'd be so you could kill him?"

He blinked as though awakening from a trance. His condescending smile reappeared.

"You yourself made it possible, I'm delighted to say. The night I was told you'd been hired, I telephoned him in Kentucky to warn him he needed to come get his money before you started poking around."

It began to make sense. Draper had fled in such a panic he hadn't taken the time to retrieve his money.

"I suggested we'd meet and I'd give him the photographs – no hard feelings. He jumped at the chance. It was dark, of course. I had a very large flashlight. When I gave him the envelope of photos, I pretended to drop them. He bent to get them. I hit him on the back of the head."

"Thinking he'd have his share of the money somewhere in his car. But all you found was his safety deposit key."

"You've taken enough of my time already."

Hill raised his voice to the Kirkmann brothers.

"Shoot her or tie her up. I don't care which."

Gus looked at his brother, then at Hill.

"You do it."

Wildman spoke softly.

"I'm quite willing to die, Miss Sullivan. As long as you kill this bastard."

Hill's gun began to waver uncertainly between me and Wildman.

"It's what I'm paying you for!" he snapped at the Kirkmanns. "What's wrong with you? It's three against one!"

"Do the math again," said a voice behind me.

FORTY-SEVEN

Only well-ingrained discipline kept my head from jerking around. Hill's eyes jumped, but he kept the gun in his hand aimed at Wildman.

The voice belonged to Rachel Minsky.

While the men's attention was fixed on her, I eased closer to the tires.

"My, my, James," Rachel chided. "You've been a naughty boy."

Hill looked livid. He brushed at his collar. He liked order, a commodity that was slipping away.

I hadn't been able to see Rachel, only hear her. Now she strolled into view. She'd probably come through a door in the wall behind me. The dark fur swaddling her from head to knees would have blended nicely into shadows. In addition to her usual hat and coat, her hands were tucked inside a matching muff.

"What the hell are you doing here?" I asked through clenched teeth.

She was just enough ahead of me that I could see the side of her face without looking away from the three armed men.

"Weren't you listening just now? I'm evening the odds."

At the moment she looked more like a liability than anything else, standing there with no trace of a weapon. Then again, I couldn't see Rachel Minsky walking into a place she didn't expect to leave.

Her light steps angled in my direction.

"Hold it right there, girlie," snapped Brutus.

She stopped.

"That pile of dirt owes me money." She nodded toward Hill.

He'd turned some to watch her, eyes burning with outrage. His gun no longer pointed directly at Wildman's head, although it could return in an instant.

"You told me you'd gotten your money back," I said.

"Only half. Draper was supposed to bring the rest the day he disappeared. I knew from some of your questions you'd figured out who his partner was – or were close. I've been following you."

"I hope you brought your boyfriend."

"I don't need him when I'm properly dressed."

She spared me a look. Her eyes were glittering. I hoped I read her correctly. I hoped she'd understand me. Wildman's life depended on it. Thrown by our chit-chat, the Kirkmanns were juggling their attention between us. Hill opened his mouth to speak, as distracted as he was likely to be. I shifted my weight to my heels.

"Then the only thing I see left is deciding who dates whom," I said.

Less than a second and she understood.

"Right."

Rachel's hand moved out of the muff. We fired at the same instant. I put one in Brutus first, then one in Gus, ducking and rocking my weight side to side as I fired. Something singed the air too close for comfort. I swung back and saw Brutus, in spite of a bleeding shoulder, drawing a bead on me. I shot him in the knee and heard him fall and drop the gun. I spun and saw Hill was down, shrieking in pain.

"I'm all right!" Wildman shouted. His chair had tipped over. He lay on his side.

Like that it was over. With nobody dead, not even the vermin. Before I could even determine the make of the gun Rachel held, she tucked it away.

The big guy I called Brutus was pushing himself along the floor, trying to get to his weapon. I went over and kicked it out of his reach. Picking it up, I gave him a tap on the head to put him to sleep for a nice long time.

The guy with the bandaged pinkie had a bad enough hole in his chest to keep him from making trouble. Hill appeared to be suffering equally from wounds in chest and crotch. He was mostly unconscious.

Rachel and I pulled Wildman and the chair he was tied to upright again. He'd been planning, and pushed himself over when he saw Rachel's gun emerge.

"I can cut you loose – call Rogers to come and get you before I call the cops," I said. "It might look better if they found you like this."

He nodded.

"Thank you – both of you."

I gave Rachel an inquiring look. "Were you here?"

"I already told you I don't care for cops."

"One of the Kirkmanns must have hit Hill in all the confusion," I said. "When I rolled that tire." I'd never gotten close enough to shove it, but I would on the way out. "Or maybe a wild shot from the kid that ran. And that dark-haired woman they think they saw was somebody who stuck her head in. Maybe a girlfriend."

"Yes, that's how I remember it," Wildman said. His hawklike eyes were sharp and hard.

To make sure no one put too much stock in whatever Vern said, but mostly because it was satisfying, I stepped behind him and gave him a whack on the head. I told Wildman I'd call his house and ask them to send his lawyer.

"When the cops arrive, tell them the shoulder I hurt last week got roughed up again and I went home," I said. "I'll be in tomorrow to give them a statement."

"And if it's convenient, please stop by for breakfast," said Wildman.

His sister and I were on good enough terms now I figured that might be safe.

FORTY-EIGHT

Rachel and I walked out into falling snow, thick, fluffy and clean.

"That one place you shot Hill made it look kind of personal," I said.

She smiled her inscrutable smile.

"Pearlie will have called this in," she said. "As soon as he saw we were both standing. He didn't like playing it that way, but he follows orders."

Our feet crunched on the cinder path leading out to the street. In the distance I caught the first faint wail of a siren.

"There's a place not far from here where we could have a drink," Rachel said. "Warm up without being bothered. You could make your phone calls. They serve a good corned beef sandwich."

"The drink sounds good," I said.

My DeSoto had never looked better. I turned up my collar.

Rachel noticed. She gave the muff she held a self-satisfied pat.

"You know," she said, "you really should consider fur."

The End

ABOUT THE AUTHOR

M. Ruth Myers is a former reporter and feature writer for daily papers including *The Journal Herald* (Dayton). Her novels have been published in foreign translations as well as in English.

Ruth's time at the word processor allows her husband to climb on the roof with untied shoelaces, and the cat to sprawl on the kitchen table without reprimand.

Her new series featuring private eye Maggie Sullivan began with the novel NO GAME FOR A DAME.

Get better acquainted with Ruth and enjoy free samples of upcoming novels at her website
http://www.mruthmyers.com

Drop her a note at her Facebook author page or follow her on Twitter at @mruthmyers.

CPSIA information can be obtained
at www.ICGtesting.com
Printed in the USA
LVHW112239250719
625423LV00001B/121/P

9 780615 732619